Shadowmen

The War Scroll Series
Book 2

J.B. TUCKER

This work of fiction is purely imaginative and created for entertainment purposes only. Any resemblance to real persons, living or dead, or actual events is purely coincidental. The author has taken creative liberties in constructing the narrative, characters, and events within this piece. The intent is not to represent or reflect any real-life situations, individuals, or occurrences.

ISBN: **979-8-9908355-0-4**

First Edition

Cover art by MeLisa Stone
Copyediting by Twisted Whisperings Press and Editing

www.jbtuckerbooks.com

To my husband who supports my literary addiction.

To my students who give me the voice and guts to follow my dreams.

Everybody is a moon and has a dark side they don't show to anyone.

Mark Twain

Chapter 1

Luca

Luca stood in front of the tall windows of his apartment that overlooked the busy city. He frowned at the bright white lights emanating from the sprawling White House in the distance, a den of vipers.

Many of the major cities in the world were influenced by the Shadowmen in some way or another, but in Washington, D.C., they were everywhere, cowering in the shadows, whispering their lies as they rubbed shoulders with old, fat congressmen at upscale bars. And now, they had the ear of the President of the United States. It wasn't the first time they'd positioned themselves so well, nor would it be the last. The thought left him feeling bone-weary.

Luca turned away from the window, tucked a white pressed shirt into his slacks, and slipped on a black tailored jacket. With quick, sure hands, he tied a Windsor knot at his throat and let the white silk tie fall into place. The room surrounding him was pristine, lacking both dirt and color. His D.C. apartment wasn't as quaint as the one in Paris had been, but at least he didn't have to worry about his neighbors. A pair of piercing blue eyes set in a heart-shaped face came to mind, derailing his focus. He shook his head hard. *No distractions tonight*, he thought. After what happened in Paris, so much was riding on him being at his best.

Procuring tickets to the Presidential Inaugural Ball had been easy enough. Luring out the Shadow positioned near the newly elected President would be a bit trickier. Normally, he'd have Arin and Alena by his side, but he'd asked to go it alone this time. Less conspicuous, he'd told Ms. Delgado and Mr. Daiko when they'd given him the assignment. He hadn't seen or spoken to Arin or Alena since the bombing two months before. It was the longest they'd been apart since Abbott formed their little band of misfits. The truth was, he wasn't ready to see them yet. He couldn't risk hearing one of them say *her* name. Arin would berate him again for being an idiot, and Alena would likely say something nasty about Kirie to sway Luca against her. Either way, the effect would be the same. Besides, they had plenty to do in the wake of the Center bombing.

No distractions, he reminded himself.

An Aston Martin pulled up to curb outside the lobby of the high-rise apartment building. A young man in a valet uniform stepped out and handed the key fob to Luca, who then pressed a large bill into his hand. Luca drove off toward the National Building Museum in a streak of silver. He parked in the large pay lot and stood waiting in the long security line out front of the stately building. Straightening his tie, Luca breathed deeply and commanded his racing heart to calm. It immediately complied. He couldn't rush this assignment. Without the right amount of patience and finesse, he'd blow his chances at success.

Passing through security was uneventful, as Luca knew it would be. After all, he didn't need weapons to be dangerous. The four-story walls surrounding the inner hall were illuminated with red lights, and white gossamer fabric draped above from balcony to balcony. Tables covered with the presidential seal were spread across the floor between tall, stately pillars. Dignitaries and donors in fine clothing mingled, some congratulating themselves on their recent success in the election and others bemoaning their loss.

Luca rolled his eyes at their naiveté. The entire election had been rigged from the start. All their rallies, fundraisers, and money couldn't have changed the outcome. Stronger forces than the American dollar were at play.

Scanning the crowd, Luca spotted the newly elected President. Men and women surrounded him like a muster of preening peacocks vying for attention and praise as they congratulated him on his win, each seeking to gain favor in the new administration. The President, shorter in person than Luca would've expected, shook each of their hands with a practiced smile.

Luca walked around the room, conversing with the occasional

donor or governor who was always looking to make a new connection. All the while, he kept an eye on the President-elect, searching for his shadow. Luca had come prepared to play the part of a campaign leader, someone with no real power or influence and, therefore, beneath anyone's interest. Each new suitor moved on to bigger conquests after only moments of meeting the lowly grunt.

It was when the orchestra began to play that he finally spotted her. To the left side of the stage, where the President and First Lady danced the traditional First Dance, was a middle-aged woman dressed in a black sheath and simple black pumps. She was average to the extreme, with short brown hair, and simple features. Nothing about her stood out, at least not to the average person. To Luca, however, she looked like spilled ink on a white shirt. The darkness radiated around her like a sinister halo.

There was an almost feral possessiveness in how she watched the President as he danced with his regal wife, like a predator studying its eventual prey. Getting her alone would be difficult but not impossible. He'd have to be careful not to underestimate the female shadow. Getting close enough to the President to become his Chief of Staff was quite the trick. *I have a few tricks of my own,* Luca thought with a wry smile.

As Luca made his way toward her through the crowded room, he let his mind fill with the memories of his past, from his time with Donovan in the dark London streets. They flashed through his mind like an old-time movie reel—killing an innocent for the first time—hours and hours strapped down in a hard chair in front of a small, flickering screen—stalking a young Bright One through a darkened, foreign street—he let them all free from the box he fought so hard to keep them locked in.

As the memories washed over him, Luca let the darkness take over and force the light out just like Donovan trained him to do *before*—before the Society of Light found him—before they rescued him. His heartbeat irregularly as the last bit of peace and hope seeped out of him like lifeblood from an open wound. His stomach turned over as he willingly embraced the darkness.

Now it was his turn to stalk *his* prey.

"Excuse me," Luca said, tapping the woman on the shoulder.

She turned to him with a sour expression, upset at the intrusion. "Yes?"

"Hi," Luca said, clearing his throat like a nervous teenager. "I'm a recent Harvard graduate and was fortunate enough to head up Mr. McCallister's campaign headquarters in Boston. I just wanted to meet the woman lucky enough to work with him every day." Luca gave the woman a bashful smile.

She assessed him from head to toe. She must've liked what she saw because a lecherous smile spread across her face. "Well then, I suppose I should congratulate you on a job well done. We did very well in the state of Massachusetts."

"Yes, ma'am." Luca ducked his head as if embarrassed by the praise.

"What did you say your name was?" Her eyes raked over him,

drinking him in.

"Fredrick Mason, ma'am," Luca reached out a hand, and they shared a cold handshake. Luca subtly transferred a bit of his darkness between their joined palms, and the older woman let out a low sigh. It was almost too easy.

"I'm staying at The Regis tonight. Why don't you meet me at the bar on the first floor around eleven, and we can talk about your bright future in politics."

"Really?" Luca said with raised eyebrows. "Thank you! I'll see you tonight."

"I look forward to it," she said, biting her bottom lip slightly.

It took about thirty minutes for Luca to drive to The Regis and charm the girl at the front desk into telling him the Chief of Staff's room number and another thirty seconds to pick the lock. She was staying in a double room suite that showed little sign anyone occupied it. With gloved hands, Luca searched under the bed, behind chairs, and in the closet with no success. Not even a suitcase. Lying on the desk near the window, however, was a small laptop. Luca lifted the lid and powered it on. He checked the time on his cell and swore under his breath. 10:36 PM. The woman was likely already on her way to the bar.

Hacking her security took longer than he wanted; it was 10:57 PM before he was in. Three files sat brazenly on the computer's desktop. Luca shook his head; the woman had too much trust in her "secure" password. The first file held pictures of the President in various compromising . . . positions. Each picture featured a different girl, one younger than the last. It was the perfect collection to bribe oneself into a powerful position.

The second folder was a bit more interesting. It contained Blueprints of various historical buildings worldwide, including The Paris Pantheon. Luca swallowed hard, pushing memories from that ill-fated night to the side. *No distractions.*

He attempted to break into the last file, but the encryption was on another level. Luca's gut told him this file was significant. He slipped a memory stick into the laptop and checked the time again. 11:26 PM. He was out of time. He quickly transferred the files onto his device and slipped the drive into his pocket just as the door opened and the woman walked in. Luca stood up from the desk and faced her.

"What are you doing in here?" She barked at him. She dropped her briefcase onto the nearest chair and put her hands on her hips. "Who let you in?"

"I let myself in," Luca said in a chilly tone. "Tell me, *shadow*, what are your plans for the president?"

The woman shook her head, chuckled once, and locked the door behind her. When she turned back around, her flat hazel eyes had darkened to black orbs. As she stared at Luca intensely, the lights in the room stuttered and dimmed until they went completely out. A smile spread across Luca's face, and his arms tingled in anticipation.

"Who sent you," she said in the darkness. She sounded closer to him than before, though he didn't hear her move. The tactic was meant to scare and confuse him, but Luca was unaffected.

"Sorry, Dove, I'll be asking the questions tonight." In one swift movement, Luca reached out and grabbed the woman by the neck and lit up the room in a sudden flare of brightness. Pure, white light exuded from every inch of his skin, chasing the shadows into the far corners of the room. The hand he had wrapped around her neck was blue in hue, hotter, and more intense than the rest of him. Her skin sizzled under the heat of it.

"You! How did you . . ." She rasped.

"Now, now. We've already established that I'm in charge tonight. Tell me what I need to know, or I'll fry you where you stand. What are your plans for the President of the United States?"

The shadow clawed at his hand and glared at him with hate and fury as she struggled to breathe. The air rippled and tendrils of black smoke rolled off her. Luca raised his left hand and shot a lightning bolt past her face, slicing off a large chunk of her ear. The sickening smell of burnt skin filled the air.

"I'm not in the mood for your little tricks tonight, Shadow. You'll answer me now or I *will* turn you into dust."

"I've heard of y-you, Luca Durant. The b-brightest light in millennia. But," *gasp,* "there's a darkness in you too, little lightning boy. I can t-taste it." She ran her tongue over her dry lips and moaned.

"I'm flattered." His stomach soured. "The list. What's it for?"

"They say there's one even brighter than y-you," she continued, sucking in a shallow breath. "He'll find her, and he'll extinguish her light ssssslowly." She gave a reedy laugh.

The paint on the walls began to melt as Luca squeezed her neck tighter. He lifted her off the ground so they were eye to eye. "You tell the devil when you meet him in hell that I'll burn anyone who tries."

She let out a choked scream as Luca's light intensified. In seconds, she was nothing but a pile of dust at his feet. He stared down at his dirty shoes in disgust, not at the demon he'd banished from this world, but at himself. He hated how natural it felt to use the darkness inside him. If there was ever any physical proof that he didn't deserve Kirie, there it was.

Bit by bit, he locked the dark thoughts, the hate and despair he'd unleashed away in its box, and light began to seep back into him. The light was hesitant, like it didn't like what he'd done–like it didn't approve. He'd acted just as Donovan had taught him to— without mercy. No matter how hard he tried, he'd never erase the stain Donovan had left on him.

Kirie's voice echoed in his head again for the hundredth time, *"I deserve better."* She had no idea how right she was. Luca had been a stain in her bright world. He should've never gotten so close to her. Even as he thought of Kirie, he could feel the heat of her light on his skin, making him shiver. But that was all he could allow himself, memories.

Luca shook his head and stepped away from the pile of ashes at his feet. Disappointment and self-loathing swirled in his chest as he turned and walked out of the hotel room. He should've gotten more out of her. He would have if only he'd held his bloody temper. Slipping his hand into his pocket, Luca wrapped his fingers around the memory stick. He may have thoroughly hated himself for the night's work, but at least he wasn't walking away empty-handed.

Shadowmen

more out of her. He would have if only he'd held his bloody temper. Slipping his hand into his pocket, Luca wrapped his fingers around the memory stick. He may have thoroughly hated himself for the night's work, but at least he wasn't walking away empty-handed.

How like a winter hath my absence been

From thee, the pleasure a fleeting year!

Sonnet 97

by Wiliam Shakespeare

Chapter 2

Kirie

I'd never liked winter. The increased space between the sun and earth always left my body feeling colder, more run-down. I wrapped my jacket tighter to my body and lifted my face to the slanted sunlight peeking over the skyline. I soaked in its weakened rays and thought of spring. It was March, so brighter days were only weeks away. A slight warmth blossomed in my chest, and I held onto it.

A lone snowflake floated lazily down from the sky and landed on my cheek, melting almost instantly. Unbidden, the image of my mother standing in the falling snow outside our two-story home in Colorado filled my mind. She was smiling at me, her hazel eyes so bright and full of life, and the familiar stab of grief pierced through my center.

I wrapped the end of my long braid that lay over my shoulder around my palm. I never left it down anymore; it got in the way of training, but I couldn't bring myself to cut it. It reminded me of my mom's hair, a shared trait that somehow made me feel closer to her. With each passing day, the sting of her murder lessened slightly, but it was like a scar, an inseparable part of who I'd become.

After the Paris bombing, all surviving Society members were whisked away to various Centers across the globe for safety. My fellow students and I were sent to Rome for further training. Arin, Alena, and all other fully trained Agents of Light (including Luca, I assumed) were put on "active duty" after the attack, which meant they were shadow-hunting. I didn't quite know what that consisted of, but I could make an educated guess. The thought left an ashy taste in my mouth.

"Hurry *up*, Kirie!" the tiny girl with an angry, scrunched-up face yelled back at me. Her arms pumped wildly as she sped-walked ahead of me through St. Petersburg Cathedral's crowded courtyard. "If we're late for class, I'm telling Bert it's *your* fault!"

Aonani and her mother lived in the same apartment building as I did in downtown Rome, so the little monster and I rode together to The Center every day for training. The Society put me up in a one-bedroom flat with a minuscule kitchen. A far cry from the one in Paris. It was small, clean, and unlike Alena's Paris flat in every way. It was also generally quiet . . . with one tiny, black-haired exception.

Every Sunday afternoon, Aonani would knock on my door with a board game in hand. "Play with me, Kirie," she'd demand. "I'm bored, and Mommy said she needs a break." I could understand why. Aonani always wanted to play games, and she played to *win*. I let her because it was better than the alternative. Nothing was scarier than a tiny Hawaiian Agent of Light throwing a fit.

"Ok, Aonani. I'm coming," I sighed good-naturedly. I followed in her wake. She was a minnow carving a path through a school of trout.

Centuries ago, the Rome Center of Light was located in an annex attached to St. Peter's Cathedral, but with the crowds of visitors numbering in the thousands each day, the Society relocated the Center underground.

As Aonani and I wound past the long line of people waiting in front of the stately entry and made our way over to the secret side entrance, I prepared to see Bert. No matter how hard I'd tried to make my French trainer happy, nothing I ever did was good enough for him. All my life I'd prided myself on being a good student. I was your typical teacher's pet. It was what made me . . . well me. Disappointing a teacher made me question my very identity. I actually hated Bert a little for it.

We stood before the discrete security keypad set into the cream stone wall, and Aonani pressed her ID against its smooth surface. The light turned green, and the nearly invisible door popped open with a soft hiss.

"Watch out," Aonani said. I held the door open as she elbowed her way past me. She bounced down the short hallway that was lined with security guards dressed in black. Each had discrete bulges on their hips that I knew to be firearms. Ever since the attack on the Paris Center of Light, security had tripled at all the other locations around the world. Bert said it wasn't a matter of *if* the Shadowmen attacked again but *when*.

All the underaged trainees, like Aonani and me, were training double time in response to the increased threat, hence the dark circles under my eyes. The Society was expecting a wider-range attack soon and wanted everyone to be ready. I wanted to be ready, too, but my thighs and biceps wanted a day off.

Aonani stopped at the elevator and began pushing the call button over and over. As it descended, she sang a Disney song in her tiny Tinker Bell voice. She may be able to kill a person ninety-nine different ways, but she was still a little girl. The elevator arrived, and we climbed in.

The subterranean complex felt much like a large office building with marble floors, twenty-foot ceilings, and a honeycomb of hallways and meeting rooms. I still got a thrill every time the elevator doors opened to the central hub. The power-filled room lay directly beneath St. Peter's Chapel and was similar to the War Room in Paris, full of energy and advanced technology. However, unlike the ultra-modern version in Paris, this command center had a more artistic, lived-in vibe. It felt as if it could be Leonardo Da Vinci's living room if Da Vinci had been a futuristic war general.

Filling the open space were priceless pieces of Renaissance

paintings and furniture. And like the stately building above us, frescos were painted onto artistically domed ceilings. I wondered if the artist of each was one and the same. Despite the old-world décor, the ultra-advanced tech filling the room would still amaze and confound any Silicon Valley billionaire.

To simulate natural light for regeneration, The Society developed special light bulbs that mimicked the sun's rays. The lights were placed behind faux windows that not only made the building feel like it was above ground but also replenished Agents of Light's energy. I had to confess, even I forgot we were underground.

"Bonjour," Aaron called from the reception desk as we stepped off the elevator. Aaron had been another transplant from Paris. I often wondered what happened to the previous receptionist who had occupied the position before the Paris bombing. Never daring to ask, I simply smiled and waved politely as we continued on.

Like always, the War Room was a beehive of activity. I searched for any signs of urgency or distress on the agents' faces, but thankfully it was business as usual. For now. It was only a matter of time before that changed. The thought of another attack—one *underground*—made me shudder.

Aonani skipped in front of me down the long hallway leading to the training room like we were going to church. She happily danced through the frosted glass doors without a thought, but I had to take a deep breath before following her in. The training room still horrified me a little. I never truly felt comfortable being surrounded by walls lined with lethal weapons.

"Kirie! Aonani! Tu es presque en retard!" Bert yelled as I walked through the door. Bert still demanded that we speak only French during training sessions despite the fact that we were no longer in Paris. He refused to speak any other language, though I knew he must be fluent in many.

"Je m'excuse," I apologized with a low bow. It didn't matter that I *wasn't* late; I would always fall short of his incredibly high expectations. I used to wonder if there was anything I could do right in Bert's eyes, but I quickly learned to apologize and try harder.

The whole crew was there, lined up by height. Eden whispered "bludger" to me in her Australian accent as I took my spot next to her. Not knowing what bludger meant, I just shrugged it off. I could handle Eden. She had a long way to go to be as mean as Alena. Plus, I found her desperate efforts to become our instructor's favorite student entertaining. Bert didn't play favorites, so all her perfect aim, eye batting, and hair-flipping were in vain.

Dawn, the tallest in the group at 6'1", stood at the end of the line. As we began the warm-up stretches, I looked back and waved good morning to her. She gave me a warm smile before closing her eyes and following Bert's commands on point. Her movements were like a perfectly synchronized symphony. I sighed in envy. My body had grown stronger since my training began, but I had a long way to go to catch up with my younger classmates.

"Plus rapide!" Bert barked at the group as we ran through our warm-up exercises, a mixture of kickboxing and taekwondo. Each of us nodded and pushed harder. Sweat dripped down my face and into the corners of my eyes, making them sting from the salt. *You can do this.* Positive affirmations had become my best friends.

After the warm-up, we ran through the usual self-defense drills before splitting up to work on our specialties. Eden headed straight for her bow and arrow. Dayton and Dawn favored the bayonets and Aonani had a talent for explosives. I dragged my feet toward the throwing knives, carefully avoiding Liang as he did a complicated dance with his longsword.

When I first started training, Bert had me try every weapon in the room. Ironically, I immediately showed a talent for knife-throwing. Despite the hours of drills, though, the image of Donovan's knife sliding across my mother's throat filled my mind every time I picked one up. I didn't see that changing any time soon . . . if ever.

After our morning sessions, the younger students rode to a nearby private school together and would return for our afternoon training. I stayed back and worked one-on-one with Bert. I envied my younger classmates for their ability to attend school, and not just because they got a break from my overbearing instructor. I missed *learning*.

Last fall, Abbott contacted the principal at my high school in Colorado who agreed to let me graduate early. He could hardly argue with Abbott's request since I had a 4.5 GPA and more than enough credits to graduate. Since then, I'd received several acceptance letters from Ivy League universities worldwide. Now, it was simply a matter of choosing a school–likely one near a Center of Light–and waiting for the fall semester to start.

Waiting and training.

Every day.

All day.

I also missed having the time and freedom to study biophotonics with Parisxxxi8. It had been my obsession before my world fell apart and reformed itself into a mess of shadowy stalkers and knife-throwing practice. It wasn't that I didn't think it was cool to have great reflexes and move faster than any normal person could. It was just…there was so much more I wanted to do with the light inside me than learn to decapitate a man twice my size.

Bert *insisted* that I train eight hours a day, seven days a week, so I could catch up with the rest of the group since I started so late. According to Society standards, I was practically an old lady at age seventeen, at least when it came to combat training. In any other situation, I may have been considered too old for training. But, somehow, I had become a priority . . . an exception.

"Encore!" Bert snapped.

I pulled my hand back and brought it forward, rotating at the waist like he taught me. The dagger sang across the training room and sunk into the target with a low thunk. I missed the center by two inches.

"Pas bien." *No good.* "Encore!" He told me this at least ten times every hour.

I held back a groan. My shoulder muscles screamed for rest. "Oui, Maitre Bert," I said dutifully. Any other response would have earned me extra time with the knives.

We moved on to strength training, followed by speed and agility training, a never-ending cycle of torture. I'd never been a prisoner of war, but I'd imagined it felt something like this. Strangely, I'd learned very little about my Light ability since coming to the Rome Center of *Light* three months prior. Bert said I would eventually be assigned a special Light tutor and to shut up and be patient, so I stopped asking about it.

When our combined afternoon training was blessedly done, I met my bodyguard/driver at the curb outside of the cathedral, and he drove me back to my apartment. Jaques, an over-muscled, middle-aged bald man with tattoos snaking up his neck, was my constant shadow. He wasn't nearly as scary as he appeared, and I even enjoyed his company occasionally. Still, I craved my independence.

It had taken weeks to convince Jaques that I could walk up to my building from the car alone without getting attacked by a Shadow. Even then, he waited faithfully at the curb until I came back down the next morning. Every. Single. Day.

We pulled up to my building and I waited for Jacques to search the area before giving me clearance to exit the car. I thought it was ridiculous. There was no way the Shadowmen had followed us to Rome. The Society had made sure to take extra precautions. But I didn't complain to Jaques since it wasn't *his* fault he was stuck babysitting me.

In my apartment, I sat in the middle of my bed, logged onto my usual medical chat board, and checked my messages. Parisxxxi8 and I stayed in touch after the science project we'd been working on in the fall went bust. But my science chat board friend had been MIA for a whole week, the longest he'd gone without messaging me back, and I worried that I'd said something wrong and chased him away. I opened my inbox and smiled at the new message from him. Finally.

> Parisxxxi8: Sorry for the delay, Luv. I've been out of town on holiday.

> Brightgirl101: No worries. Did you get to lie on a sun-filled beach at least? I hear sunlight can be very rejuvenating.

My heart got up and sprinted out of my chest when three little blinking dots appeared in the message box indicating he was writing.

> Parisxxxi8: That it can. Actually, I was in the States for a few days. It made me think of you.

My hands hesitated over the keyboard. Though many of our conversations still focused on the latest scientific developments in biophotonics, they'd gotten a bit more personal in the past few weeks. After I lost everything in Colorado, and then again in Paris, he'd become my best and only friend, one of my last connections to my old life. Still, I didn't want to ruin our relationship by getting too personal.

> Brightgirl101: I thought of you, too.

I regretted my response the moment I hit the enter key. So cringy.

> Parisxxxi8: I'm honored. Things have been bananas at work lately. Our little chats have kept me going.

He had no idea. I put a hand over my mouth, wiping away the grin that had blossomed on my lips. I reminded myself, not for the first time, that Paris could be a fifty-year-old pervert living on his mother's couch. I didn't even know his real name. I just couldn't quite convince myself, though.

> Brightgirl101: Want to talk about it?

> Parisxxxi8: I'd rather put my hand in a blender, thank you. Let's talk about you. Have you given any more thought to recreating your X-ray machine? An idea like that is worth revisiting, isn't it?

Paris had been pressuring me to recreate the one I broke at my high school science fair back in Colorado for several weeks. He was right, of course. My light-powered X-ray machine was worth recreating. I still believed in the work I'd been doing before the Shadowmen showed up and wrecked my life. I thought about asking Bert for a day off to work on it and instantly laughed out loud.

> Brightgirl101: I know. I know. I'm just too busy with schoolwork to think about another project. I'm exhausted.

I sighed, feeling a little guilty for the small lie. I wished I *had* been busy with schoolwork instead of battle training.

> Parisxxxi8: Don't forget to take time for yourself.

Brightgirl101: Not all of us can just take a holiday like you.

It must've been nice to get away from work for a while.

Did you do anything fun?

He was slow to respond, and I worried I'd been *too* sarcastic. When I saw he was typing again, I released a sigh.

Parisxxxi8: Let's just say it was an enlightening trip. I've got to run, but I'll check back in tomorrow. Night, Luv.

The happy bubble inside me deflated a little, and I cursed my sarcastic nature.

Brightgirl101: Oh. Okay. Thanks for letting me vent.

Parisxxxi8: At your service *tips hat

I inhaled deeply and snapped my laptop shut. Lying back onto my bed, I fell into an exhausted sleep.

Chapter 3

Luca

How **much longer** until you've broken through the encryption?" Luca asked. He hovered over a greasy-haired boy perched in front of a row of computer screens. Numbers and symbols flashed across the monitors in quick succession.

"Could be a week. Could be a month," the hacker said with a shrug as his skinny fingers danced across the keyboard.

"No good. I need it today," Luca said in a clipped tone.

"Dude, chill," he said, pausing to take a bite of a blueberry pop tart with sprinkles on top. Luca's lip curled in disgust. It was his fifth one that day. "This isn't your average Instagram password. Shit like this takes time."

"Well, make it take *less* time," Luca snapped. He loomed over the boy like a dark tower, eyeing the offensive excuse for a pastry as the hacker placed it back down on a thin paper plate.

The boy gave Luca side-eye before turning back to the row of screens. The artificial light reflected off his oily, unhealthy face. "Who'd you say you got this file from?" The boy feigned nonchalance as numbers and characters flashed across his face like a pimply disco.

"I didn't," Luca snapped, arms over his chest. The hacker pinched his lips.

Luca tapped his foot at an impatient tempo and studied the boy. He had spiky red hair that looked like it hadn't been washed in days, and the spatter of amber freckles across his long nose gave him the appearance of a child. He couldn't be older than sixteen.

The hacker shifted uneasily under Luca's heavy scrutiny. "Look, man, you might as well come back later. Hovering over me like a freaking vulture isn't going to make me work any faster."

"No thanks, mate. I think I'll wait right here." Luca planted his feet shoulder-width apart as if rooting himself to the stained concrete floor. He couldn't risk the hacker opening the file and seeing what was inside while he was gone.

"Dude, suit yourself," he said over his shoulder. "Just back off me. You're freaking me out."

Luca let out a deep sigh and reluctantly stepped back. He carefully lowered himself onto a green couch pressed against the gray cement wall that probably hadn't been cleaned since the seventies. The basement of the boy's mom's place was cold, dark, and damp—all the things Luca hated. He'd been down there with the young hacker for twelve hours straight, and he could already feel his energy waning from the lack of sunlight. There was no helping it though.

Luca leaned back and let his mind wonder, the creaking metal springs digging into his back. The mission in D.C. had left him shaken. He didn't like letting the darkness inside him dictate his actions. He'd been in control of it for years, and it irked him that he'd lost control. But that shadow had mentioned Kirie *by name*. She'd revealed that not only was The Order aware of Kirie's existence, but they also knew of the sheer magnitude of her power. The Shadowmen would not stop hunting her until she was dead. A cold fury had taken over and he'd lost himself, confirming what Donovan always said; Luca was irrevocably stained by darkness.

The night before, Luca had been able to download the files from the woman's computer onto a thumb drive before he fried it and left it in a molten mess in the hotel bin. But one of the files was heavily encrypted and beyond his hacking ability.

That morning, he'd found an internet café and searched the dark web for a high-level hacker. Surprisingly, the odorous teen over there came highly recommended. The little bugger was expensive too.

There were agents within The Society, of course, who could've easily broken the encryption faster than this boy could. If Arin had been there, it would've already been done. Luca knew he couldn't give the thumb drive to The Society. Not yet. For the past several months, he'd sensed something wasn't quite right within its ranks. The bombing in Paris had only confirmed his suspicions that there was a traitor hidden somewhere deep within The Society. Luca suspected that the information on the thumb drive could turn the tides of this godforsaken war, and he needed to know what it was before it got into the wrong hands.

Painfully long hours passed as he waited in the damp, cell-like basement. Luca left only to use the restroom and refuel his energy. It was well into the second day when the boy let out a whoop in celebration. Energy flared inside Luca as he sprang forward, hovering over the boy once more.

The hacker jumped out of his seat and backed away from Luca, wide-eyed. "Whoa! How'd you do that?"

Luca cursed himself silently. He hadn't meant to move so fast. "Do what, mate?"

"You *literally* flew across the room just now," he said, pointing at the empty couch.

"Maybe you should lay off the Red Bull, kid. You're going bonkers."

"Sure . . . whatever, man." The hacker watched him wearily as he pointed to the screens. "I, uh, broke through."

"Wonderful." Luca leaned toward the computer bank and reached for the thumb drive, but the boy knocked his hand away. A shadow rose in Luca, and he fought to tamp them down.

"Whoa, payment first," the hacker said.

"Of course," Luca said through gritted teeth. With a forced

slowness, he returned to the couch and reached into his black bag. He pulled out a thick stack of green bills. "Thirty thousand. All large bills as requested." Luca handed the stack of bills to the boy.

He flipped through the bills with a greedy smile on his face. "Yeah, about that." He hitched a thumb at his computer. "This encryption was deep-level shit, man. Cracking it took more effort than I'd expected."

The restless shadows responded to Luca's irritation. "What's your point, mate?"

"The price just went up." He slapped the stack against his palm. "It's going to cost you another $20K."

This kid has no idea who he was messing with. Unfortunately for the boy, his inner light was running low, leaving him susceptible to the darkness beneath the surface of his calm exterior. As if they could smell the boy's greed, dark tendrils began writhing under Luca's skin, begging for release. The lights started to dim, and a chill filled the air. He knew what the boy would see: dark eyes, shadowy whisps hugging Luca's tall frame. The boy's computer screens began to flicker on and off, and he almost felt bad for the little delinquent as terror filled his face. Almost.

With wide eyes, the boy backed away like hunted prey. "You know what? $30K is perfect." He turned to his computer and quickly removed the thumb drive, handing it to Luca with shaky fingers.

"Cheers, mate," Luca said with a sideways smile. He tucked the drive into his jeans pocket and touched the computer. The machine gave a pop and sizzle, and a string of foul words spewed from the boy's freckled lips as smoke curled up toward the popcorn ceiling.

Shadows surged inside Luca once more, and he knew he needed to get into the sun as soon as possible to re-energize his waning light. Without a backward glance, Luca slipped through the mildewed basement window and up through the spider-webbed window well.

It was late afternoon when Luca checked into a seedy hotel in small-town Virginia. It was a single-level establishment that looked and smelled of bad deeds. He sat at the small wooden desk next to a queen bed covered in a stiff, polyester cover that reeked of stale cigarettes and sausage breakfast muffins.

Luca opened his newly acquired computer and plugged the thumb drive containing the hacked files into the USB slot. He clicked open the hacked file, ignoring the others. There were several folders within the file. The first one contained a road map and black-and-white pictures of a rolling desert. The labels and defining characteristics on the map had all been redacted, with no signs or labels on any of the photos.

Luca closed the file and moved to the next. This file was a bit more interesting. It contained copies of emails to and from various high-ranking government officials on the United Nations Security Council. They were all addressed to the same recipient: "UNKNOWN." He opened the first email, which was dated April 2, 2015.

TO: UNKNOWN

FROM: karrighan.john@us.gov

SUBJECT: None

All went as planned. The framework has been laid. I did as you asked. Now it's your turn.

John K.

United States of America

Secretary of State

The next one was dated July 10, 2015, just days before the United Nations Security Council had signed a comprehensive agreement on the Iranian nuclear program in Vienna.

Luca vividly remembered watching the news as the controversial deal had been made. Of course, The Society had long been suspicious of Iran's nuclear ambitions since darkness often thrived within totalitarian and theological governments. They'd searched for signs of Shadow's involvement in the deal, but none had been found. Yet.

The next email was from an Italian representative.

TO: UNKNOWN

FROM: d.maughn@esteri.it

SUBJECT: None

It took some convincing, but France is on board.

Where is the proof of life you promised?

Dominica M.

High Representative of the Union for Foreign Affairs and Security Policy

There were dozens of similar emails. Each country in the alliance was represented. As the dates progressed, the emails became increasingly more desperate. Someone, presumably the unknown recipient of these letters, was holding something over each of these dignitaries, and it all led back to the Iranian nuclear deal. Luca sat back, trying to understand it all. On the surface, it didn't make sense. The primary purpose behind the uranium deal was to impose more regulations on their nuclear production, not leave it open for more.

Luca moved on to the third file. It contained pictures and nothing else. The first picture was of a modern mine shaft. Again, there were no defining details. It could've been any mine in the world. The next several photos showed a large, cavernous room full of unmarked crates--whole stockpiles of crates. Vexation churned like sour milk in Luca's stomach as he thought of the many things that could be in those crates. Yet, there was still nothing in any of the photos to indicate *where* or *when* they were taken.

The fourth file contained just one image: a map of the world. Big red dots littered its surface. London, Paris, New York, Mumbai, Tokyo—every major city in every country worldwide held the ominous red mark. Luca sat back in the creaky wooden chair and placed his hands over his face as all the pieces clicked together in his mind. The mines, the stockpiles, the emails, and bad deals . . . all of it began to paint one horrible picture in his mind. Bile rose to his throat. It was a strike plan.

Luca pulled his phone from his pocket and called Abbott. He answered on the second ring.

"We need to talk right away."

"I'm not in a secure location," Abbott replied in a low voice. Luca knew that meant Abbott was within hearing distance of people he didn't fully trust.

"Understood. Meet me at our rendezvous spot. Tomorrow at noon."

"I'll be there," Abbott whispered. He paused for a moment. "Luca, they're wondering why you haven't checked in yet. You need to be debriefed. If you wait any longer, it will only make them more suspicious of you."

The Society knew all about his time with Donovan. He'd had to recount every gruesome detail after Abbott had recovered him in London all those years ago. Ultimately, they'd accepted him into The Society—with reservations. Though he'd shown "great promise," some within The Society still didn't fully trust him. Daiko had been watching him closely for years. And Luca had been watching *him* right back.

"I need you to check in for me. Tell them the mission was unsuccessful. Tell them the shadow attacked me, and I had to neutralize it. Tell them I was injured in the process and was unable to recover any useful information."

Abbott sighed on the other end of the phone. "That isn't going to satisfy them for long. You need to come in, Luca. Soon."

Luca squeezed his eyes shut and pinched the bridge of his nose between two fingers. "I can't just yet. I'll explain everything tomorrow."

"Fine." Abbott sighed again. "Tomorrow."

The line went dead and Luca dropped the phone on the table. As he began closing the files, Luca noticed he'd overlooked one. It contained a single email. Like the others, this one was sent to the same "unknown" email account. The sender, however, was a mystery as well, and although the body of the email contained few words, Luca felt each one like a knife to his heart.

TO: UNKNOWN
FROM: *restricted*
SUBJECT: None

Upper-level, Pantheon
Do it before 6 AM

Luca looked at the date. It was sent on the same day The Paris

Center of Light was bombed. Bile rose in his throat. Someone had revealed the Center's location. Who? His fingers flew across the keyboard as he traced the email's origin. Ten minutes later, he slumped back in his seat. The email came from inside The Paris Center of Light itself.

Chapter 4

Kirie

"**Bien,**" **Bert called** out. He was met with a chorus of relieved sighs and groans. By the time Bert finally excused us for the night, it was later than usual. My eyes blurred as I gathered my things in my black duffle bag and traded my training shoes for ballet flats.

As I zipped up my duffle bag, my thoughts strayed to my life back home in Colorado, as they often did. At that very moment, my old friends were probably shopping for prom dresses and looking forward to graduation. I pictured Rylie and the kids I'd gone to school with all my life walking across the stage on graduation day. The hole inside me left behind after my parents' murders widened slightly at the thought.

I'd been *that* student my entire life—the one who was more

excited about graduation than senior ditch day, parties, or school dances. Graduation was an important milestone. For years, I'd envisioned myself on stage in a cap and gown with an acceptance letter to Harvard in my back pocket. And in that vision, my parents would be there cheering me on in the audience.

This list of things that Donovan had stolen from me continued to grow. I shivered as his scarred face filled my mind, unbidden and unwanted. His flat, dark eyes were always there when I closed mine, a constant reminder of the dark things that hunted me.

Aonani left with her mom as the rest of us packed up our gear for the night. Eden, Dawn, Liang, and Dayton stood grouped near the door. Dawn waved me over, and I paused momentarily before joining them.

"We're going to dinner," she said in her deep Zimbabwean accent. "Would you like to come with us?" I'd come to love Dawn. Being near her made me feel warm and peaceful, like lying in the sun. Eden, on the other hand . . .

Dayton stood next to Liang, and the two pulled out their phones and texted each other stupid GIF videos. They peered over each other's shoulders and laughed at their comedic geniuses. Brilliant Agents of Light or not, pre-teen boys would be pre-teen boys.

Dayton glanced up from his phone and smiled at me. "Yeah, Kir, you should come with us. It'll be awesome."

It had been a long time since I'd gone out. Bert had ensured that I was either too busy or in too much pain to have anything resembling fun since coming to Rome. The old Kirie would've pulled her hair over her face and made some excuse to stay in. But I wasn't that girl anymore. I'd grown comfortable with my younger classmates; I even *liked* being in their company. Well, most of them.

"I'll have to bring Jaques," I said with a shrug. "But, I'm game."

"I'm okay with that," Eden said a bit too quickly. I suppressed an eye roll. The young girl had a thing for older men, it appeared. She was trouble with a capital "T."

"What kind of food are you guys thinking?" I asked.

"Pizza. What else?" Eden said sarcastically. Since her first day in Rome, Eden had become obsessed with Italian pizza.

"Kirie, attends une minute," Bert called out to me. The boys raised their eyebrows at me and dramatically oohed as if I were being called to the principal's office. I groaned softly, hoping that Bert couldn't hear.

"You're being summoned, Your Highness," Eden said. Sarcasm dripped off her words like poison from fangs. She threw her gym bag over one slim shoulder and stalked out the door.

Clearly, she wanted it to be *her* name Bert had called. I wanted that, too. I'd just spent the entire day being tortured by the man, and my body hurt from my head down to my pinky toes, but saying no to Bert would be stupid and suicidal. So.

"You guys go on," I sighed. "I'll catch up with you."

"Cool. I'll text you the location." Dayton said, barely looking up from his phone.

Dawn gave me a sad smile, and Liang smacked me on the

shoulder. "Catch you later," he said with a Mandarin lilt. "Good luck." On his way out with the others, he threw me a peace sign. I waved to their backs and turned to meet Bert in the middle of the room.

"Oui, Masteur Bert," I responded, bowing.

"Votre nouvel instructeur lumiere est arrive," he informed me. My heart jumped in my chest. I'd been assigned a Light Trainer! Finally, I was going to do something other than training how to kill a person. Before I could think, I clapped my hands together and bounced on my toes like an excited toddler. At Bert's stern expression, I cleared my throat and put my traitorous hands behind my back. Heat flushed my face, scorching my fair cheeks.

"Vous devez le rencontrer dans salle de conférence un dans dix minutes." *You're to meet him in Conference Room One in ten minutes.*

"Oui, Masteur Bert," I said, trying to hide my excitement and completely forgetting any thoughts of dinner.

"Bien. Vous êtes excuse." He waved me off with his hand as though I was nothing but vermin. As I ran out of the room, though, I looked back and saw the hint of a smile on his face.

Finding the right conference room amongst the others in the vast subterranean complex took several minutes. Finally, I found a door plaque with "Conference Room 1" written in Italian. I pushed on the brass handle of the heavy wood door and stepped inside. In the center of the elongated rectangular room, a long table with a white marble top sat surrounded by dark brown leather rolling chairs. A faux window at the far end displayed a realistic picture of a Roman setting sun.

I must've arrived early because the room was empty. Feeling slightly awkward, I sat in one of the leather chairs and waited. A clock on the wall ticked loudly in the silence, punctuating each second with an exclamation point. It was five long minutes before the door handle turned, and a middle-aged man walked into the room.

His commanding presence instantly struck me, though nothing about his appearance screamed power. He wore a light-colored linen shirt over loose slacks. His blond hair, the color of corn husks, hung in waves across his forehead, and his bright blue eyes were striking against his tan skin. His attire was effortlessly casual in an expensive sort of way, giving him the look of a wealthy Italian vineyard owner on his day off.

I took a fortifying breath and slowly stood to greet him. When I moved forward and raised a hand to him, his eyes widened, and he stepped back. He stared at me like I was an apparition coming to life, his tan face draining of color. He clutched a hand to his chest, bunching the fabric of his shirt in his fist.

I rushed forward with my arms out, suddenly concerned for the older man's health. "Sir, are . . . are you OK?" I asked.

He blinked rapidly. "Pardon me. You just . . . you look like someone I used to know."

"Oh . . ." I said lamely, unsure what else to say.

He smoothed the front of his shirt and cleared his throat. "Please pardon my rudeness. Let's begin again." He raised his hand to shake mine. "My name is Finn Bellamy."

When our hands met, a low hum of energy passed between us. It was warm and strangely familiar. I dropped his hand, feeling even more confused.

"I'm one of the leaders of The Society. I believe you've already met my colleague, Mr. Daiko." I shrank back from both his stare and the mention of *that* man's name. I hadn't seen Mr. Daiko since that first day at the Paris Center of Light. My stomach soured at the thought of that unpleasant meeting.

"Um, yeah. I have," I say, feeling wary, fearing Mr. Bellamy would be like Mr. Daiko in his methods. "You aren't going to do that mind probe thing on me again, are you?" I folded my arm over my chest in defiance. I would never let anyone do *that* to me again.

He put his hands out in front of him as if to pacify me. "Oh, no. Of course not. I have no need to. If Abbott says you are trustworthy, that's good enough for me."

"Well, Mr. Daiko must not have felt the same way." I let sarcasm spill into every word. I was still angry and sickened by the older man's rape of my thoughts and memories.

Mr. Bellamy continued good-naturedly as though he hadn't caught my tone. "Mr. Daiko and I govern The Society, so to speak, along with a woman named Ellen Delgado. She and Mr. Daiko are still in Paris dealing with the fallout from the bombing, so I've offered to see to your Inner Light training."

"Really?" I said, taken back. "Why you?"

He gave an easy laugh. "Would you prefer someone else?"

"Oh no! Sorry. I meant . . . well, you're the leader of one of the world's oldest and most powerful organizations. Do you usually tutor new members like me?"

"Well, Kirie, to put it bluntly, no. I don't. We have full-time Light Instructors for that purpose. However, you're a special case. From what I understand, your light is unique. I'm here because some see great potential in you."

"Why me?" I asked.

"Why not you?" he asked. I had no answer to that. He continued, "From what I understand, Mr. Abbott has taught you a bit about the War Scrolls, am I correct?" I nodded *yes*. "Good. You might remember, then, that the scroll speaks of seven great battles between the Children of Light and the Children of Darkness."

"Yes. Each side wins three battles, and the Light wins the seventh."

He nodded. "Exactly. Then you'll remember that the scroll also prophecies that during the last and final war—the one that decides the world's fate—those with special abilities will emerge on both sides to aid in the fight."

I thought back on Luca and his miraculous capabilities to heal and Ciara's ability to suck the life out of your very being with her black eyes. I shuddered. I knew just what he meant. "People who can harness the powers of light and darkness and use them as weapons. People like us." I motioned between the two of us. "But haven't people like us always existed? Aren't we *all* the prophesized ones?"

Mr. Bellamy nodded his head. "Agents of Light and Darkness alike have been on the Earth since it was formed, and all have held some level of power. The battles between the two have been long fought. In the final hour, a very limited group of *truly* gifted people will emerge to tip the scales. People with abilities far beyond anything the world has ever seen before."

"And you think *I'm* one of those people?"

"Maybe," he said, searching my face again. "To be honest, I'm not quite sure. What I *do* know for certain is that the Shadowmen believe you are." Mr. Bellamy looked at me with a somber expression. "Kirie, if indeed you're one of these special cases, you, and the very few like you, will play a key role in the rise or fall of Darkness on the earth."

The power of his words ran deep through my core. Its truthfulness burned inside me like a flare in the night. I'd felt the same conviction that day in the Paris coffee shop when Abbott told me who I truly was. I exhaled, releasing some of the heavy emotion pulsating inside me. "Okay. No pressure."

Mr. Bellamy laughed lightly. "Don't worry. I'm here to teach you how to use your light to defend yourself and those around you. I have no doubt you'll do well." Mr. Bellamy motioned toward the table. "Shall we get started?"

"Of course, Mr. Bellamy," I said, feigning confidence. I walked to the nearest chair and sat down. He took the one on the other side.

I studied Mr. Bellamy from across the table, searching for an ulterior motive or duplicity. Though he didn't *seem* creepy like Mr. Daiko, I still wasn't ready to trust him on sight.

"First, please call me Finn. Mr. Bellamy makes me feel old. Now, I want you to put your hands on the table, palms up," he instructed, placing his palms on the table as an example.

I laid the backs of my hands onto the cool marble top. Goosebumps spread across my skin, and I repressed a shiver. "Good. Now, I want you to close your eyes and envision a happy image. Something that makes you feel warm and safe. It could be a sunny beach, a favorite food, or the embrace of a loved one." His voice took on a slow, rich tone like dripping honey. "Hold that image in your mind and let its warmth surround you. Let it seep into your skin. Feel the energy of that light, like a living soul."

I fought the urge to open my eyes and searched for the warmest thought I could pull from. Instantly, my mother's face came to mind. Thinking of her beautiful face hurt in a bittersweet way. I imagined that her never-ending love and devotion were a blanket covering me, keeping me protected and warm. Energy began to spread through my limbs. My skin grew hot, warming the stone marble beneath my outstretched arms.

"Good. Now imagine pulling that feeling into yourself, directing it toward your chest."

I imagined embracing the blanket against my heart, and the energy responded readily, traveling from my limbs to my torso. I imagined my mother's smell, a mixture of vanilla perfume and laundry detergent. In my mind, I held her to my chest, soaking in her warmth. The heat in my chest grew stronger until it became a living thing inside me. It grew quickly. Too quickly. Soon, it pressed insistently against my ribs, like a caged animal begging for release. Within moments, it was too much to contain.

I cried out as if in pain. As if from a distance, I heard Finn call my name. I tried to hold it in, but my control slipped, and I felt the energy burst free from my chest. My eyes flew open, and Finn cried out. Brilliant light brighter than the noonday sun filled the room, chasing away even the most minute shadows from their corners.

Finn stared at me with wide, incredulous eyes. He'd moved several feet from the table, whether from awe or fear, I couldn't tell.

"Incredible," he breathed.

The space around us ebbed and flowed with pulsating light as though inhaling and exhaling. I gazed down at my normally pale skin, now shining like gold, reflecting sunshine, and rubbed my arms as if I could wipe the golden light away, but the raw energy remained. I stared at Finn in panic, feeling completely out of control.

He held his hands out. "Kirie," Finn said with a slight tremor in his voice. "You're alright. Try to take a deep breath. Breathe in from your nose and out through your mouth."

I did as he said.

Breathe in.

Breathe out.

Breathe in.

Breathe out.

After a few moments, the light dimmed and my erratic heart rate slowed. The warmth in my chest slowly diminished until it was just a feathery touch.

Finn cleared his throat. "Well, that was . . . *enlightening*. Excuse my pun." His light laugh contrasted with the tension around his mouth and eyes. I was unsure of what to say, so I stayed silent.

He studied my face with friendly curiosity before asking, "If you don't mind my asking, what were you thinking about? It must've been something very important to you for you to produce that level of response."

Tears filled my eyes, the emotion still raw. I whispered, "I thought of my mom." I looked down at my hands still outstretched on the table and pulled them into my lap, feeling suddenly cold.

Finn cleared his throat. "Yes. Abbott told me about the loss of your parents. I'm sorry you had to go through that. Do you mind telling me what they were like?"

I gave a short kind of laugh. "My mom was your typical helicopter parent." I rolled my eyes. Instantly, I felt bad for the jab, true or not. "She was beautiful. And kind, too. Everybody loved her." A tear escaped from the corner of my eye and traveled down my heated cheek, evaporating quickly. "I was lucky to have her."

Seemingly uncomfortable with my tears, Finn shifted in his seat and asked about my father.

"Barry?" I said, wiping my eyes. "He was just my stepdad. We weren't super close, but he loved my mom—a lot. So," I shrugged my shoulders as if that was answer enough.

Finn peered down at his own hands on the table and asked, "And your birth father?"

"He died before I was born," I said, shrugging again. "I don't know his name, but I think he was an Agent of Light like us."

I thought of the letter my mother wrote to me before she'd died, still sitting on my bedside table back at home. It was the first and only time Mom had acknowledged my power. She'd come clean about how my father hadn't died from cancer and how he had power over light like me.

Since coming to Rome, I'd wondered if my father had trained here, too, and if, as a boy, he walked the same halls I did every day. It was a ridiculous notion. I'd never met the man and knew nothing about him beyond what Mom had written in that letter. Yet, I couldn't help but look for his ghost in the people and spaces around me.

Finn stood. "Well, I can honestly say the rumors were not exaggerated. Given your magnitude of power, I believe we should start each lesson with mind exercises meant to teach you control. We'll begin each night after you finish with Bert."

I nodded, half excited to finally gain control of my power and half exhausted just thinking of the extra hours of training. "Finn?" I began.

Finn "Yes, Kirie?"

"There's something about what we do here that I just can't

work out in my mind."

"Yes?" He raised his eyebrows in question.

"If the Society of Light is all about freedom and enlightenment, why are they training us to fight with axes and assault rifles? Doesn't hand-to-hand combat take us back in evolution, not forward? Aren't we . . . I don't know . . . sinking to their level?"

Finn sighed and sat back in the leather chair. "In theory, you're right. In an ideal world, the Shadowmen wouldn't exist, and we wouldn't have to fight them at every corner. But they do, and we do." Finn sighed again and looked down at his folded hands resting on his lap. "We're at war, Kirie. Ignoring the fact and holding tight to our lofty ideals of enlightenment and peace will only ensure our defeat. When we win this final war, when the shadows have been vanquished, we'll be free to build the society you imagine. But until then, we fight with *all* the tools in our arsenal."

My chest tightened. Ever since I was little, I wanted to make the world a better place with my scientific discoveries. I wasn't made to be a fighter. Killing Cole after he attacked me tore me up inside. It didn't matter that it was in self-defense or that I hadn't meant to stab him with his own knife. His blood would forever be on my hands.

"What if I'm not meant to fight? What if, when the time comes, I'm unable to pull the trigger, so to speak?"

Finn nodded thoughtfully. "There was a time when I felt as you do. I wanted to marry, get a job, have a few kids . . . live a normal life. None of us asked for this war, yet we can't escape it. Believe me, I tried. The Order will not stop until all light in the world is extinguished and darkness reigns once more. The Shadowmen will not rest until we're all dead. There's nowhere you can hide where they can't find you. Your light cannot be hidden."

Those words . . . they were strikingly similar to the ones spoken by the voice in my dreams. A cold shiver raced down my back.

"Well," he finally said, somewhat abruptly, "I won't keep you any longer tonight. We'll begin again tomorrow." He led me to the door and held it open. "Good night, Kirie," Finn said and disappeared back into the conference room.

Chapter 5

Kirie

Aonani and I arrived early at the training center the next day at her insistence. She wanted extra time to work on the throwing stars before Bert arrived. To her great irritation, he'd insisted she was more suited to blowing things up than throwing sharp objects.

"Nobody puts Baby in a corner," she'd said that morning at my door, fists on hips. I doubted she even knew the origin of her quoted proclamation, but I agreed to go with her all the same.

I brought my laptop and quietly read the latest reports on light therapy while Aonani threw razor-sharp stars at a moving target along the practice wall. Dayton was the first to arrive for class.

"What happened to you last night?" he asked. He set down his gym bag and began stretching his arms and legs, swinging them wildly.

"Sorry. I forgot to text you that I couldn't meet up. I had my first light lesson last night." I couldn't help but say it with a smile.

"Soooooo, they finally got you a tutor?" he asked, one arm stretched over his chest. I nodded. "Who is it? Hammond? Ashland? Perez?"

"Hey!" Aonani said, anger etched into her tiny, brown face. "Why didn't you tell me you got a tutor? Huh?"

I considered lying about the whole thing. Clearly, having one of the leaders of the Society as my trainer wasn't standard procedure. It wasn't going to win me any brownie points with my classmates. Eden already thought I received special treatment, and that was a badger hole I did *not* want to crawl down.

"No, actually. His name is Finn," I said, opting for his first name to throw him off.

A look of confusion crossed Dayton's round face. "Finn? I've never heard of a Light Trainer named Finn."

Liang entered the room and set his bag on the floor next to Dayton's. Dayton looked back at him and called, "Hey, Kirie's got a new Light Tutor. His name is Finn. Ever heard of him?"

Liang shook his head. "Is he new?"

"No. I'm pretty sure he's been around a while," I replied, averting my eyes.

Dayton cocked his head to the side. "Really? Where's he from?"

I thought back on our meeting. I'd detected no accent in his voice the night before. "I think he's from the States." I shrugged.

"I didn't ask."

Aonani began collecting her throwing stars from the wall. "Is Finn his last name?"

I shrugged again and bent down to tie one of my training shoes. From the corner of my eye, I saw Dawn and Eden walk in.

"What are you blokes going on about?" Eden drawled, throwing her training bag into the ever-growing pile. Next to her, Dawn began kicking off her street shoes.

"Kirie's got a new Light Tutor. We're trying to figure out who he is," Dayton said.

"What is his name, Kirie?" Dawn asked in her deep, calm waters voice. She sat down on the floor and began stretching.

"She says his name's Finn, but I've never heard of the guy," Dayton said for me. I began tying my other shoe, head down.

Eden folded her arms over her chest and popped her hip to one side. "I've never heard of a tutor named Finn. Are you sure you didn't get his name wrong?"

"Pretty sure," I replied.

Having tied both shoes thoroughly, I reluctantly stood and faced the group.

"Perhaps Finn's a nickname," Liang offered. He flipped a pair of long swords behind his back. "What's his last name?"

"Um, Bellamy," I said quietly, hoping my voice wouldn't carry. Liang's swords stilled midair.

It was like an EMP had gone off in the room. Complete radio silence.

"Wait!" Dayton put his hands up, shattering the silence. "You mean to tell me that Mr. Finn Bellamy, leader of the entire Society of Light, is *your* Light Tutor."

"Wicked!" Liang said with an excited smile.

Eden dropped her arms and glared at me. "You're such a liar, Kirie. Mr. Bellamy doesn't have time to train aged-out newbies like you."

I sighed. "Believe what you want Eden. It doesn't really matter to me."

"Dude!" Dayton hooted and bounced on the tips of his toes like a bird on a powerline. "What's he like? Does he look like Superman? I hear he can fly!"

"Shut up, grub," snarled Eden, turning on Dayton. "Kirie's just lying to get attention." She turned back and leveled me with a red-hot glare. The literal heat of it bent the light around her like a desert mirage. I stepped back, feeling the threat in her surging energy. "Like you don't get enough attention already."

"Ladies, ladies! You're both pretty," Dayton said. Liang continued twirling a pair of long swords in front and behind himself, apparently enjoying the show.

"I honestly don't have time for your jealousy, Eden," I said with a sigh.

I didn't see it coming. One moment, Eden stood several feet away, and the next she hurtled toward me. Before I could react, she knocked me to the ground. I rolled away from her before she could gain the upper hand. Dawn called out Eden's name in warning, but the hellcat was past reason.

"I am NOT jealous!" She spit the words at me like a cobra.

I rolled to my feet as Eden blurred toward me again. I spun away from her forward movement, only barely dodging a roundhouse kick to my stomach. Eden was fast, but so was I. Using the defensive techniques Bert had taught me, I deflected her onslaught of fists and kicks. I blocked her leg just before it made contact with my skull and failed to see her right fist before it collided with my ribs. The air rushed out of me in a *whoosh* and I doubled over in pain.

"Yes!" Eden hissed in triumph.

Heat surged through me. *I'm done putting up with her attitude*. From my bent-over position, I charged toward her, catching her in the middle and lifting her into the air. I didn't realize how much energy I'd put into the movement until it was too late. Eden flew across the room, slamming into the mirrored wall. It shattered into sharp, tiny pieces, falling around her like confetti as she slid to the ground.

A wave of stunned silence washed over the room, and Eden stared down at the glass around her in confusion. Little beads of blood seeped from tiny cuts all over her exposed skin.

"Oh, shit," Dayton said, breaking the silence.

Dawn rushed over to Eden and began checking the stunned girl for injuries.

"That was so *cool!*" Aonani cried, clapping her hands together. "Kirie, I didn't know you could do that. Did Finn teach you to do that? Can he teach me how to do that? I want to do that."

"I'm sorry," I said in a small voice. I couldn't feel my legs and arms.

Eden pushed Dawn's hands away. "I'm fine. Just let me get up."

Bert entered, calling the room to attention. He calmly surveyed the damage with a frown. "Explique," he barked.

No one moved. No one spoke.

Bert turned to Eden, eyebrows raised. Eden raised her chin and stabbed a finger in my direction. "Kirie threw me into the wall, Maitre. She started it," she said in French, as was required in Bert's presence.

The room thawed instantly, and everyone began talking all at once.

"*You* started it," Dayton said, pointing a finger at Eden.

"That's not right," Liang objected.

"Nuh, uh!" Aonani bellowed, tiny fists on hips.

Dawn hummed low in her throat in quiet protest and stepped away from Eden.

"Silence!" The room grew still once more under Bert's anger. I barely dared to breathe. He turned to me and leveled me with an intense stare. "Explique!" he demanded.

I slid a glance at Eden, who glared at me from her place on the ground. Bert caught the exchange and leveled her with one of his own, this one far more dangerous. Eden seemed to shrink into herself and I felt a twinge of sympathy for the poor girl.

"I apologize, Maitre," I said in French. "I didn't intend to throw Eden across the room." I hoped this answer would suffice, but

Bert simply put his hands on his hips and waited for the rest. My eyes strayed to Eden again, strangely hesitant to expose her part in this.

"Se concentrer sur moi," Bert snapped, pointing at his eyes with two fingers. *Focus on me.*

My shoulders dropped in defeat. There was no going to war with Bert. He always won. "Eden was upset about my new Light Tutor. She attacked me, and I tried to defend myself." I sighed and pointed to the shattered wall of mirrors. "I honestly didn't mean to throw her into the wall," I repeated.

Bert asked Eden if that was true, and she reluctantly nodded, still sitting in the glittering remains for our fight.

Bert tisked disapprovingly and ordered the others to go to school early. Practice was canceled. Dawn patted my shoulder as she left, filling me with a bit of her warm energy.

Bert called for a healer who examined Eden and me for any permanent damage. Diagnosis: we'd live. Our trainer gave each of us a broom and left us to clean up the mess. I had a feeling we'd be on cleaning duty for the foreseeable future.

We worked in silence; the only sound in the room was the swishing of the broom and the broken glass pieces tinkling as we swept them into piles. Eden kept her back to me. I could feel her anger toward me, like standing in front of a roaring fire. But I also felt sadness there too, amidst the hate. Suddenly, I felt sympathy for the younger girl. Her petty jealousy just made her seem so broken, so small. Perhaps she was.

But broken or not, we'd be training together, and I didn't want to be a part of this one-sided war she'd been waging against me. I stopped sweeping and looked over at Eden with a neutral expression, testing the waters. Feeling my stare, her back tensed and she glanced up from her work and sent me a petulant glare. I sighed, deciding to be the bigger woman.

"I don't want to fight anymore, Eden. Can we just call a truce?"

"I don't know, are you going to stop parading around like you're the Queen of England?" she said mockingly.

"You know what? I didn't ask for any of this. I didn't *want* any of this. I'm just trying to figure out who I am and what I'm even doing here. I wasn't brought up in The Society like you. This doesn't come naturally to me."

"I guess it doesn't hurt that you get special treatment. It's like none of us exists now. You suck up all of the attention."

I dropped my broom and put my hands on my hips. "Would you just stop? I don't care about attention. In fact, I'd rather be left alone."

Eden rested her chin on the end of her broom and spoke softly to the floor. "I know. I know you don't care. But that just makes it worse, you know? You come in here, and it's like you're all anyone's talking about anymore, and you don't even appreciate it."

We stood in silence for a moment, not knowing what else to say.

"Look, I really didn't mean to throw you across the room you like that."

Eden rolled her eyes at me. "Yeah. That's the other problem with you. You're too much of a goodie-good." She turned to me and waved a hand in my direction. "All that potential, and you don't even want to use it. This isn't playtime. We're training for *war*, Kirie. People are going to get hurt. Better the other guy than you."

"I know. It's just hard to remember that we're the good guys when we're learning fifteen ways to use our gifts to kill." I gestured to the walls lined with weapons.

"Stop being stupid. Do you think the Shadowmen care if you're the good guy? What happened in Paris was just the beginning. Things are going to get worse. You fight, or you lose."

Her argument had merit. It was the same one the others had used on me before. It just didn't *feel* right to me. Was violence the only way to stop the shadow from spreading? The Society held history's most brilliant minds in its ranks. Couldn't they figure out how to stop the darkness without resorting to violence? Sure, we were talented fighters, but did that mean that was the only tool in our arsenal?

Abbott once told me about the Enlightenment and using knowledge to free people. Yet, we're going to war with our fists and super-shining lights like cavemen with torches. Perhaps things had gotten so bad that that was the only option left. But, hadn't governments used that rationale in the past? Wasn't the result always a lot of dead bodies?

"Eden, have you ever been on a mission?"

She shook her head. "They just let us do the baby stuff. We're not allowed to go on any of the exciting missions until we're at least eighteen. It's total rubbish. I've been training for this since I was a little tike."

Donovan and Ciara's faces filled my mind, and a chill ran up my spine. I could go a hundred lifetimes without running into them again, and it still wouldn't be long enough. I thought about how Ciara choked me with my own hair back in that Paris courtyard, and I felt like throwing up. After Donovan slit my mother's throat in front of me, he and his henchmen did all they could to kill me. They were the most despicable assassins in The Order, the shady organization to which all Shadowmen belonged. Their tactics were particularly cruel and depraved.

"You don't want to fight Shadowmen anytime soon, Eden. Trust me."

I waited for a snide response, but it never came. Eden was suddenly ultra-focused on sweeping the floor. By now, everyone in The Society knew my story, and I supposed even Eden had a limit to how petty she could be.

I cleared my throat and changed the subject. "I've never asked you about your family. Are they still alive?" Normally, this would have been a ridiculous thing to ask, but in The Society, it was a practical question.

"My parents are back in Australia with my little brothers," she said to the floor.

"That's pretty far away." I thought of my Mom. Before she'd

died, she'd never let me leave her sight. Mom would've freaked out if I moved half a world away without her. "I bet they miss you."

Eden gave a rude snort. "They think it's *awesome* that I'm here. It's like I'm off at some boarding school they don't have to pay for."

Instinctively, I felt the ground beneath us grow shaky once more. I moved forward cautiously, not wanting to break the fragile truce we'd built. "Do they come to see you often? I bet they're excited to come see you in Rome now that we've moved."

"Nah. They're too busy with the little ones to worry about me."

"I suppose it's hard to travel with kids. But I'm sure they miss you," I said reassuringly.

"You can be so naïve, Kirie." She rolled her eyes, but the usual venom in her voice was gone. "They couldn't *wait* to be rid of me, honestly. I was only five years old when my powers came in. I couldn't even watch The Wiggles without lighting up like a torch. It totally freaked out my folks. They said I was unnatural. I think if The Society hadn't shown up to collect me, my parents would've burned me for being a witch." She finally set the broom down and sat, leaning against the concrete wall. "So, no. They don't come for visits."

We sat in silence for several beats. What was there to say about that, really? Then Eden added, "You know, you're not the only one who lost her whole family. At least your parents didn't choose to leave you behind."

And it all clicked into place—why she had such a chip on her shoulder and had to be the center of attention. She was as alone in the world as I was, only she didn't have to be. My heart hurt for this petty, mean girl. Would I have reacted the same way she had if my family had abandoned me? Probably not. But I supposed I could see why she did.

"Kirie! Tu t'entraineras avec M. Bellamy aujourd'hui," Bert yelled in French. The day just got brighter. I would take light training with Finn over cleaning any day.

"Oui, maitre Bert!" I bowed and waved to Eden. "I'll see you later."

"Later," she said in a mocking sing-song voice. I stuck my tongue out at her, and as I turned away, I caught the edge of her smile.

Chapter 6

Kirie

I grabbed my bag and ran down the hallway to Conference Room One. As soon as I entered, I back-stepped out and read the plaque beside the door, convinced I'd entered the wrong room. It was the right number, but the table and chairs were all missing. The empty rectangular room had a strange, abandoned feel. Finn walked in behind me. "Oh, good. You're here. I wanted to get an early start today, so I had someone remove the furniture this morning."

My heart did a little flutter in my chest. What kind of lesson required removing all the furniture? Finn must've seen my pained expression because he laughed. "Don't worry. It's just a precaution. We'll be working on control today and I didn't want you to worry about breaking anything."

I ducked my head, and my cheeks heated in embarrassment. "I guess you heard about this morning, then."

"Yes, well, word travels fast down here," Finn said dismissively.

I put my hands over my furnace-hot face and groaned at the thought of all those agents gossiping about my dangerous lapse in control. "I'm never going to be able to show my face again," I said between my fingers.

Finn laughed again. "Don't worry too much. I accidentally broke another kid's arm when I was in training. Learning your limits is part of the process." He gestured to the floor. "Now, have a seat, and we'll get started."

We sat facing each other in the center of the empty room, knees crossed. "Close your eyes." I complied, feeling awkward. "Now, in your mind's eye, summon your thought of inspiration." His words bounced off the walls.

Luca's face appeared in my mind unbidden, and I shivered. My memories of Luca—when I was too weak to block them—were . . . complicated. They were like my memories of my parents in that they always carried a bittersweet mixture of joy and loss. However, the ones of Luca were infused with the addition of *hope*. Hope that our paths would cross again. Hope that the girl on the other end of that phone wasn't his. Hope that what we'd shared meant as much to him as it did to me.

Hope was its own kind of torture.

Oddly, that strange connection between us hadn't diminished in all the months we'd been apart. In fact, it'd grown stronger than ever, full of compelling energy. Cautiously, I opened myself to it. It responded to my power instantly, flaring to life. I grasped onto the line of energy as if it were a rope and held it tightly.

The room's temperature instantly rose, and I knew I was outwardly projecting my light. Goose bumps spread across my exposed arms, where my heated skin met the cooler air.

"Now, pull your power back. Slowly."

As I tried, the energy pushed back, amplified by the invisible cord that connected me to Luca's energy. The additional power twined with my own and pulsed through me in waves. Like a caged animal, it searched for release. A light above popped and shattered, and glass sprinkled onto the ground around me.

"Pull back," Finn repeated.

"I can't!"

Pop! Another tiny explosion of glass. The walls began to vibrate, and the air around them stirred.

"You can," Finn said in a firm tone. "You're in control of your mind and body. If you believe that you can, you will."

I repeated the word "calm" in my mind, but the pressure continued to build, searing my insides as it demanded release. My connection to Luca fed the growing power inside me. It was as though it would implode. With a cry, I let go of the connection, and the energy diminished. I tamped down what was left, and my heated skin cooled. With a sigh of relief, I opened my eyes.

"See, *you* are in control," Finn said hesitantly as if he wasn't sure.

Whatever that conduit of energy was, I knew it was dangerous because tapping into it nearly crushed me. I wondered if Luca, wherever he was, felt my presence just then. Had he experienced the same surge in energy when I accessed our connection? I would likely never know.

Finn and I practiced taming my power every day, and by the end of the week, the furniture was moved back into the room. On Friday, I found Finn waiting for me at the head of the table. We said our hellos and I sat in the armchair to his right. On the table was a long silver dagger, thin and finely crafted. Despite having trained with throwing knives for over an hour that day, the sight of the double-edged blade made me shrink back.

"I thought we'd do something different today. What do you know about your light power, Kirie?" Finn asked. I couldn't stop staring at the knife in the middle of the marble conference table. The newly fixed lights above gleamed off its perfectly polished surface.

I looked up, meeting Finn's ever-patient gaze. "Um. It has the power to move objects, eliminate darkness, light things on fire, break glass . . ."

"Good. But you're missing one important thing," Finn replied. "Light can *heal*."

"Oh yeah. That." I recalled the moments when Luca's energy was inside me, stitching me back together, and my face grew hot. I blinked and focused again on the knife, hoping Finn didn't notice the color rising in my pale cheeks.

Finn picked up the knife. "Today, you're going to practice the art of healing." Without warning, he extended his left hand and slid the knife's blade across his palm. I squeaked in surprise, not quite believing what he'd just done. With wide eyes, I watched a tiny crimson pool grow on the white stone tabletop as blood dripped over the edge of Finn's palm.

Finn extended his bleeding hand across the table. "Now, try to use your energy to heal my hand."

I leaned back and shook my head. "I don't know how. Shouldn't we have gone over how it's done first?"

"This isn't something you can study in books, Kirie. It must simply be practiced."

I placed my hands over my mouth and nose, blocking out the coppery scent filling the room. "I can't do this," I whispered between my fingers.

"Yes, you can. It's the most natural thing in the world for you to do. It's like running or singing. Your body's made to do it."

I shook my head again and looked away. Finn sighed. "I'm sorry; this must be very triggering for you."

I heard a rustling noise and looked back to see that Finn had pulled a cloth out of his pocket and pressed it to his palm, soaking up most of the blood. He then wiped the blood off the table, leaving reddish-brown streaks behind. "You must push past your discomfort." His voice was firm, but not unkind.

I nodded and took a deep breath. "Ok. Tell me what to do."

"It's simple. Just place your palm over mine," he instructed.

I reached out a shaky hand and placed it lightly over his. His skin was warm and sticky from the drying blood. My stomach soured, but I forced myself not to shrink away.

"Next, close your eyes and bring to mind a memory that brings you happiness."

I thought of Rylie this time, a safer option. It was a memory of one of our many sleepovers in her backyard. We decided to camp out on her trampoline that night. Instead of sleeping, we'd stayed up all night giggling and staring at the stars. The sky had been crystal clear. Countless stars and galaxies stretched as far as our eyes could see like a million glittering diamonds. It was one of the only times I could remember not being afraid of the dark.

"Now, gather your light into your center and let it grow in strength and brightness," Finn instructed in the calming tone of a yoga instructor.

It came easily, growing into the center of my chest. The warmth made the hairs on my arms rise, and I shivered slightly.

"Good. This time, I want you to direct that energy down your arms and into the tips of your fingers."

As always, the energy resisted initially, wanting to burst from me in wild waves. I furrowed my brow and concentrated on directing the energy from my core to my arms and then my fingers as Finn had directed. It obeyed.

I peeked through my closed eyelids and saw that my fingertips glowed slightly.

"What do I do next?" I asked.

"Transfer the energy from your palm to mine. Your light will know what to do."

As I did as he instructed, new images began filling my mind. Places and people I'd never seen before played across my vision. My mother suddenly appeared. She looked years younger than I remembered. She was standing on the beach, smiling back at me. Reaching out, she beckoned me toward the water that was so vast and blue. I could smell the salt and feel the breeze on my hot skin, but that was impossible because I'd never been to the ocean before. My mom refused to leave the safety of our small Colorado town. My heart rate picked up as I began losing control of my energy. These couldn't be my memories.

"Focus, Kirie," Finn said, his voice strained.

I shook my head. The images washed away like sand, and I was back in the conference room. *What had just happened? Where had those memories come from? Could I see the past now? Light couldn't do that, could it?*

"Let's try again," Finn said, pulling me from my turbulent thoughts.

I cleared my throat. "Sorry."

I shifted in my seat and filled my mind again with the image of the diamond- studded sky. My fingers heated with energy once more, and I placed them over his gaping wound, my mind firmly fixed on Rylie and the stars.

"Good. Try again." I released the energy cautiously, allowing it to flow slowly into his wound. With my eyes still closed, I focused on controlling the flow for several more minutes when Finn finally said, "Kirie, open your eyes."

I did as instructed and stared in wonder as the skin on his palm stitched itself back together. The blood-covered skin was whole, unmarred from the blade.

"Oh my gosh," I whispered. I let my now heavy hand rest on the table. Every muscle in my body was suddenly mush.

Finn gazed from me to his hand and then to me again. The pride on his face was like sunshine on my own.

"Well done! I haven't seen a student heal on their first try since Luca came to us." My smile dropped. Finn pulled an alcohol wipe from his back pocket and cleaned his blood off the stone surface, completely oblivious to the effect the name he mentioned had on me. "You're truly a special young lady."

"Thank you," I said through a yawn.

"That's enough for tonight. Healing takes a lot of energy, and you're going to feel very tired for the next few hours. I'll have them bring a car to take you back to your apartment."

I nodded slowly, and the room swam. I laid my increasingly heavy head on the cold stone tabletop as Finn called for the car.

They cannot scare me with their empty spaces

Between stars – on stars where no human race is.

I have it in me so much nearer home

To scare myself with my own desert places.

"Desert Places"
by Robert Frost

Chapter 7

Luca

Luca **waited for** Abbott along an empty stretch of beach on what he liked to call "Recovery Island." Back when Luca was new to The Society, he suffered severe symptoms of PTSD. The things Donovan showed him, the things he made him do, had broken his young mind, leaving him . . . unstable. Little things would set him off and he'd shoot bolts of light into the floors and walls. So, Abbott had created a place for them to meet when Luca needed to calm down and regroup. It was where Luca learned how to be human again.

Recovery Island was the brightest place on Earth that Abbott could find, a small, deserted island off the Florida Keys that could be accessed only by boat. There, Luca could misfire without harming others and recharge his energy stores in a bright and quiet place. Over the years, Abbott taught him how to control his emotions and fears on that tiny stretch of land. Luca learned to hone his light, to heal with it, and to lock away the darkness. Abbott had pulled Luca from the brink of darkness more often than he could count in those early days.

A small hill stood in the center of the rocky terrain. Luca climbed to the precipice and sat, peering out at where the Atlantic and Caribbean seas converged. On one side of the island lay a serene and transparent ocean. On the other, a turbulent sea, dark and unsettled. Luca and the island were the same. Somewhere in between light and darkness. Though he'd come a long way, some stains couldn't be removed.

Luca's eyes were drawn to the clear blue water of the Caribbean—the exact color of Kirie's eyes. He let himself remember, just for a moment, the feel of her lips under his own, the touch of her warm hand in his. Never in all his life had Luca felt so connected to the light as when he'd touched Kirie. Even now, he could feel their connection, straining and insistent. The distance, it seemed, merely increased the pull toward her like an overstretched rubber band.

Luca felt a sudden tug in his center, and the connection flared to life. Hairs standing on end, Luca sat up, looking in the direction the connection pulled him—toward Rome. The energy that bound them together grew stronger, and for one insane moment, Luca thought he could smell her vanilla perfume. His internal light strained to grab onto the invisible cord, to strengthen the power building between them further, but the connection suddenly lessened, returning to its dormant state. Luca let out a sigh and raked his hands down his face. *What'd that been about?*

A low hum in the distance pulled Luca from his thoughts of Kirie. He stood and gazed out across the azure sea. A red and white speedboat sped toward him on the Caribbean side of the island. Abbott. As the boat sped toward the island, the placid water beat a steady rhythm against the boat's hull. Abbott pulled up behind Luca's smaller craft and waved.

Luca returned the wave as he walked down the hill and into the warm sea. Abbott threw a rope to him, and Luca steadied the bow as the older man climbed over the side and into the water, soaking his red and white Hawaiian shorts and a floral button-up shirt with salt water. Luca snorted at his mentor's ridiculous attempt to "dress the part." He suspected Abbott's habit of "*over*dressing the part" was his way of being satirical.

Once the boat was secure, Abbott followed Luca up the beach. The hot, coarse sand scratched the bottoms of their bare feet as they walked. They sat side-by-side beneath a palm tree in silence for several minutes in mirrored positions, folded arms over bent knees and feet buried in the sand. A warm breeze blew over the island and the tree fronds painted dancing shadows along the white sand.

"I assume your mission in the States was a success," Abbott finally said, breaking the silence. His voice tilted up at the end in question.

"Depends on your definition of success, I suppose," Luca replied. His stomach soured as he thought of the data he'd recovered from the dead shadow. For the first time since Abbott had dragged him off the filthy London streets, his faith in The Society was truly shaken. It was as if the ground he stood on had turned to quicksand.

"I discovered The Order's final plan of attack. They're going to destroy every major city on the planet."

"By what means?" Abbott's voice shook slightly.

"Nuclear weapons. The files seem to suggest they will acquire a massive stockpile of uranium very soon. It won't be long before they have the means to carry out their plan."

Abbott swore. "Was the location of the bombs in those files as well?"

"There are a few grainy pictures of an unmarked desert but nothing else. There are likely thousands of deserts that fit its description. Finding the right one will take time. Time we might not have."

"But we have to try. Our techs can use satellites to track movement and heat signatures in deserts across the globe simultaneously. Don't worry, we'll find it."

Luca shook his head. "No. We can't take this information to The Society. Not yet."

"What is it you're not telling me, son? Why bring me out here in secret instead of reporting your findings to the appropriate channels?"

Luca looked out at the dark and moody Atlantic. He picked up a stone and threw it toward the water, stalling. He didn't want to put words to it. He didn't want to make it real.

"What is it?" Abbott urged.

Luca closed his eyes. "I found an email within the shadow's files revealing the location of The Paris Center of Light. When I traced the IP address of the informant . . ." Luca took a deep breath before continuing. "It came from a computer inside The Paris Center of Light. It was sent just *hours* before the bomb went off."

"Damnit," Abbott said, rubbing a hand over his forehead with more force than necessary. "Do you know whose computer it came from?"

Luca shook his head. "That's the thing. The email was sent from a computer that hadn't been used in weeks. The agent assigned to it was out on maternity leave at the time."

"Smart. And more proof that it was an Agent of Light."

Luca turned to Abbott, holding onto a childish hope that his mentor would fix things as he'd always done. "What should I do? Tell me what to do."

"Well, first, you need to check in," Abbott said. "Soon."

"What should I say? I can't go running my mouth that we have a traitor in our midst now, can I? The mole could be anyone, and we'd lose our advantage."

"Give them as little information as possible, just enough to avoid suspicion. We need to tread lightly going forward."

"Come on, Abbott. You know I'm a piss-poor liar. They'll see right through me."

"Then take some time off. It's been years since you've taken a vacation. No one would notice if you took a few days to yourself."

Luca shook his head and let out a sarcastic laugh. "And instead of lying on the beach, I'm to find a random mine in a random desert using only a grainy photo?" Abbott nodded. "Brilliant," Luca said, digging his feet deeper into the sand.

Abbott ignored his tone. "Precisely. In the meantime, I'll search for the mole. I have more access to The Society's internal workings than you do."

"And if I happen to find the location of the mine? What then? We can't trust telling anyone in The Society without potentially tipping off the informant. The Order will get wind of it and go underground, and we'll be back to square one."

"Then we assemble a team of trusted agents and we go stop a nuclear holocaust before our cover's blown."

Luca threw another rock at the turbulent waters. "That simple, eh?"

"When has this job ever been simple, my boy? We'll do what has to be done to save this planet from utter darkness. It's what we're made to do." It was an old sermon of Abbott's, one Luca had written into his soul.

"The Society will have our necks for this."

Luca didn't care much about his own neck, but Abbott would go down with him. Good intentions or not, The Society was an organization of rules and regulations. Going rogue was grounds for dismissal from its ranks, and disgraced agents didn't last long in the world alone.

"It's a risk we must take."

84

I had a dream, which was not all a dream.

The bright sun was extinguish'd, and the stars

Did wander darkling in the eternal space,

Rayless, and pathless, and the icy earth

Swung blind and blackening in the moonless air;

Morn came and went—and came, and brought no day,

"Darkness"

by Lord Byron

Chapter 8

Kirie

It was dusk when I exited through St. Peter's hidden side entrance to meet my driver, Jacques. A frown tugged at my lips when an empty curb met me. Strange, he'd never been late to pick me up before. I sent a quick text to Jacques, who quickly responded that he was nearby. I slid my phone into my back pocket and folded my arms over my chest, bouncing up and down on my toes while I waited.

The door behind me squeaked open. I turned, and Mr. Daiko, co-leader of The Society of Light, walked toward me. He wore a perfectly tailored black suit and shiny black shoes, the perfect picture of a powerful man. The hairs on my arms stood on end as he joined me at the curb, standing a bit too close for comfort. I held my arms tightly at my sides and faced the street.

"Hello, Kirie," he said in his thick Mandarin accent.

"Sir," I said with a nod. "I didn't realize you were in Rome." If I had, I'd have avoided him at all costs.

His eyes formed slits as his cheeks lifted in an unconvincing smile. "I've only just arrived. I met with Mr. Bellamy tonight and he told me your light training is going well."

"I'm glad he thinks so," I said lamely, hoping he'd soon move on to wherever he was headed.

Mr. Daiko turned and placed a hand over my shoulder, his grip firm and pressing. A chill ran through me, and it took all my strength not to shrink away. "You have great potential. Everyone will be watching to see what you do."

"Oh," I say, shifting slightly under his grip. "I'll try not to disappoint them."

He dropped his fake smile and increased the pressure on my shoulder. "However, I must warn you. Beware. There'll be some who will wish to see you fail." His words sounded more like a threat than a warning.

A black luxury sedan appeared around the sharp corner, its tinted windows reflecting the streetlamps like a shiny black beetle. Relief flooded through me. Jacques to the rescue. The car pulled up alongside the curb, and I pulled free from Daiko's grip.

"Well, this is my ride. It was, um, good to see you," I lied.

"It was my pleasure," he said with a slight bow.

Pulling the back door open, I slid across the cold leather seat into the darkened car. I could feel Mr. Daiko's eyes follow me as the car pulled away. When we neared the corner, I glanced back. Mr. Daiko hadn't moved from his spot on the curb. A shiver ran through me. There was something off about that man. I couldn't understand how Finn worked alongside that creep for all these years. The two men couldn't be more different. Perhaps the third member of the presidency, Ms. Delgado, evened them out.

As St. Petersburg shrank in the distance, my stomach began to rumble, and all thoughts of Daiko evaporated. I'd forgotten to stop for lunch and dinner. I was *starving*. I thought of the prospects back in my tiny kitchen and nearly cried. Crusty bread and hard cheese weren't going to cut it tonight.

"Can we stop somewhere and grab food?" I asked Jacques as a sharp hunger pang assaulted my abdomen. It felt like my stomach had resorted to eating itself from the inside out.

Jacques didn't even bother to look over his shoulder at me. "No stops. The Society is still on high alert, and my orders are to deliver you to and from home. No exceptions."

I scooted forward in my seat and put my arms around the passenger headrest. "Please, Jacques? I haven't eaten all day." I was met with a firm jaw and a low grunt like a dog sounding a warning. "We could stop at Satiricus. It's on the way, and we can get it to go." Another grunt, this one with a little more bite. "I'll buy you a pizza," I said in an innocent sing-song voice, hoping to tempt him with food.

Jacques finally turned slightly toward me; the streetlights outlined his firm profile. "Margherita? With extra basil?"

I tried—and failed—to hide my smile. "Whatever you want."

Jacques parked along the curb of a white stone building. Tables and chairs were set in front of black-framed windows. I'd smelled the delicious aromas from Satiricus Restorante as we drove back to my apartment after training each day. My mouth watered at the thought of finally tasting the food responsible for the nightly temptation. Jacques turned around in his seat to level me with a glare. "Don't talk to anyone. Don't use the bathroom. Just get in and get out, you got it?"

"You act like I'm headed into a war zone," I said, digging my wallet out of my duffle bag. "It's going to be fine."

"I mean it, Kirie. No messing around, okay?" The sincerity in his tone robbed me of my retort. It was easy to forget that we were, in fact, in a war zone and that the normal world no longer existed for people like me. Perhaps it never did.

"Okay, Jacques. I'll be right back." I reached over the seat and patted his shoulder before slipping out onto the sidewalk.

The restaurant was warm and filled with clinking plates and chattering patrons. Marble columns were set at intervals throughout the room, and green plants hung from the ceiling amidst bronze chandeliers. Mirrors lined the walls and reflected the light, making the long, small rectangular room appear grander. Simmering herbs and garlic permeated the air so thickly that it was as if I'd stepped into a giant steaming bowl of pasta. I'd been living on salad, bread, and cheese for months, and my stomach seemed to rejoice at the promise of real, hot food. A pretty girl about my age greeted me from a host stand. "Ciao. Come posso aiutarti?"

"I need to order food to go," I responded in Italian.

"Bene." The girl pointed to a counter off to the side of the dining room. "Puoi ordinare laggiu."

"Grazie," I said with a smile. A young man stood behind a computer screen atop a light-colored marble countertop. He gave me a nod and handed me a leather-bound menu. Bruschetta, caprese, lasagna, it all sounded amazing. Bert and Finn had worked me hard that week and I seriously needed the calories. I considered ordering one of everything. The leftovers would feed me for weeks. Jacques made me promise to be quick, though, so I quickly ordered two pizzas: a quattro formaggi for me and a margarita with extra basil for Jacques. The server pointed to a padded bench near the to-go desk and said it would be about twenty minutes.

From my place on the bench, I was able to see most of the lightly busy dinner crowd. Conversations in different languages filled the space with life and energy. I let it soak into my skin. It wasn't nearly enough to replenish my empty stores—between Bert's and Finn's lessons, I could barely keep my eyes open—but it helped take the edge off of my fatigue.

I sent a quick text to Jacques, letting him know how long the food would take and that I wasn't dead yet, and settled in to people-watch while I waited. Since the restaurant was so close to St. Peter's Basilica, most diners were tourists. Nearest to me sat a French family of three. A young toddler with rosy cheeks and messy hair stuffed a napkin in her water and kicked her feet against the base of her highchair while her parents discussed the art they'd seen that day. The toddler threw the soaked napkin on the table and let out an ear-piercing scream. The young mother leaned over and patiently put a hand over her mussy head and shushed her lovingly. The obvious affection in the mother's eyes sent a stab of grief and anger through me, and I had to look away.

At the next table over, a man sat with his back to me. I hadn't noticed him sitting there before; it was as if he'd simply blended in with the environment. Perhaps it was his utter stillness. When I reached out with my energy into the room, there was a void where the man sat, like he had little or no life. A chill ran down my back. I didn't *see* any shadows surrounding him, but still.

The man turned his head, and our eyes met. I half-expected them to be black, but they were simply a muddy brown, not particularly outstanding or menacing. Everything about the middle-aged man, from his short, trimmed hair and average build, was ordinary. Briefly, our eyes held before I glanced away, embarrassment flooding my cheeks at being caught staring. I pretended to study my nail beds for several minutes before daring to look up again. When I did, the man was gone. Feeling uneasy, I searched the crowded dining room but saw no sign of him.

"Mi scusi signora," a male voice said. I turned to see the server holding a bag of food. All thoughts of the strange man fled from my mind, replaced by happier thoughts of fresh Italian food.

I jumped up from the bench and took the bag from his hands. "Grazie!"

Holding the hot food close to my chest, I rushed to the car still waiting at the curb. I slid into the backseat and let the heat from the bag warm the tops of my sore legs. I was worn to the bone from training and all I wanted to do was sit on my tiny couch at home and eat pizza.

The sun had gone down, leaving deep shadows in the sedan's cab. "Sorry it took so long," I said to my straight-backed bodyguard. Jacques stared straight ahead, offering no reply, likely upset that our detour took so long. I pulled the Margherita pizza out of the bag and leaned over, setting it on the front seat. Still, no response. Shrugging, I laid my head back against the headrest. I was too tired to worry about Jaques's bad mood.

I let my mind wander as I stared out the front windshield. I thought of my 6:00 AM alarm. I could almost hear my muscles begging for mercy. If the Shadowmen didn't kill me, Bert's training lessons certainly would. There was a sharp turn ahead where the road met the River Tiber. A stone graffiti-covered wall separated the raised road from the river, more than twenty feet below. *Strange. This isn't our usual route.*

"Where are we going?" I called to Jacques. Still, no response. I set the bag of food aside and sat upright. My scalp tingled in warning.

As we approached the sharp turn in the road, the car began to accelerate toward the stone barrier. I leaned forward in confusion. "Hey. What's up?" I asked, hoping Jacques was just trying to scare me as punishment for making him stop for food. Still, he sped up.

"Jacques! Stop!" I yelled as the graffitied wall grew closer.

The driver's side door flew open, and the driver threw himself out onto the street. I watched in mute horror as the man landed blithely on his feet on the paved cobblestone. Time slowed as the car passed him. The man from the restaurant—not Jacques— smiled at me as the car careened toward the barrier.

Unprepared for impact, I was thrown forward against my seatbelt, the edge cutting into the skin of my neck. I became weightless as the car sailed up and over the stone barrier and began free-falling the twenty feet to the water below. The front bumper collided with the water's surface, and I was thrown forward again, the sound of the crash loud in my ears. I gasped for air as the car bobbed up and down like a buoy a few times before it began sinking into the murky river.

Frigid dark water rushed in at my feet, quickly soaking my training shoes and pants. In mere seconds, it covered me to my waist and then to my chest. My head pounded with the rhythm of my erratic heartbeats as my numb hands struggled to release my seatbelt. It gave way just as the water reached my chin. I sucked in one last deep breath as the frigid river water surged over my head.

Panic and desperation took over as the inky black water swirled around me. Instinctively, my center began to warm, and my hands lit up, casting an eerie green glow inside the submerged car. I found the door handle and pulled, but the pressure against the door sealed it firmly shut. I bent my knees to my chest and kicked against the glass window unsuccessfully. My legs were limp spaghetti noodles as I kicked it repeatedly. Black spots filled my vision. My efforts slowed. It was useless; I was going to drown.

As the darkness closed in, I didn't see a flashback of my life, like in the movies. I saw my mother's face, pleading for me to fight. I reached a hand out to her, but her face dissolved into the dark water and was replaced by Finn's. His kind blue eyes begging for me not to give up. But after enduring months of constant fear and grief, my body was worn, and I had little left to give. My outstretched hand became limp. And just as my body ate up the last of the oxygen, Luca's face finally appeared.

I'd forbidden myself from thinking about him during my waking hours, leaving my obsession over him to my dreams. At the end, though, it was his face my dying mind wanted to remember. The connection between us, the one that I never could ignore nor deny, pulled taut. The murky river faded away, and we were together again under the Paris streetlights. Luca was leaning in for a kiss. I could almost feel his arms around me, warm and strong. His vivid green eyes held mine as he lowered his head. But just as our lips were about to meet, Luca jerked back, his perfect features twisted into a mask of horror. *Kirie, FIGHT!* he yelled. His voice echoed in the water-filled cab, forcing me back to reality.

Red-hot energy gathered from somewhere deep inside me, growing by the second and begging for release. My mind and vision cleared as light filled the car's interior. The panic that clouded my mind faded, and I knew what I had to do. I pulled my legs behind me and raised my palms to the window. Searing bright light burst from my hands, shattering the glass and blasting the door from its hinges. I swung my arms behind my back and used the last bit of energy inside me to shoot myself out of the car. I broke the surface with a gasp and treaded water as I sucked in the air. The water surrounding me was hot and bubbly like a jacuzzi.

The energy left me all at once, and I laid back, letting the slow-moving current take me toward the river's edge. I reached for the sidewalk, and the rough concrete scratched my palms as I struggled to find something to hold on to. I grasped at the thin branches of a copse of bushes growing along the walkway and held on. Shivering and gulping in the frigid air, I struggled to catch my breath as reality sank deep into my skin.

A shadow found me in the middle of Rome. But how? Even *I* hadn't known I'd be in that restaurant. The attack *couldn't* have been planned. What then? I'd run into a shadow by horrible coincidence? The odds were incredibly slim. The whole thing felt like a setup.

My swirling thoughts turned to Jacques, and shame washed over me. I had no way of knowing if he was alive or dead, and it was all my fault. I never would've run into the shadow If I hadn't insisted on stopping. If I had just *listened* to Jacques . . .

Cursing myself, I mustered my remaining energy and pulled myself up over the edge of the concrete path, using the bushes as leverage. My arms buckled underneath me, and I fell chin-first onto the cement river walkway. I grunted and flopped onto my back. My body wanted to stay there and sleep forever. Still, I needed to find another light source to re-energize my energy cells, preferably before the shadow who drove the car into the river came looking for a body.

As I lay shivering on the pathway, pebbles dug painfully into my shoulders and scalp. I shifted my weight, and my eyes wandered upward, giving me an upside-down view of the riverwalk above. Tall stone walls lined either side of the river, and I could see no staircase leading to the street level. I followed the line of the wall with my sore head, and my eyes caught on a dark figure leaning over the barrier's edge. A man obscured in darkness stared down at me. He held something in his hand.

Light glinted off the shiny metal, and I realized it was a gun a mere second before he fired. I rolled sideways, and the bullet hit the ground just inches from my head. With a yelp, I rolled back into the river and dove beneath the murky water. Bullets rained down around me like an underwater hailstorm. A sharp sting ripped through my bicep. Bubbles obscured my vision as I screamed.

I stayed below the water's surface, using the river's current to carry me away from the Shadow, coming up for air for only moments at a time. The sound of gunfire soon faded into the distance. Still, I stayed low in the river's center, knowing the Shadow would surely follow.

Several hundred feet downstream, buildings rose from the center of the river. Lights shone from the windows like an ocean liner rising from the riverbed. I wiped the water from my eyes and shook my head, momentarily wondering if I was seeing things. *This must be Isla Tiberina.* It was a small plaster village constructed on a tiny island located in the center of the river, as old and full of history as the city surrounding it. I'd seen Isla Tiberina from the road a hundred times before but had never had the time to visit.

The river carried me beneath the bridge connecting the island to either side of the river. At the island's tip was a concrete platform a few feet above the river's surface. I felt a sharp sting in my bicep as I pulled myself onto the river rocks at the platform's base. Pebbles and sticks stabbed into my frozen hands and knees, and I bit my bottom lip to keep from crying out. I turned back and searched the darkness for the Shadow. He was nowhere to be seen, but I knew better than to feel relief. Cars and pedestrians passed by, and the sounds of normal city life surrounded me in cruel irony.

Several feet ahead, a couple strolled along the walkway surrounding the island's buildings. I considered calling to them, but I didn't know if the Shadow hid on the bridge above, poised to shoot. I couldn't risk putting anyone else in harm's way. I waited until they passed before pulling myself over the platform's edge. A grassy knoll led upward to a three-story terra cotta building complex. Trees and bushes lined the wall's interior, providing a verdant barrier from the riverwalk.

I stumbled up the hill and huddled among the bushes. I heaved in cold breaths as I took stock of my injuries. The accident had jarred my neck and my chest hurt where the seat belt had caught me, leaving behind heavy aches. There was a stinging sensation in my left arm, and when I reached below my ripped jacket, my fingers came away wet with warm blood. I carefully ran a finger across the length of the wound, fearing the worst, but the cut was shallow. Thankfully, the bullet had just grazed me.

Wet clothes clung like icy curtains to my trembling body, and I shook so violently that I could hear the chattering of my own teeth. On instinct, I rubbed my hands up and down my arms, trying to regain some circulation in my limbs, but the movement only sent red-hot pain through my injured arm. I needed to call for help before I froze to death. If I could just make it to one of the island's buildings without being seen, I might be able to find a phone.

A chill swept into my little hiding place. Shifting forward onto my knees, I swung my head back and forth, searching for the Shadowman that must certainly be near, but saw nothing. The Roman city life hummed around me, undimmed by any physical shadow. I peered around me again not trusting my instincts as I could feel a creeping Darkness attempting to take over my mind. My body shook harder as its inky fingers slithered up my frozen shoulders and into my scalp. Gasping, I realized the darkness wasn't *near* me, it was *inside* me.

This darkness was deeper than any Shadow I'd encountered in the flesh. And it was *familiar*. Its presence slipped into my mind and took control of my senses. In my weakened state, I was utterly powerless to stop it.

I was again at the edge of that vast ocean, bare feet in soft, white sand against a harsh black backdrop. A desperate knowledge that

I was alone in this forsaken place crashed down on me.

The voice, bottomless and vast, spoke to me with the strength of a thousand waves crashing in an endless cave. This was not the presence of any mere Shadowman, but something far more ancient and sinister. It was the voice from my dreams.

You cannot hide, Bright One. Your light shines to the furthest corners of the universe. It calls to me. I see you always.

My shaking stilled and my body turned as cold and hard as marble. My eyes slid shut and my sense of self began to descend just as it had months before. I pushed back against the slippery tendrils pulling at my consciousness, and screamed out, "Get out of my head!"

Your efforts are in vain. I am eternal. Endless. I have fought many battles. You will never win. Now is the day of my retribution. Now is the day I claim what is mine.

A vivid image filled my mind's eye. I was above the Earth, looking down at its blue-green surface. It appeared peaceful and serene in its stillness. Then, a vibration shook the vision, and giant mushroom clouds sprung up across the planet's vast surface. There were dozens of them—no *hundreds* of them—popping up like tiny puffs of smoke.

The scene changed. I saw horrifying scenes in quick succession like an old-time movie reel. People on crowded streets running. Screaming. Faces burnt. Skin melting. Luca, kneeling in a pile of ash, his skin melting down his face like wax on a candle.

Different cities—all the same—millions of people and millions of screams. Then darkness and wailing and nothing else—nothing but the absence of life . . . the absence of light. The nothingness stretched on without end. Its vastness stole my breath away.

This is what is to be, The Void said in echoey triumph. *My kingdom rightfully restored.*

"No," I cried, throwing my frozen hands out as if to somehow push the images from my mind. My palms scratched against the thorned twigs of the bush in front of me, but I barely registered the pain.

It is the end foretold by many. It is the world's end. It is your end. Your light will cease to shine, for I cannot bear to see it.

Across the endless ocean, I felt a pull, as if I was being tugged by some unseen rope. My sluggish mind struggled to push it away from me, but the magnetic force only strengthened. I opened my swollen, tired eyes, but there was nothing there but the dark, windless sea. The tugging at my center continued to strengthen, refusing to be ignored. I closed my eyes again and focused on the incessant pull.

In my mind's eye, I saw a pure gold chain. Its shining surface cut through the darkness like a spear and stretched through the mists of darkness to where I knelt in the sand. I reached out with my frozen hand and grabbed onto its warm, smooth surface. The chain hummed with energy, strong and familiar, filling my empty places with peace and yearning. I held on, and it pulled me back from the edge of the precipice.

Slowly, my limbs regained feeling, each scratch and bruise

fighting for attention.

Familiar sounds of the city rushed back in all at once, anchoring me to the Earth again. The blaring horns and rushing river water were welcome sounds. The warmth of the echo of that connection replaced the cold hopelessness the Void had brought with it. I pressed my cheek against the cold stone pillar and sobbed for the memory of the devastation, the memory of Luca's melting skin.

As the vision drained from my mind. I sagged into the bushes, sharp branches tangling in my wet hair. Memories of another night came rushing into my tired mind. It was a night like this. I was cold and huddled behind shrubbery while a maniacal Shadowman hunted me in the night along the side of a road. Like that night, I was acting like a frightened bunny stalked by a fox. I was *hiding in fear*.

NO! Anger coursed through me. I was no longer that weak little girl I once was. I was stronger now. Neither The Void nor the Shadowmen would back me into a corner with fear and intimidation. I gritted my teeth in determination and got up.

Chapter 9

Kirie

aked branches clawed at my hair and skin as I crawled out from the bushes, but I barely felt their sting. I hobbled around the building at the island's tip and read the words "Ospedale Fatebenefratelli" on a plaque above one of the doors. I was tempted to hobble through the automatic sliding doors. Although a hospital was exactly what I needed, going inside would put all the patients at risk. I would be better off being healed by someone from The Society anyway. I just had to survive long enough to get in contact with them.

I stumbled down the concrete walk to the other side of the island's main building. There was a church attached to the backside of the hospital, perhaps so that people could pray while their loved ones fought death just down the hall. How morbidly convenient.

Like many of Rome's buildings, this church's front door was lined by stately Roman columns, and history was etched into every inch of the plaster building. In front of the church's entrance was a monument shaped like a column topped with a cross that sat in the middle of a cobblestone courtyard.

I scanned the other plaster buildings surrounding it, searching for a quick energy source. I was dangerously low, and although the ambient electricity that flowed through all things was usually enough to keep my levels up, I'd never been so empty. I needed a more direct source. I considered sneaking into one of the surrounding buildings, but I feared absorbing the residual energy from the lights and electronics there would take too much time.

Examining the buildings, a bright red and green neon sign shaped like a cross caught my attention. It was attached to the front of a building on the other side of the street. Its harsh blinking light strained my sore eyes. The juxtaposition between the modern and the ancient was jarring to my tired mind. The energy from the sign pulsed in ebbs and flows like a living, breathing thing, and my empty cells yearned for the electricity. I found myself walking toward it, as if in a trance.

A sense of unease crept up my spine as I walked across the street leading to the sign. I paused and looked around. I stood in the middle of a stone bridge that extended to the left and right, connecting the island's center with the surrounding city streets. I felt exposed, like a deer in an open field during hunting season. I needed to avoid open roads.

Heart pumping, I hurried across the bridge to the red and green neon sign. Its garish light cast a sickly light on my pale skin. My eyes caught on an electrical cord running from the sign's base down the building's plaster exterior wall. I'd never siphoned energy from such a direct source before, but there weren't any alternatives. I picked up a sharp stone from the roadside rubble and began cutting through the black wire. The rock shook in my trembling hands and I struggled to hold onto it.

Just as the plastic gave way, the temperature around me began to drop. The rock slipped from my trembling fingers, and I spun around, searching the darkness for the threat I knew to be there.

On the other side of the river, shadows began to gather like a storm on the horizon. Streetlights sputtered out as they slithered across the bridge in their non-corporeal forms. The lone Shadowman from the restaurant had clearly called for backup, and they were moving quickly. My shivering increased. I thought of my cell phone sitting in my training bag at the bottom of the River Tiber and nearly cried in frustration.

Icicles formed on my wet sleeves as I touched the exposed wire and began siphoning the raw, unfiltered electricity. Energy coursed through me at an alarming speed. Too much. Too fast. My cells filled to bursting and I gritted my teeth against the onslaught.

From behind, an ice-cold hand slipped over my mouth. The corpse-like skin pressed down hard, crushing my lips against my teeth. I jerked and a warm metallic taste filled my mouth. Letting go of the wire, I reached back and grabbed the Shadow's face with both hands. The excess energy pulsing violently through my veins needed no encouragement or direction as it burst from my skin into his, unmitigated in its flow. The Shadow had little time to react or even scream and the smell of burnt skin quickly filled the chilly night air. I lost my grip on the Shadowman's face as his heavy body thumped to the pavement at my feet. I slapped my hands over my mouth, vomit rising in my throat. The Shadow's face was black and unrecognizable. *I think . . . I think I killed him.*

The city around me descended into darkness as if a curtain had been pulled. I spun around and came face-to-face with a wall of complete living darkness. An eerie stillness filled the air, muting the wind and city sounds. Shadows filled the small courtyard in front of the church and the surrounding buildings and businesses had gone dark. I squinted into the advancing Shadows and saw over a dozen undefined figures amid the darkness. My heart beat out a heavy rhythm in my throat.

Stumbling away from the charred mass at my feet, I channeled the energy inside me into my hands like Finn showed me and shot bolts of light into the shadows. Several Shadowmen stepped out of the way, creating a break in the line. The chaotic street across the river broke through in a burst of noise and light like the moon peeking through passing clouds in a veiled sky. Unharmed and undaunted, they stepped back together, closing the gap.

I raised my palms again and fired a quick succession of bolts into the group. A few cries rang out, but the line of shadows continued to advance. I turned and began running across the bridge leading to the opposite side of the river, but was cut off by a group of shadows, materializing from thin air.

To my right was a staircase covered in bright graffiti leading back down to the river. Taking the steps two at a time, I again found myself at water level. I sprinted down the pathway surrounding the island's base, the sound of the river growing louder with the beat of my racing heart.

The pathway led to the opposite tip of the island. I rounded the corner and was cut off by a rolling cloud of shadows. They advanced on either side, forcing me back. I tripped off the edge of the walkway into the frigid water, landing hard on my tailbone in the sharp rocks.

The river was shallow there, only a foot or two deep, like a watery extension of the island. Stacked rocks surrounded the collapsed base of an ancient bridge, creating a kind of flooded platform. The center pylon was ringed by crumbling age-stained steps leading to a center keyhole, like the dais of a medieval throne room. Trees and bushes filled the space, creating a scene straight out of a King Author movie.

I pulled myself up the steps toward the cutout in the pylon, hoping to use its sidewalls for protection. The Shadowmen quickly surrounded my hiding place on all sides, hovering above the water like a thick fog. As I began pulling my energy into my center, a shadow burst from the group. Small feminine fingers reached for me. I strained backward, nearly falling from my raised position. Bone-white hands clutched the front of my shirt and tugged me forward.

I curled my fist and struck out at the female Shadow, but she was still shrouded in darkness, and my hand went straight through her noncorporeal form. Wrapping her fingers around my throat, the Shadow pushed me into the stone column at my back. My skull ground into the stone behind me and its rough edges cut into my scalp. I pushed the pain away like Bert taught me and tried to focus my excess energy. Heat flooded my vision, and the stone beneath my skin became hot, my light expanding and burning holes into the dark night. The Shadow holding me grimaced, her teeth grinding together audibly as she squeezed my neck tighter, clearly hoping to strangle the light out of me before I had the chance to destroy her.

When my center felt the strain of the force, I focused my energy on the woman. The Shadow screamed with a voice like a wraith. Her cries abruptly cut off as her skin turned a glowing black like molten lava, and her hand released my neck as her charring body fell into the river with a splash. I gasped in a breath and looked down at the charred mass floating in the dark water. My body shook. I'd killed again. I glanced up in time to see dozens of shadows rush forward.

An ear-splitting crack filled the air, and a flare, bright as a lightning bolt, collided with the shadow nearest me. Several more bolts of light shot toward the advancing group of Shadowmen. I strained my neck to see where the bolts were coming from, but I couldn't see over the railing from my position below the bridge. I centered my light in my palms and shot out into the wall of darkness. My light was joined by many others, lighting up the night.

A beam of bright white light shot past me, hitting an approaching female Shadow to my left squarely in the chest. She shrieked and fell to her knees in the shallow water, clutching her blackened torso, a twisted mess of anguish and hatred on her face.

Out of the darkness, another semi-solid Shadow rushed toward me with incredible speed. I raised my burning hands, but I was too late. The Shadow fully materialized and rammed into me, sending us both tumbling down the rock steps. My back hit a sharp rock as we crashed into the shallow river water, and I felt warm blood leak from the wound into the frigid water. The Shadow's black eyes stared down at me with unveiled hatred as he tore at my clothes like a rabid dog.

A light appeared above him, creating a halo around his head like the moon during an eclipse. With a grunt, his body went limp, and he fell forward, landing on top of me and forcing my head below water. I squirmed beneath his dead weight, sending red-hot pain through my already bleeding back as it scraped across the sharp river rocks. I pushed my way free of his body and surged toward the water's surface. The icy air burned my lungs as I sucked in great gulps.

I stumbled away from the base of the bridge, my feet sending sprays of water in every direction. I looked up again. From this vantage point, I could see a line of figures along the bridge's crumbling stone railing.

Bert, my classmates, and several of the older agents I knew only by sight were there. I even thought I saw the top of a short brown-haired girl's head. My stomach lurched. *Aonani.*

In the center of them all was Finn. He shone brightly, a lighthouse in the darkest storm. His vibrant blue eyes blazed like a summer sky on fire. His gaze was trained on the Shadows below with a frightening intensity. My breath caught in my throat. Gone was my laid-back trainer in khakis. Finn was as terrifying as the sun.

"Kirie! look out!" Dawn, of all people, leaned over the railing, light shining off her skin like an aura. Her brows were knit in worry.

"Wha . . ."

A thickly muscled arm wrapped around my neck from behind, cutting off my air. A feeling of black despair rushed into my veins at our touch as the Shadow held me firmly in a chokehold. Gritting my teeth, I pushed past the forced lethargy and let my training take over. I stepped to the left and thrust my right arm down into the Shadow's groin. He groaned and bent forward. I swung my fist upward, hitting him square in his downturned face.

The Shadow cried out in pain, and a spatter of warm liquid coated the back of my neck. His arm loosened just enough for me to drop out of his hold. With outstretched hands, I rolled onto my feet, sending a blast of light at the Shadow. He cursed and fell off the shallow platform back into the rushing river, arms pinwheeling.

I reached up and wiped my neck. My stomach turned when my hand came away covered in crimson liquid. My vision began to blacken around the edges as I stared at the Shadow's blood.

"Reste Vigilante," Bert yelled down to me. His angry command snapped me from my stupor. I shook my head and swung around to face my attackers.

The Shadowmen had surrounded me in a U-shaped formation. I took a deep breath and centered my energy. I raised my palms and released the energy in concentrated rays like Finn taught me. The Shadows morphed between smoke and solid form as they dodged the bolts of energy coming from above and below the bridge.

A female Shadow rushed toward me, vaporizing as a beam of light shot from above. It passed right through her, the light reflecting off the black particles that made up her Shadow form. When she materialized again, her right arm was raised toward the bridge. *The Shadow has a gun.* A resounding *crack* rent the air and a high-pitched scream came from the line of agents. I looked up. Eden leaned over the edge, her face bleeding and contorted in pain. Bert shot another round and caught Eden as she began to fall.

Eden had been *shot.*

"NO!" I yelled.

I swung back around and fired multiple bolts at the armed female Shadow, but she dodged them easily, morphing in and out of physical form quicker than I could gather and release my energy. With each change, she moved closer to me. I stepped back, hands still outstretched but less sure.

Bolts of light and gunshots volleyed back and forth as the circle of shadows tightened around me like a noose. The dark mass grew with each passing second until dozens upon dozens of shadows surrounded the bridge. Pretty soon, our energies would run out and we'd be forced into hand-to-hand combat with the massing shadows. We were outnumbered and outgunned.

I swung around, searching for something to use as a weapon, but I was surrounded by nothing but water, river rock, and Shadowmen. I jerked to a stop, the solution becoming obvious. *We are standing in water, and I'm made out of electricity.* I had to act fast.

I thought of my mother's face. As my body began to warm, I soaked in the energy expended by the other agents' bolts, pulling it into my center. It built until there was no more room to contain it–until I was nothing more than exhilaration and pain. The chaos surrounding me became white noise, as I kept the vision of my mother front and center in my mind.

With my glowing palms facing down at my sides, I sank into the water, my knees hitting the river stones just below the surface.

And I let go.

Purple and blue beams streaked through the river water in all directions like a lightning-filled sky. Light filled my vision. The Shadowmen standing closest to me dropped before she even had the chance to scream. One by one, the shadows fell, screeching and sizzling in the electrified water. The smell of cooked flesh filled the air.

It was over quickly.

Energy thoroughly spent, I stumbled to my feet and nearly fell back over. My vision was blurry, and my limbs felt boneless and numb. I'd never expended so much energy at one time before.

The night was silent save the sound of the rushing river.

I shook my head, and as my vision cleared, a horrific scene materialized. Dozens of bodies surrounded me, bobbing on the surface of the water like dead fish.

I turned away and vomited into the river.

Chapter 10

Kirie

I was a monster.

A hideous, dangerous, monster.

And a coward, too. Because instead of facing what I'd done, I ran. Up the hill and away from the rushing river full of charred bodies.

I stumbled up the graffiti-covered stairs, across the courtyard, and through the tall green paneled doors of Basilica di San Bartolomeo. Falling into one of the wooden pews, I let my head fall back against the backrest, unable to hold it upright any longer. Above me, centuries-old paintings surrounded by gilded trim decorated the ceilings, each displaying cherubic men and women draped in flowing robes. My eyes swam with emotion and the paintings morphed into something darker. Instead of angels and saints, I saw men and women screaming, their skin turning black as they fell back into the river. My body shook as I remembered the masks of horror on the faces of my classmates and fellow agents as I fled the scene.

I imagined that at any moment, senior agents would storm the chapel and demand punishment, or at the very least, my expulsion. Surely what I'd done was forbidden by some Society code of conduct. Killing without restraint or a clear target must've been against some *moral code* at least. I'd released my energy into that water without restraint, without control, killing everyone in my path. There was no place for me within a society determined to save the world's *humanity*.

The heavy wooden door creaked open, and a gust of cool wind blew down the aisle. Goose flesh prickled across my skin, making me shiver. I briefly considered running from the inevitable reprimand, but I couldn't summon the energy. *Let them find me. I don't care.*

A lone figure appeared in my peripheral. I recognized Finn's energy, and I rolled my head along the back of the pew to face him. He sat several feet away, silently staring toward the altar. I wanted to move away from the kindness and warmth radiating from his strong and steady frame—I deserved neither after what I'd done—but my body was too limp and hollow.

"Go away," I said in a voice full of gravel, sounding like the monster I was.

"I had to check on you," Finn said, warmth and patience in every word.

I swiped a stray tear from my face with a limp hand. "I'm fine. I just need to be alone right now."

He sighed and leaned back against the wooden bench, smooth and shiny with age, seemingly determined to make himself comfortable. Fine. Damn him.

We sat silently in the damp stone chapel for several long minutes. Candles atop metal candelabras flicked along the aisle, tossing dancing shadows across the walls, but I felt none of the light's warmth.

"Are they going to kick me out now?" I asked, breaking the silence.

"Who? The Society?" He let out a short, humorless laugh. "No. In fact, I believe we owe you our gratitude. You took out dozens of Shadowmen tonight. All on your own. I've never seen anything like it."

I shook my head, refusing to accept praise for my actions. My braid, heavy with river water, flipped over my shoulder. I reached up and held onto it with one hand.

"I k-killed all those people. Fried them until they turned black. *I did that.*" My voice broke on the last word. Self-loathing swirled inside me like black sludge.

"Kirie, those men and women were trying to kill you. Their whole purpose in life is to rid the world of light. That includes people like you and me. It's your duty to fight back. This is a *war,*

Kirie. Casualties are a given." He said the ugly words kindly.

Fury rose in me, hot and strong. "I never wanted to go to war. I never wanted to kill people, no matter how awful they are. I wanted to go to college and study science to *heal* people. I. Don't. Want. This!" I yelled.

My words crashed into the ancient walls like waves. Finn sat stone still beside me, seemingly content to let me rage. But the fight was already draining out of me, and self-loathing quickly covered me in its dark blanket once more.

"Did anyone else get hurt?" I whispered. I replayed the scene in my mind. Had Bert been in the water when I let my energy go? Had Eden? Dayton? Did Aonani make it safely back to her mother? If I'd hurt her . . .

Finn shook his head, his blond hair falling across his forehead. "No. Agents of Light absorb energy, remember. If anything, you energized the group." His joke fell flat on the shiny stone floor. I let it lay there to die. A modicum of pressure lifted from my chest, though, knowing my friends were okay.

"And Jacques?" I asked. I held onto the end of my braid with a tight fist, pulling on it until my scalp stung. River water dripped onto my lap.

Finn's eyebrows dropped low as if they'd suddenly become too heavy to carry and foreboding dread settled over me. "They found his body in the alley behind the restaurant," he finally said.

It was as though a bomb detonated inside my chest, shrapnel shredding my insides. I covered my face with my hands and rocked forward. Ugly sobs tore through me. They echoed through the chapel, bouncing off the gilded walls and back to me as if to affirm my guilt.

My fault.

My fault.

My fault.

So many deaths, so much loss, simply because I existed.

"Kirie," Finn said, scooting near and putting a comforting hand on my back. I shook him off and I turned on him with a glare.

"Don't you *dare* say it. This is all *my* fault, and you know it. Jacques didn't want to stop for food, but I convinced him it would be safe. *I killed him. Me!*"

Finn sighed and dropped his hand. "No, Kirie. The Shadow killed him."

I shook my head back and forth until it swam. "He told me it was too dangerous. But I wanted pizza, Finn. *Pizza!*" My voice broke and I whispered, "He died because I was stupid, selfish, and childish, and . . ."

"Stop!" He commanded, the steel in his voice stopping my breath. "Jaques's death is NOT your fault. Rome has been crawling with Shadows for months now. It was just a matter of time before one or more of our agents ran into one."

"But it didn't have to be Jacques. That's on me," I said, sniffling pitifully.

"Kirie, listen. Once they found and destroyed the Pantheon in Paris, they began patrolling every historical building throughout

Europe, hoping to find another Center. That's why they could gather such a large force to the river so quickly. They were already here."

I pressed my lips into a hard line and looked away.

Finn let out a frustrated sigh. "I know this is hard to believe right now because you're so full of self-loathing, but this is bigger than you."

Fresh shame filled me. He was right. I was the most selfish and self-centered monster that ever walked the earth. And my weaknesses were hurting others.

"I think I need to resign from The Society," I whispered.

"Kirie . . ." he sighed.

"No, I mean it. I can't do this anymore. I obviously can't control myself and I don't want to keep hurting people. You need to let me go."

"I can't," he said shaking his head. "You won't be safe on your own. I *can't* let you go."

"I thought I was free to make my own choices. Besides, why do you care where I go? You have legions of Agents at your beck and call. Why do you need *me*? I'm just one person."

Finn sighed and ran his hands down his face. "Look. There's something I need to tell you."

I folded my arms over my chest, guarding myself again from more unwanted absolutions. Finn gazed up at the painted coffered ceiling as if praying to God. Finally, he said, "I knew your mother."

I turned toward him fully, genuinely confused. "What?"

Finn looked a million miles away, his blue eye reflecting the painting above like twin mirrors. "I knew the moment I saw you. It was like staring at a ghost."

My throbbing head spun, unable to find solid ground in this strange conversation. "What are you *talking* about?"

His eyes flickered down to meet mine briefly before reaching for the ceiling again. He swallowed hard. "You look so much like her." The words came out in a whisper.

"Finn, you're not making any sense," I said, rubbing my eyes.

His eyes dropped to the floor. "I, uh, took the water bottle you left behind after practice last week to a lab."

My swollen brain ached from the whiplash his words were giving it. "My water bottle? W-why?"

"I needed a DNA sample."

I shook my head and squeezed my eyes shut. "I d-don't understand."

"It was a match. 99.9 percent." Finally, he looked at me, and it was there, in his tortured, hopeful expression. I began to put it all together. The beach blond hair, Ocean blue eyes that matched my own. An energy that felt so familiar—like family. The images I'd seen of my mother, younger and playing in the surf when I healed Finn's cut—those had been *his* memories of her, not mine.

My hands lay limply in my lap.

No.

It wasn't possible.

99.9 percent.

Too much.

Too much.

Tears ran rivers down my face, creating tiny pools in my upturned palms. Was he saying . . . Finn? My *father?* Incoherent thoughts flitted through my mind like a canary in a cage. My mom's letter. A beach boy with the gift of light. Shadows stalking him. No dead body.

My father?

"M-my mom t-told me my father died," I stammered.

"That's what I led her to believe," he said.

Not dead. Just gone.

I balled my tear-soaked hands into fists. Fury took over as I thought of all the precautions my mom had to take to keep me safe—all that worry, all those years of not really living—hiding from the world. He left her to raise me on her own in a world full of hunters made of shadows. It cost her her life.

"I should explain," he began, hands out in surrender.

My voice rose, cutting him off. "How could you do that to her? To me? What kind of man leaves his pregnant girlfriend alone to fend for herself?"

Finn's face crumbled, and it was like watching a great monument turn to rubble. "I left The Society to be with her. I thought that I could hide from what I was and live a normal life with the woman I loved. I was convinced I could make it work. But when the Shadowmen showed up, I knew I couldn't hide from The Order forever. As long as Claire was with me, she was in constant danger. I had to let her go."

My hand itched to slap him. How dare he act like the wounded hero? "What about me? Didn't you think your *child* needed protection? Didn't you wonder if I turned out to be like you?"

He shook his head, brows tightly pinched. "I didn't know Claire was pregnant. I never would've left her if I'd known."

I pressed my hands to my face. Tears leaked through my fingers and down my chin.

"Look, I know you must hate me right now. I hate myself, too, a little. But I want you to know I loved Claire more than I can express. I've never loved anyone since. I would give anything to have those years back, to see you grow inside her, hear you say your first words, take your first steps, to watch Claire mother my child. But I can't," his voice broke. "All I can do is ask for your forgiveness and a chance to be a part of your life going forward."

I kept my hands over my eyes, unable to look at him. Finn was my father. I had a *father*. After all the loss and grief, I didn't know how to process the thought that I was no longer an orphan. I didn't know how to feel about a man who left my mother when she needed him most, regardless of his good intentions. I was lost. Utterly lost.

"I'm sorry. I've dropped a lot on you. My timing is less than ideal, I know. You don't have to say anything. I just . . ." Finn signed. "After all you've been through, it didn't feel right to keep the truth from you."

The bench jostled as Finn stood. "I've asked one of the senior agents to take you home so you can get cleaned up and rest," he said, sliding into his "Head-of-The-Society" authoritative tone as easily as one slides his arms into a suit jacket. I wanted to punch him for it. "Given what has happened here tonight, I've decided to call for a regional meeting. It'll be held in the central conference room tomorrow morning at ten. All members are required to attend."

The heavy doors creaked open again, and a woman in her early fifties stepped into the chapel. Her black combat gear was drenched, presumably from being in the river. My face began to heat in shame and embarrassment, knowing she must have witnessed my lack of control. Finn nodded once to the agent and walked down the central aisle and out the ancient doors into the starless night.

"I'm here to escort you home," the woman said, eyes averted. She couldn't even *look* at me.

I stood and followed her to a black sedan waiting in the courtyard. I slid into the backseat and laid my head against the window, watching the city lights fly by as we drove back to my apartment. Just hours before, it was Jacques behind the wheel. It all felt surreal, a deranged, funhouse version of my life where everything went sideways. A living nightmare I couldn't wake up from.

The car slowed. I lifted my eyes to my building, barely registering that I was home. *Home.* Whatever that meant.

"Someone will be there to pick you up in the morning," the

Agent said, glancing back at me only briefly in the rearview mirror.

"Thanks," I mumbled and stepped out of the car.

She waited until I was in the door before driving away. I somehow made my way up the stairs to my bedroom on numb legs. I threw myself face-first into my covers and fell into a dreamless sleep.

Chapter 11

Luca

Luca took Abbott's advice and went on "holiday." Fewer questions that way. He found a short-term beachside rental in the Florida Keys. It was close to his island and as far from the frigid northern states as one could get without crossing borders. He hoped the warmth and light would keep his agitated shadows at bay.

The thatch-roofed bungalow he'd rented for the week was as picturesque as it was private. Luca sat at a wicker desk in an open-air office facing the Atlantic Ocean. Seagulls squawked happily outside the open doors, and sunlight played on the water's surface, casting rippling shadows into the room. His dark hair curled at his neck, soaked in humidity and sweat.

Luca's laptop was in his carry-on bag by the door. It wasn't safe to use Society-issued devices while doing clandestine work, so he'd purchased a laptop from an electronics store in town using cash that morning.

The golden Florida sun rose and fell through the open doors as he poured over the D.C. files he'd stolen from the shadow. A discarded plate of Ropa Vieja he'd ordered from a local Cuban restaurant sat beside his elbow, mostly untouched. The spicy beef had cooled in the night air as Luca zoomed in on a satellite image of yet another Iranian mine. His eyes ached from staring so long at the small, low-resolution screen.

The emails from the stolen files created a patchwork picture of a complex plot. It was clear that The Order intended to bring the world to its knees with a massive nuclear attack. It was a plan many years in the making. Like The Society of Light, The Order played a long game. Dignitaries and politicians worldwide had been pulled into its dirty dealings, *most* of them against their will.

The emails also revealed that the controversial 2015 Iranian deal had been a ruse orchestrated by The Order for the sole purpose of gaining access to large amounts of uranium without the UN and other world powers noticing. The grainy pictures hidden inside the encrypted files showed images of the mine where the exchange would take place. Unfortunately, there were no identifiable markers Luca could use to pin down an exact location.

This was problematic since Luca couldn't go strolling through each of the ten mines spread across Iran without giving himself away. If he mucked this up, there would be no second chances.

He'd have one go of it. Luca would have to be 100% sure he had the right mine before he made his move. Time was running out.

The sun had risen over the ocean and climbed high in the sky when Luca found a date hidden among the dozens of emails sent between various world dignitaries and "Unknown." The Order would transport the stockpile of uranium on February 15th. Two days from then.

He clicked through the photos yet again and paused on an exterior shot of the mine. In the far left corner of the shot, was the edge of a sign. It was such a small thing, so he'd missed it before. Luca zoomed in and saw a sweeping line of blue paint. Cropping the image, he did a reverse image search. Nothing valuable came up.

He tapped the trackpad on the laptop with his forefinger as he thought. His gut told him this small detail was significant, and his gut was rarely wrong. Luca did another image search, this time of the gates in front of each of the mines. Fifteen minutes later, he found something. Saghand, a mine just southeast of Tehran, had a white sign stretching across the road. On it was blue script. Luca enlarged the two photos, comparing the lines and dimensions of the blue paint on each. They were a perfect match.

"Finally," he sighed, leaning back in the office chair. He found it.

Luca stood for the first time in hours and stretched his aching back. He paced across the tiled floor, sand sticking to his bare toes as he considered his options—a mission like this required backup, preferably three or four agents plus more for tech support. That would be fine and dandy if it weren't for the fact that this wasn't a sanctioned mission.

The Society still had no idea Luca had recovered the file from the Shadow in D.C., and since he hadn't identified the traitor who leaked the Paris location yet, he didn't know who to trust. Luca stopped pacing. That wasn't entirely true. He felt a sharp pain in his gut. He could trust Abbott, Arin, and Alena with his life. Had, in fact, many times over.

The weight of the world dropped on his shoulders and Luca slumped down in the office chair, dropping his heavy head in his hands. Destroying several hundred pounds of highly flammable uranium in an underground mine would be dangerous to one's health. Luca knew this would likely be his last mission. He'd already made peace with that. Not many Agents of Light lived long lives anyway. Luca had already outlived his entire family and lost his own soul years ago. He was ready and willing to give his life to ensure The Order did not prevail in the end. Any agent would.

But he would also give his life to protect his adopted family. How could he ask them to go on an unsanctioned mission with no backup and little to no chance of survival? And yet, how could he not, given the alternative? If the mole got wind of his mission, they'd alert The Order and the opportunity to stop them from getting hold of the uranium would be lost.

So, that was it.

It was the world's survival for his life and the lives of nearly everyone he loved. A shitty bargain.

But when had life ever played fair with Luca? Kirie's face materialized in his mind for the one-millionth time since they'd parted in Paris, and his heart squeezed painfully. The moment he'd met Kirie, he'd felt a bone-deep connection with her. He still did despite the days and oceans between them. Just in the past twenty-four hours or so, he could've sworn the connection had grown stronger. He'd felt emotions that weren't his own—fear, desperation, and grief, but only for an instant. Then the intense sharing of energy dissipated. It left him questioning his own sanity.

Kirie unsettled Luca. She made him *think* things. Things like maybe there was more to his future than darkness and death. For a short time, she'd even made him imagine a future full of love and light—with her.

Luca was surprised to realize that until that moment, he'd still been holding out hope that the two of them would find a way back to each other. The loss of that little bit of hope was crushing. He'd never again feel the pull of their shared connection. Never again touch his lips to her warm, full mouth. Never encounter her soul-healing light.

Luca curled his hands in his hair and screamed, "Fuck!"

It was unfair. He'd never had a chance at a normal, healthy life. None of them had. Even Kirie. With all her mother's efforts to hide her away, she'd still been stripped of her home, safety, and peace. Fuck the Shadowmen, too, for that. Tears rolled down his face, mixing with the humid, salty air. Luca curled into himself and let the pain of disappointment pierce through him like a thousand tiny knives.

It was the sound of waves that eventually brought Luca back to himself. He dried his face and straightened his shirt. And because he was a weak man, Luca turned to his low-quality laptop and logged onto the medical chat board he'd been frequenting for the past year. Like always, his heart sped up in anticipation of connecting with Kirie again. His hands shook as he typed.

Parisxxxi8: Hey. You up?

Luca stewed in anticipation and self-loathing as he waited for Kirie to respond. An AI algorithm had flagged her as a possible Bright One early last fall when she began logging on to medical chat boards and asking overly intelligent questions for a high school senior. Abbott tasked Luca with the initial contact. Luca had no idea then that Brightgirl101 would fundamentally change him. He could instantly feel an abnormally strong connection despite having only met her online.

When they'd boarded a plane heading to Colorado, Luca felt their connection grow as the miles separating them shrank. He'd been nervous to meet her, afraid he might instantly give himself away as Parisxxxi8, so he'd sent Arin to stake out the science fair in his stead. He'd pressed Arin for details that night, but his descriptions lacked substance. "She was hot, bro," he'd said, "but a bit insecure for my taste." Luca had never wanted to punch his brother more.

Luca waited for thirty minutes, but there was no response from

Brightgirl101. He glanced at the clock and rolled his eyes. It was 10:30 PM in Florida, which meant it was only 4:30 AM in Rome. She was probably still asleep. Luca ran a hand down his face. He wasn't thinking straight these days.

Luca's phone lit up, making him jump. Abbott's name appeared on the screen. He swiped his thumb across the phone's surface and put it to his ear. "I have news," Luca said, dreading the conversation awaiting them.

"Tell me," Abbott said in his no-nonsense, "I'm the father," voice Luca rarely heard him use anymore.

"Meet me in Tehran tomorrow after the meeting. Bring Arin and Alena. I found the uranium."

"I see." Abbott sighed heavily. "We'll be there. We have much to discuss." The line went dead.

Luca had a long list of regrets. Killing innocents, endangering the lives of the only family he had left, and not killing Donovan when he had the chance were a few. How strange it was that not seeing Kirie again, not saying goodbye to a girl he'd hardly known, topped the list. Luca squeezed his eyes shut and let the shushing ocean waves comfort him. He tried to content himself with the memory of her. It wasn't nearly enough.

Chapter 12

Kirie

The meeting was held in a large auditorium deep within The Rome Center of Light. Dozens of rows of chairs stretched across the wide-open space. Like the other rooms in the subterranean compound, this one was lined by brightly lit windows emitting solar light. Instead of modern landscapes, however, these windows displayed rich digitized landscapes of Rome as it once was. Stately columns and domed buildings surrounded by green rolling hills and golden lanes were reminiscent of paintings by 17th-century artists like Gaspard Dughet. I wouldn't have been surprised if that was exactly what they were.

A stream of agents flowed into the room. Men and women had traveled from all over Europe. I could only guess they'd jumped on their private jets to arrive mere hours after receiving the summons.

I stood in the back corner, holding up the wall. I'd left my hair down, needing the weight and comfort of it. I wore it around me like a veil, hoping to hide my face from spectators. Still, their gazes found me. My face grew furnace-hot as their eyes pressed in on me. News of the river attack had traveled far. It was even featured on the morning news, though the story's particulars were doctored. According to the perky morning news reporter, a tree branch fell on a live electrical wire, knocking it into the river. No casualties were reported, of course.

I stared high above their heads, refusing to meet their gazes. Did they fear the little monster in their midst? Did they know I was also responsible for Jaques's death? My legs itched to run away to some dark corner of the world to wallow in my self-hatred.

Finn sat at the front of the room in a high-backed velvet chair atop a platform. He appeared at ease in his position of power, wearing it casually like a pair of flip-flops.

The word "father" echoed in my head like a pinball bouncing against the walls of my mind. I studied the details of his face. Was there any part of me that was him? Perhaps his nose? His chin? His power? Why, after knowing I had a living, breathing father, did I still feel like an orphan? I tore my eyes away, not having the energy to process this new development.

A striking Hispanic woman with salt and pepper hair sat on Finn's right side. Straight-backed, chin lifted, the older woman exuded confidence that spoke of power and experience. Ms. Delgado, I assumed. The third leader of The Society of Light.

To Finn's left sat a man wearing a dove grey power suit and a self-righteous scowl. Mr. Daiko. Unlike Finn, Daiko wore his elevated position like a gilded crown. He surveyed the growing crowd with the air of a king inspecting his loyal subjects. My skin crawled at the sight of him. Something about Daiko didn't sit right with me. I still hadn't forgiven him for entering my thoughts and memories without warning or permission for the "safety of The Society." Justification or not, I'll never forget how violated I'd felt.

Abbott entered through the large double doors and quickly found my hiding spot. I let out a little sigh when I saw him. After The Society and Shadowmen began to suspect I was a Bright One, Abbott acted as my fake AP US History teacher back in Colorado. He represented a small piece of the home I'd lost, and I found some comfort in his presence. Though I hadn't seen him in months, we'd kept in touch via texts.

Abbott gave me a solemn nod and, somehow sensing I needed space, stood a foot or two away from me along the wall. Though he didn't say a word, I felt his silent support coming through his energy. I let my hunched shoulders relax a little.

In the back row, not far from where we stood, Dawn, Eden, Dayton, and Liang sat huddled together. They whispered to each other excitedly, likely still hyped from the night before—their first mission. Anyone with eyes could see they were a unit. Connected at the shoulders, they were a solid chain of support and camaraderie. It seemed the fight on the river had brought them even closer. My stomach tightened at the sight of them. I trained with them, sure, but that didn't mean I was part of the group's DNA. And after what I'd done, I knew I never would be. I was a freak among freaks.

Several seats down, Aonani sat with her mother. She bounced up and down, kicking her little legs impatiently. I smiled despite myself. At least the little fireball hadn't been hurt in the fight. It was the one ray of sunshine in my otherwise crappy life.

The final arrivals trickled just before 10:00 AM and the heavy wooden doors were shut tight. Nearly every seat was occupied. The sheer number of agents close enough to Rome to make the impromptu meeting was staggering. I had no idea there were so many agents in The Society. I was beginning to think there was little about The Society of Light I *did* know.

Without thinking, my eyes scanned the crowd, searching for the one agent I hoped hadn't come. I held my breath when I spied a tall, dark-haired boy sitting near the front. I searched for the pull I'd always felt in Luca's presence. Though it was still there, it was no stronger than it had been in the months since we separated. The boy turned his head, revealing his profile, and my chest deflated—not Luca. I reminded myself that was a *good* thing. He was likely galivanting across the globe James Bond-style, doing God-knew-what. I couldn't care less.

Mr. Daiko stood and approached the podium and raised his palms. A hush settled over the room as he leaned forward on the podium like a pastor revving up for a stirring sermon.

"Welcome. We've assembled you here today to discuss the escalating aggression against the Agents of Light and our Centers. As you might have guessed, The Order has become emboldened by its successful attack on the Pantheon in Paris. They have deduced that our Centers are likely connected to other monuments and buildings of historical importance. And so, they are amassing in cities with rich histories across the globe, hunting for agents and clues to our other Centers of Light."

The audience's eyes were trained on Daiko with rapt attention, hypnotized by his smooth tone and provocative words.

"As you may have heard, one of our junior agents was exposed last night just blocks from this location. Within moments, dozens of Shadowmen were able to form an offensive attack." He swept a somber gaze across the room until his eyes settled on me. "Now more than ever, we must be *vigilant* in our actions. A simple misstep can lead the Shadowmen to our strongholds. We cannot afford to be careless in times like these."

Flames licked my cheeks. I flattened myself against the wall, willing it to absorb my body. It was one thing to berate myself for my own carelessness. It was a whole other thing to have one of the leaders of the world's most influential organizations publicly call me out for it.

"Thankfully, our highly trained agents were able to step in and defeat the Shadowmen with their light abilities. We all owe them a debt of gratitude."

Daiko spread his arms wide over the crowd in magnanimous praise and my mouth dropped. There was a hesitant smattering of applause, many agents having already heard about what I'd done on the river. Several heads turned toward me, confusion etched into their brows. I looked at Finn, wondering if he was in on the lie, but his attention remained on Daiko, his calm eyes giving nothing away. I quickly closed my gaping mouth and smoothed my features into a similar mask.

Once the uninspiring applause died down, Daiko continued. "Make no mistake. The enemy is closing in despite our recent victory over Darkness. They are at our very gate. We must meet them on the battlefield or face certain destruction. These are the days foretold by countless visionaries throughout human history. These are the days when light gains the final victory over Darkness!"

The crowd erupted in cheers this time, and the room surged with blinding light. The hairs on my arms stood on end as their combined energy rushed over me. Daiko basked in it like a lizard in the sun, soaking the light into his cold skin. He stepped back, allowing Ms. Delgado to take center stage.

The older woman stepped up and placed her hands on the podium. She gazed out at the agents with a solemn expression. "As you may have already surmised, we're at open war," she said in a smooth Spanish accent. "We'll need every ounce of light on earth if we're to be successful. Together, nothing can break us." Delgado swept an intense gaze across the assembly. "And so, all agents ages eighteen to sixty-five are officially called to active duty, effective immediately."

A murmur swept through the crowd like wind through a prairie. Some heads bowed side to side to whisper, others shaking in disbelief, approval, or both. My eyes found my classmates. Dayton and Liang sat on the edge of their seats, eyes trained on Delgado. Dawn and Eden sat quietly, holding hands. Eden's lips were pressed in a hard line, a light pink scar running down her face from the bullet wound the night before, and for the first time since meeting her, Dawn lacked a little of the serenity that usually enveloped her.

Ms. Delgado raised her hands again, a silent call for quiet obedience. The crowd complied immediately. "Additionally, for their safety, children under the age of eighteen are now under house arrest until further notice."

Aonani jumped to her feet, her hands in tight fists at her sides. "But I want to fight," she cried indignantly. Several heads turned her way, and a few agents chuckled goodheartedly. Her mother slapped a hand over Aonani's mouth, shushing her. She pushed her hand away and glared at the other agents, daring them to defy her. I hid a smile behind my hand.

Delgado raised her hands for quiet again, and Aonani's mother wrestled her into her seat. "Activity at local Centers of Light has been suspended for the time being. Only a select few will remain to transfer data and information to secure satellite locations." Again, a murmur swept across the room. Ms. Delgado turned and nodded to Finn. She took her seat as the light and voices in the room surged.

Finn stood and approached the pulpit. "Please remain calm," he implored. He waited as the noise died down and all eyes were on him. He proceeded with a placating tone he'd repeatedly used on me in training. "We knew this day was coming. We're well prepared for the fight ahead of us. We're the torches in the night. We don't fear the dark and we will not stop until The Order is eradicated from this earth."

Agents stood, and thunderous applause filled the auditorium, shaking the walls. The heaviness of it pressed in on me, making it hard to breathe. I slipped out of the side door and into the deserted hallway, taking a deep breath. Finn's voice faded as the door slid shut behind me. I couldn't believe Daiko had shamed me that way. Perhaps he did me a favor, crediting last night's "victory" to the other agents. Perhaps it would take some of the spotlight off me.

"Are you alright?" a male voice said from behind. I spun around and found Abbott in the hallway. My shoulders dropped.

"Not really," I said. "I'm sure you heard about what happened last night."

"I did," he nodded.

I folded my arms over my chest. "So?"

"So, what?" he asked with raised brows.

"Do you regret it?"

"Regret what?"

"Bringing me to Paris. Introducing me to The Society of Light."

His brows knit. "Why would I regret it? You're one of the most powerful agents The Society has ever seen."

"I killed people last night, Abbott. A lot of people,"

"Yes, but . . ." he began.

"I was reckless," I cried, cutting him off. "I didn't even think before I let go of my power. What if there were bystanders in the water downstream? I could've killed innocents. I'm dangerous!"

Abbott didn't blink at my confession. "Of course you are. That's what makes you an asset to The Society."

"An asset?" I laughed. "I'm a *monster*. I have all this power but I'm inexperienced and careless. Aren't you worried I'll destroy everything?"

Abbott slowly approached me like I was a cornered predator—in many ways I was. He carefully reached out and pushed one side of my hair over my shoulder with the tips of his fingers to reveal my face, then stepped back. "I'm only worried about the toll it's taken on you. What we do leaves a mark on our spirits," he said kindly. I peered down at the floor, unable to meet his fatherly gaze.

"But how can I live with myself after this, Abbott? How can I ever look at myself in the mirror again and not see a murderer?"

"By remembering what you do in the fight against Darkness allows others to remain free. You don't know what it's like when The Order's in control. You were born in a softer time when you can freely pursue knowledge and light. But what about those who are born into tyranny, slavery, and oppression? Darkness like that snuffs out a person's inner light. At times, even their will to live.

There's nothing crueler than that."

My thoughts immediately went to the disturbing dreams I'd had of The Void. They were so real, so hauntingly real. I'd lost myself in the vast darkness then. My light and sense of self had been stripped from me as had my will to fight. I knew what he spoke of more than he could've guessed.

Abbott continued. "By fighting—and yes, sometimes killing—Shadowmen, you're helping to ensure a brighter future for us all."

"I understand that. I do," I said around the lump rising in my throat. "But all I ever wanted to do was use light to heal people. All I ever wanted to do was use my gifts to make the world better."

"And you will," Abbott said, putting his hands over my shoulders. "Once this war is over for good, we're going to need your brilliance and light to build a better society."

"I just don't know if I'm strong enough to survive this war." I jabbed a finger to my chest. "I don't know if *I'm* enough."

"Listen to your inner self and follow the light. It will be enough."

I rolled my eyes and let out a sarcastic laugh. "You sound like a fortune cookie."

"If only I were as wise," he said with a wink. The doors to the conference room swung open, and agents began filing out. "I think you better head on out before your new fans begin asking for your autograph," Abbott said, hitching a thumb at a group of agents walking our way, their eyes trained on me.

"Thank you, Abbott. For supporting me."

"Always," he said with a smile. He turned and spread his arms wide and approached the agents, blocking their view of me. "What can I do for you ladies and gentlemen?"

I took that moment to escape out the side door. A new driver, this one more silent than the last, took me home from the meeting. I sat quietly in the backseat, chewing on my lip. When we pulled up to my curb, a large man stood next to my apartment door.

We wear the mask that grins and lies,

It hides our cheeks and shades our eyes,

This debt we pay to human guile;

With torn and bleeding hearts we smile,

> "We Wear the Mask"
> by Paul Laurence Dunbar

Chapter 13

Kirie

Arin stood in the shadows of my building, his massive shoulders uncharacteristically hunched over. He held a shiny black phone to his ear. Scowling at the ground, he nodded to whoever spoke on the other end. His downturned lips changed the shape of his face.

As the car approached, the frown he'd been wearing melted like a mask made of wax. He murmured something into the phone and slid it into his back pocket. I thanked my nameless driver and slid out of the car.

"Arin!" I cried and rushed into his open embrace. He wrapped me in his tree trunk-sized arms and lifted me from the ground. Arin squeezed me tightly, forcing the air from my lungs before setting me back on the pavement. I stepped back and sucked in a lung full of his masculine body spray. His sudden appearance felt like a ray of sunlight in the dark. The warmth of his bright smile surrounded me, somewhat easing my anxiety.

"What are you doing here?" I asked.

"I was summoned just like everyone else," he said, smiling down at me.

"Right," I said, feeling stupid. "I must've missed you in the crowd."

He shrugged his shoulders. "Came late. Left early."

"Oh. Okay, well come on. We shouldn't stay on the street." I grabbed his hand and led him into the cramped apartment lobby. His shoulders brushed against the walls as he followed me up the narrow staircase.

My apartment felt smaller when Arin stepped into it, his large frame dwarfing the already cramped space. Arin wandered into the kitchen and leaned against the counter as I set my keys down and took off my shoes. He picked an apple from the fruit bowl and tossed it in the air with unfocused eyes. He seemed a million miles away. I stepped up beside him and put a hand on his arm.

"You doing okay?"

He blinked himself back to the present. "Always. Why do you ask?"

"You looked upset when I pulled up. Did you receive bad news?"

He shook his head. "It's nothing to worry about." Arin stood up straighter. "So, what'd you think of the meeting this morning?

Pretty intense, huh?"

I decided to be a friend and go along with his obvious attempt at changing the subject. "It was a bit overwhelming. Plus, everyone kept staring at me."

His mouth quirked up on one side. "Yeah, I heard about what happened last night. You're an instant legend now, Kirie. You know that, right?"

I rolled my eyes. "I'm not a *legend*. I'm a *freak*."

"We're all freaks here, Kirie. You're just a bit flashier than the rest of us." He shrugged. "Own it."

"I don't want to stand out for killing people, Arin. I don't want to be that person," I pouted.

"What person? A badass who destroys Shadowmen?" Arin put his hands over my arms and squeezed. I looked off to the side, blinking away the tears burning my eyes. "They aren't good people, babe. If you hadn't killed them, they would've killed you."

"I just, don't know who I am anymore. I don't recognize myself."

"You just need a distraction." Arin put an arm around my shoulders and began leading me toward my bedroom. "And I have just the thing that will help take your mind off all your woes."

"Um, Arin. What are you doing?" I leaned back against his pull, though I would've had more success swimming against an ocean riptide for all the progress I made.

"Relax," he said, laughing at my worried expression. "I'm just going to help you pack. We're going on an adventure! You'll need enough clothes to last a few days."

"Okay, crazy pants. You know I can't go on a trip with you. You heard what Ms. Delgado said. Rome is on lockdown. They're sending agents to satellite locations."

"Man. Why are you always so uptight?" He nearly dragged me the last few steps to my bedroom door. I slid out from beneath his heavy arm.

"Uptight? The Society just declared open war!" I said, folding my arms.

Arin pinched my side as he slid past me, making me jump. I glared at his back and followed him. "Even more reason to get away."

"Be serious, Arin," I sighed, plopping onto my bed. "You know Bert. He would kill me if I missed even a *minute* of training. I barely get a night off as it is."

Arin began rooting through my tiny closet, searching for who knew what. "Then I'd say you've earned some time off. Come on, Kir. You need to have a little bit of fun from time to time."

"I have fun," I mumbled.

He snorted loudly. "Liar." He threw a black duffle bag onto the floor and opened my drawers.

I'd never admit it to his smug face, but we both knew he was right. Since moving to Rome, I'd only trained and studied with my classmates. Living on my own hadn't improved my social life either. Arin's sudden appearance only made me realize how lonely I was, how starved I was for conversation that didn't involve which type of weapons were most effective or how to blast someone ten feet into the air with nothing but my *"inner light."* I was starved for friendship, and Arin might very well have been my last real friend in the world. Besides Parisxxxi8, of course, though I wasn't sure he really counted, given that I still didn't know his real name.

He put his hands on my shoulders and leaned down until we were eye-to-eye. "Come on, Kir. Be brave."

"But Bert . . ."

"It's all taken care of." He squeezed my shoulders for emphasis, and I felt my bones pop a little under the pressure. "I talked to Bert before coming over here. He gave his blessing."

A surprised laugh erupted from my mouth. "Are you serious?" I couldn't imagine Bert agreeing to let Arin take me on a spontaneous trip.

"Serious as a heart attack," he said, grabbing my hand and pulling me to my feet.

A bud of excitement began to blossom like a Spring flower in my chest. I stamped it down stubbornly. I still couldn't believe this was happening, that I was going on a last-second trip with Arin. My life just didn't work that way. It never did, not even when my parents were alive.

"You'll need to pack long sleeves and pants. Three or four days' worth should be enough."

My heart sank just a little. So, not a warm vacation on the beach. Long sleeves which only promised more winter. I began pulling clothes from my dresser and tossing them into my duffle bag's open maw. "So. Where are we going, then?"

Arin's eyebrows rose dramatically, and his mouth spread into a wicked grin. "I'm taking you on your first mission!"

The socks I'd been holding fell to the floor with a soft *thunk*. I stared at him in disbelief. "Wait. Seriously?"

"Seriously," he said with a laugh. He smiled and clapped his hands together, obviously enjoying my response.

"But Ms. Delgado said underaged agents are under house arrest," I argued. My eighteenth birthday wasn't for several more weeks. Plus, sending me out into the field with only months of training was reckless. I'd proven that the night before. I would be a liability at best. "Did Bert *really* agree to this?"

Arin leaned against the wall. "Actually, it was his idea. I ran into your sweetheart of a trainer today, and when I mentioned that I was going on a quick mission, he suggested I bring you along. He thinks you're ready."

I searched his face for the lie I knew must be there, but his gaze was steady. For a moment, I thought I saw a shadow pass over his face, like a cloud over the noon-day sun, but it was only for a moment. A small chill raced across my skin, making the hairs along my arms stand at attention. I trusted Arin, maybe with my life. I might even love him—as a friend, of course. But none of this made sense.

Bert had spent every day of the last several months telling me how far behind I was, how I was too old to begin training, no matter how special The Society believed I was. There was *no way*

Bert told Arin I was ready.

"Uh, uh. He did *not* say that," I said emphatically.

"Have a little faith in yourself, Kirie. Everyone can see how special you are, even Bert, whether he says it out loud or not. You proved to everyone last night that you're a force to be reckoned with."

"I don't know . . ." I sighed.

Arin put his hands on either side of my face and leveled his eyes with mine. "You've got this, Kir."

I put my hands over his and closed my eyes for a moment. "Ok. Let's do this." I couldn't stop a smile from spreading across my face.

"Don't get too excited," he laughed with his hands out, palms up. "Alena's coming, too."

And just like that, the excitement building inside me popped like a balloon, leaving stinging trepidation and anxiety in its place.

Chapter 14

Kirie

I hadn't seen Alena since the day after the Paris attack. We barely said a word as we packed up our shared Paris apartment. Like all the other agents, Alena was on active duty, which meant . . . well, I wasn't totally sure what that meant besides being MIA for months at a time.

Though I didn't miss my old roommate, I'd thought of her every day since the Paris bombing. I wondered where she was, what she'd been doing, and who she'd been with. Because what if she was with *him?* Were they training together? Hunting Shadowmen together? Eating meals together? After all, they'd been a unit since they were little, along with Arin. I never dared ask Bert anything that wasn't essential for my physical training, so I still knew very little about how Agent teams worked.

My stomach dropped in with a sickening realization. If Arin and Alena were going on the mission, did that mean Luca would be there, too? I wasn't prepared for that.

Arin must've misunderstood my look of worry, because he patted my head and said, "Don't worry Kir. I'll keep you safe from the big, bad she-wolf."

I pushed his hand away, allowing the thought of Alena and Luca together to float away like smoke in a breeze. "Sorry, Arin, but I think she may be scarier than you." Despite his massive size, Arin was about as aggressive as a stuffed bear. At that moment, I had bigger worries than Alena and her mean-girl attitude. Like whether I was about to run into the first boy to ever break my heart.

I turned to my dresser and pulled out two pairs of black cargo pants. With my back facing Arin, I asked the question I almost couldn't stand to ask. "So." I cleared my throat. "Who else is coming with us on this mission?"

"I'd love to tell you, babe, but I've been sworn to secrecy."

"But you told me about Alena," I protested, tossing the pants into my duffle bag.

"I wanted you to be mentally prepared. Don't worry, I warned her about you, too."

"Like *I'm* the one we need to worry about here." I rolled my eyes and punched his shoulder as I crossed to the closet. I pulled out a few black shirts and my black Society of Light-issued jacket meant for combat training. I might as well look the part for my first assignment.

Arin zipped up my duffle bag and threw it over his shoulder. I followed him out of the apartment and back down the narrow staircase. His massive shoulders blocked the sun streaming from a high window like a total eclipse. Outside, we piled into the small economy car, and Arin sped off into early morning traffic.

We traveled to a small airport on the outskirts of Rome where a sleek jet sat at the far end of the lone runway, jets screaming ready. I laughed as Arin pulled the bags from the trunk and lifted them over his head like a ridiculous bodybuilder. I'd missed my funny friend. He had a way of making me laugh when all I wanted to do was cry—a ray of sunshine in my darkest moments.

I followed Arin up the steps into the plane's cabin, and I couldn't help but stare open-mouthed at the opulent interior. The floor was covered in plush, cream-colored carpet, with gold accents on nearly every surface. Even the cup holders were lined in gold. Along the sides were swivel armchairs made of leather, and a leather couch with red throw pillows at the back of the plane. It was like walking into an upscale magazine spread for the ultra-rich. I felt immediately out of place.

To make matters worse, Alena was already settled in the armchair nearest the door. A fashion magazine lay in her lap.

When she caught sight of me, Alena looked up at Arin and rolled her eyes. "I still can't believe you're bringing her along. The *bambino piccolo* will ruin everything," she said, her Italian accent beautifying her mean words.

Arin leaned down and pressed a kiss to her forehead. "Good to see you, too, sis." He placed the luggage down and left us to talk to the pilot, a pleasant-looking middle-aged man wearing a navy pilot suit. I wanted to beg him to stay and protect me from the she-devil, but I didn't want to appear weak in front of the enemy, so I took a deep breath and boldly faced forward.

"Hi, roomie," she said with a condescending smile.

I lifted my bag and continued past her without response, knowing from experience that it was better not to engage. Stowing my luggage in the back, I sat in the farthest armchair from Alena's. Just when I thought I'd been lucky enough to avoid conversation, Alena said in a sing-song voice, "Luca called last night."

My breath stopped. Hearing Luca's name was exhilarating and painful at the same time. Though I'd thought about him every day since that night in the hallway, I hadn't seen or heard from him.

I dropped my eyes and picked at the imaginary lint on my sweater. "Oh, yeah?" I said with a deceptively even voice. "How is he?" I knew she was trying to get to me. But like a starving animal, I couldn't help but take the bait.

She flipped her thick caramel hair over one shoulder and kept her eyes on her magazine. "Fine. He just finished an important mission and wanted to say hi. Didn't he call you, too? I thought you two were *sooo* close," she said in a sweet tone. She didn't fool me. Alena was about as sweet as a viper.

"Um, no. He didn't," I replied, determined to seem unaffected. I considered putting my new Light training to good use by lighting her hair on fire.

She knew Luca hadn't called me, and she probably knew why since she had personal experience with being snubbed by Luca. To Luca, girls were about as disposable as plastic forks—useful one moment and trash the next. But loving and losing Luca had taught me something; I wasn't like him. Sharing important things like amazing first kisses and near-death experiences was important to me. That was something I couldn't change about myself even if I wanted to. And I didn't.

"Hmmm. That's weird," Alena continued as if I were interested. "He didn't even ask about you. I guess you two aren't as close as I thought."

Knife in heart—twist. Her little barbs were predictable and shallow. Still, they hurt. Every time.

"I guess not. Thanks for letting me know he's okay, though," I said with an exaggerated smile. Kill them with kindness, right?

Right.

Arin stepped out of the cockpit as the jet engines roared to life. "Let's roll, ladies!" He said jovially, oblivious to the ice in the air between Alena and me.

Alena sat upright. "Aren't we going to wait for Abbott?"

I looked at Arin, confused by this new bit of information. I'd seen Abbott just hours ago, and he didn't mention a mission. He must've left right after our conversation in the hallway. What kind of mission would require Abbott's expertise? He identified possible Children of Light for the Society and hadn't been an active Agent for years. Missions weren't a part of his job title.

Arin shook his head. "Nah. He took an earlier flight to secure the car and hotel. He'll meet us at the airport."

I wanted to ask so many questions, but I knew it would've been a waste of breath. On the way to the airport, I'd already peppered Arin with a million questions. Where were we going? What kind of mission was it? Was I going to have to fight Shadowmen? He answered every question with the same response. "You'll have to wait and see." If he wasn't my friend, I would've throat-punched him.

Arin walked down the aisle and plopped onto the couch at the back of the plane, which groaned under his massive weight. Within minutes, we were in the air headed to who-knew-where.

For the next several hours, Alena read fashion magazines while Arin sprawled out on the couch and played games on his phone until he fell asleep. I briefly considered checking my phone for messages from Parisxxxi8 but left it in my bag instead, unsure if I was allowed to use Wi-Fi during the flight.

The only thing to read on board was Elle and Cosmo—not my thing—which meant I had a lot of time with nothing to entertain me but my own thoughts. As always, my mind strayed to Luca like a lost dog. Our first kiss in the park played over and over in my mind. Thanks—and no thanks—to my photographic memory, every detail of his perfect face was etched into my mind. His soft, full lips, full dark hair, and male-model-worthy jawline . . .

I knew it was stupid, but I didn't *want* to forget the color of his green eyes just before we kissed or the warmth of his light on my skin when he healed me. Despite the fact that he'd treated me like his sidepiece and then disappeared from my life as quickly as he'd appeared, I couldn't let him go. I still felt *drawn* to him as if tethered to him by some unseen cord, always pulling my consciousness to him.

I looked up and caught Alena glaring at me. I sighed, exasperated by this ridiculous grudge. "Seriously, what's your problem?"

She scoffed. "*You're* my problem, putana."

I threw my hands up. "I've literally done nothing to you. Why do you hate me so much?"

Alena snapped her magazine shut and leaned forward. "Because after all you've seen, you're still acting so naive," she said, waving a hand at me. "You walk around like the Virgin Mary, all holier-than-thou. But you've never known the hardship the rest of us."

"I don't think I'm better than anyone," I say, brows furrowed. "And how can you say I haven't known hardship? Donovan murdered my parents in front of me. I lost everything."

She scoffed. "Si, but *you* got something none of us did. A childhood."

I folded my arms over my chest. "Some childhood. My mother kept me locked away in a bubble."

Alena pushed out her full bottom lip. "Poor babina. Did your mama love you too much?" she mocked.

"Something like that," I mumbled, looking away from her derisive gaze.

"You should be grateful. *Mio* madre sheltered me from nothing. *Niente.*" The force of her anger was hot like a raging fire.

I shrank back into the leather seat. I could sense the pain in her words, but I didn't know how to respond. "I-I'm sorry," I said lamely. I glanced over to Arin for help, but he remained fast asleep. Traitor. I cleared my throat. "I didn't know."

Alena's hands tightened into fists. "You should be grateful," she repeated, passion rising in her tone. "Your mother loved you enough to shelter you. *Mio madre* was a broken woman. She had an affair with a married man who wanted nothing to do with a baby. He put her out like we were *nothing.*" Alena's voice shook, and her hands trembled. "We had no money, so she sold her body to feed me. The men she entertained were spregevole and often hurt her. She became used and bitter, and she turned that bitterness toward me." She lifted her eyes to mine. They swam with emotion. "You complain of being hidden all your life? There was no safe place in *my* world. When Shadowmen found me, I already lived in the darkness." Alena sniffed and lifted her chin, leveling me with her trademark glare. "So, stop acting like the vittima all the time."

Alena ripped her magazine open again and the cabin descended into silence once more. I stared at her in mute shock. I'd assumed something terrible had happened in her past for her to be adopted by Abbott. I never considered that most of her trauma came from her own mother, not the Shadowmen. Alena's scars ran deeper than I could have guessed. To her, I represented the childhood she *should've* had simply by knowing a mother's love.

And a birth father's, too, I reminded myself. I still couldn't process everything Finn had told me the night before. My birth father was *alive.* I thought of the anger I'd felt toward Finn when he told me the truth. I felt a twinge of guilt in my gut thinking about the harsh words I'd slung at him. To be fair, he *did* deserve some of my anger. Abandoning my mother was negligent and irresponsible despite his good intentions, but I had to acknowledge things could've been worse. Perhaps Alena was right. Perhaps I should be grateful that my mother cared enough to shelter me. Perhaps I should even celebrate that I still had a living parent.

Perhaps I needed therapy.

Alena extended her footrest and quickly fell asleep. I was struck by how soft and harmless she appeared in her sleep. Was it possible that she wasn't all vitriol all the time? Arin and Luca must've seen her better side to love her as they did. I guessed it would be years before she ever allowed me to see that side of her. If ever. I wouldn't hold my breath.

I pulled a blanket from one of the cupboards and snuggled into the luxurious leather seat. Despite the comfort of the cabin, I tossed and turned all night. My thoughts bounced from Luca to Finn to the upcoming mission in an unending cycle. I still had no idea where we were going or what to expect. My tired eyes burned as I glared at Arin's sleeping form. He appeared so *peaceful.* Damn him. He could've at least told me *something* about the mission, so I didn't feel so unprepared. I played all possible scenarios in my mind. Different cities, different missions—I tried to prepare myself for whatever might happen.

I drifted into a shallow sleep at some point in the night. Slowly, I became aware that my surroundings had changed. My body felt cold and wet all over, and I floated weightlessly. I opened my eyes and marveled at countless stars twinkling in the black backdrop of a cloudless sky spread out above me. My eyes followed a shooting star as it streaked across the heavens. It was radiant. Something hit my shoulder, and I looked over. It was a leg, naked and white. I gasped, and sharp river pebbles bit into my palms as I pushed myself upright. Bile rose in my throat at the scene around me. I was back on the banks of Isla Tiberina, encircled by the corpses of the men and women I'd killed. Their sightless black eyes reflected the brilliant night sky as their bodies floated closer to me. Hands, feet, and shoulders bumped into me as they bobbed in the water. I screamed, attempting to push them away, but there were dozens of them.

"Prepare for our final descent," a male voice said overhead. I bolted upright, heart racing. The river scene faded, replaced by the hum of the jet's engine and the soft leather chair beneath me. I breathed in a sigh of relief and tried to shake off the horrid dream. Arin and Alena still slept peacefully, and I envied them, knowing *I* may never sleep that soundly again.

I stood and made my way to the back of the plane. "Arin," I said, leaning over and tapping him on the shoulder. "We're here." He grunted sleepily in response.

Alena lowered her leg rest and yawned, "Finally."

My thoughts exactly.

Though I better understood her motives, I was more than ready to put some space between Alena and me. I swear I could feel hot waves of hatred still rippling off her. I wondered if hate fire was one of her Light gifts.

Arin finally sat up and rubbed his eyes with ham fists. His eyes met mine. "Mornin' beautiful." His sleepy smile could light up Time Square. I felt a strange twinge in my stomach in response. Although I preferred guys who were tall, dark, and brooding, I couldn't deny that Arin was a fine specimen. I mentally slapped myself. *Nope. Not going there.*

"Gross, Arin." Alena pretended to gag.

"So, are you finally going to tell me where we are? Or, I don't know, tell me what the mission is?" I asked, ignoring Alena.

"No, ma'am. That's Abbott's job," Arin said on a yawn.

Once the pilot touched down at our "super-secret" destination and the hatch opened, Alena rushed off the plane like it was on fire. I looked around, wondering if her temper had, in fact, set something ablaze.

"Don't worry," Arin had said after she stalked off, "she'll warm up to you. She's just threatened by you."

An astonished laugh burst from my mouth. "How could I possibly be a threat to *her?* She's the most beautiful and self-assured female I have met in my life . . . and she knows it!"

"Kirie, you're a lot scarier to a girl like Lena than you know. For starters, you're also beautiful . . ." I opened my mouth to protest, but Arin cut me off. "*And* possibly the brightest light the Society has seen in recent memory—you know, besides Luca," he said, waving his hand dismissively. "Of course, she's threatened by you."

"If I'm 'so bright' then how come Bert acts like I'm a total imbecile? He's constantly saying what a disappointment I am to him." I pouted.

"Oh, Kirie." Arin shook his head and chuckled. "That's just how Bert shows he cares. He's hardest on the ones he sees the most potential in. He's pushing you to be better. And it's working. Look how much you've changed since Paris."

I glanced down at my rumpled shirt and jeans. "I guess. I do work out about seven hours a day, so my arms are a bit more toned." I flexed my arms for Arin, making him laugh. "But anyone could do that."

Arin shook his head. "That's not what I meant. Just look at you." He placed his heavy hands on my shoulders and looked me up and down. "Your chin is up, your shoulders back, and you no longer hide behind your hair." He reached behind me and tugged at my braid. "And Bert must be making you do a ton of squats because you're fillin' out those pants quite nicely." He made a show of staring at the back of my jeans.

"Oh my gosh, Arin," I say, punching him in the arm.

"Whoa!" He rubbed the spot where I'd hit him. "That almost hurt."

"Like I said, I've been training," I said haughtily with my chin in the air.

"See," Arin said, pointing at me. "That's what I'm talking about. You're more confident now. It's super hot."

I rolled my eyes at him. "You're ridiculous." But I couldn't help but beam under his praise.

Arin's smile dropped, revealing the same sadness I'd seen in Rome. Instead of covering it up and deflecting like I'd expected, his shoulders and lips drooped. He searched my face with a desperate expression.

"Hey. You okay?" I ask, putting a soft hand on his bicep. I was beginning to worry there was something truly bothering him. I could feel his anxious energy in the muscle beneath my palm.

"Just nervous about the mission, I guess." Arin took a deep breath and straightened his shoulders, pinning his trademark smile back onto his handsome face. "Come on, babe. Abbott's waiting."

Abbott was indeed waiting on the runway when we stepped off the plane. He was standing in front of a stretch limousine wearing a tailored suit and aviator sunglasses. I had to admit, now that he'd dropped the nerdy teacher act, he was kind of badass . . . for an old guy. Alena must've been in the limo already because she was nowhere to be seen. The driver collected our bags and stowed them in the trunk.

When Abbott saw me, he turned and frowned at Arin. "Arin? What's this?"

I looked up at my friend, confused. Arin didn't tell him I was coming?

Arin shrugged. "Bert asked me to bring her along."

Abbott raised his brows. "Arin, a word." He grasped hold of Arin's arm and steered him away from me. I tried to listen to their hushed conversation but could only pick up the tone of Abbott's strained voice. He was worried. About me? About the mission? I couldn't tell. Perhaps I should've listened to my gut and stayed in Rome.

When they returned, Abbott let out a heavy sigh and clapped Arin on the shoulder. "Good luck, my friend. He's going to kill you."

"What's going on? Who's going to Kill Arin?" I asked.

"Don't you worry about that now," Abbott said. "Let's get to the hotel."

I glanced around, trying to guess where we'd landed. We were in a big city, that was clear. Brown smog hung over the city skyline, and the familiar sound of traffic hummed in the distance. Gray, snow-topped mountains surrounded us on all sides. Buildings stretched from the valley floor to the lofty foothills, their lights barely showing in the early evening dusk. It reminded me of Rockies-based cities like Denver and Salt Lake City. Unlike the Rockies, however, nothing about the dry, pungent air and strange city sounds were familiar. I instinctively knew we were a *long* way from home.

"Shall we, my dear?" Abbot raised an arm toward the limo, and I followed Arin in. Alena was sitting in the front near the dividing window, staring at her phone. I sat across from Arin in the back, and Abbott climbed in last, moving his way past us to sit across from Alena. She looked up at him and gave him a sweet smile, and for a moment, her face held no sarcasm or malice. I was taken aback by how much that tiny smile changed her face.

"Could you please tell me where we are now?" I asked Abbott. "Arin refused to tell me anything."

"That's because *he* didn't know."

I turned and glared at Arin, who put his hands up in mock surrender. That punk played me. Abbott chuckled a little. "I apologize for the cloak-and-dagger routine, but it's necessary for your safety and the safety of the mission. We're in Tehran, Iran."

"Iran?" My mouth gaped like a trout. As far as being out of my comfort zone, this one was a winner.

Ignoring my outburst, Abbott pulled a large duffle bag out from under the bench seat and began pulling out muted-colored fabrics. He checked their tags before handing them to Arin, Alena, and me.

"Please, put these on. We'll arrive at the hotel in about forty minutes."

I watched curiously as Arin and Alena pulled long tunics over their clothes. Alena's long-sleeved tunic was red and yellow paisley and had a high, modest neckline. Of course, the color looked stunning against her caramel-colored skin. Arin's black tunic came with a matching pair of loose pants. He put them on over his jeans. I unfolded the muted orange fabric on my lap, and something fell onto the limo. "What's this?" I asked, picking up what appeared to be a long scarf. It was made with rich, cream-colored fabric. I rubbed the silky texture between my forefinger and thumb. It was clearly expensive.

"You didn't expect to walk the streets in Iran looking like that, did you?" Alena said, rolling her eyes. "With *your* hair, you'd be arrested within an hour."

My face burned from my obvious mistake. It was against the law in Iran for women to be in public with their hair showing. I felt stupid for not instantly recognizing the hijab for what it was. I wanted to point out that I didn't even know I was in Tehran until two minutes ago, but I didn't want to sound childish.

Alena expertly wrapped her light-yellow scarf around her hair and under her chin. I watched her movements and then twisted my own long hair into a bun at the base of my neck, wrapping the fabric around my head like Alena had. Although the hijab was light and silky, it felt strange to have something covering my head and neck. But, if it didn't bother Alena, I wasn't going to show my discomfort.

We drove through bustling city streets. Cars and buses wove in and out of the traffic-filled lanes without fear or courtesy. Even though he was driving a stretch limo, our driver seemed to believe he was a racecar driver with unlimited lives. I held onto the seat cushion and prayed we'd reach our destination, whatever that was, in one piece.

As we neared the city's center, we drove down a street lined by tall, terracotta-colored brick buildings and a building that looked strikingly like the Seattle Space Needle. Things in Iran were so different from what I knew, yet also similar. It was as if there were tiny threads everywhere that tied us all together as a human race. All you had to do was look to see them.

The street descended into a giant underground tunnel crossed by another highway. As we drove through the dimly lit tunnel, the limo's interior grew quiet, darkened by the heavily tinted windows. I held onto the seat cushion a little tighter. Although I'd come a long way from that little girl who was afraid of the dark, I was relieved when we finally emerged on the other side of the tunnel.

Fifteen minutes later, the driver parked along the curb of a tall modern building. Arin stepped out first, and the rest of us followed. I played with my hijab nervously, suddenly self-conscious as our driver retrieved our luggage from the trunk. He handed us our bags, climbed back into the driver's seat, and drove away. As a group, we turned toward the hotel's entrance. Standing in front of the sliding doors was a tall, lean boy with eyes the color of a vibrant forest.

What.

The.

Hell.

I held my breath and scooted closer to Arin, trying to hide behind his tall form as Luca walked over. *Luca was here!* Arin must've known he would be. Of course, he did. I glared up at him, but his eyes were pinned on his friend. Arin shifted back and forth on his heels, nervous energy radiating from his body. He needn't have worried about Luca's reaction to me being there because *I* was going to be the one to kill him.

Luca approached Abbott and the two shook hands. Luca visibly relaxed when their hands met, as if he'd been waiting anxiously for him to arrive. He nodded to Alena and Arin. Clearly, he'd been expecting them too. It took him a moment before Luca's eyes found mine. The air jumped out of my lungs, and into the air where I couldn't catch it.

I'd imagined the moment when we'd run into each other again a million times. I'd expected some awkwardness, perhaps a few sarcastic remarks from either him or me, depending on the daydream, but I could've never dreamt of the pure look of hatred on his face.

When he finally spoke, his words were like slaps to my face. "What the hell is *she* doing here?"

Chapter 15

Luca

Arin was a dead man. A corpse walking. Darkly clouded thoughts of violence and rage swirled inside Luca like a debris-filled cyclone. The urge to give in to its seductive pull, to get wrapped up in those feelings of vengeance and hate, was getting stronger by the day. It didn't help when Arin pulled shit like this. Kirie had no part in his and Abbott's plans and Alena never would've willingly brought Kirie anywhere, let alone a mission. This *had* to be Arin's doing. The bloody bastard.

Luca almost didn't see her standing on the sidewalk in front of the hotel earlier. She'd been on Arin's far side, hidden by his giant bloody body. His initial emotion upon seeing her was no small amount of shock, but that quickly melted into something uglier, more urgent. She shouldn't be there when things were so crucial and dangerous. He'd rather she be anywhere else in the world. He was going to *murder* Arin for bringing her.

When they were finally alone in their hotel room, Luca swung to face Arin who was poised, feet apart and fists at the ready as if already preparing for combat. Luca wasn't sure it wouldn't come to that.

"Don't be pissed, bro. It was Bert's idea. He told me to bring her along."

Luca pushed further into the room. Arin stepped back in sync as if the two were partners in a deadly dance. "Bollocks! I swear, mate, if this is your sick way of trying to get me to face my issues, I'm going to . . ."

"Whoa!" Arin said, his large hands held in surrender like flesh-colored stop signs. "It's true. I went to the mandatory meeting—a meeting you *conveniently* missed I might add—and ran into Bert. He asked me where we were headed next. I told him the three of us were doing a standard security sweep, thinking that would be the end of it, but Bert told me to take Kirie along." Arin shrugged his shoulders, straining his shirt.

"You've got to be kidding me," Luca growled and took another step forward. The *last* thing Kirie needed was to be put in *more* danger. He wanted to punch a hole in something. He'd settle for Arin's face.

"Hey. What was I supposed to say?" Arin threw back at him, this time standing his ground. The two boys stood chest to puffed-out chest. "That Kirie couldn't come because we were actually going on a rogue mission that wasn't sanctioned by The Society? You know I couldn't blow our cover like that."

Luca didn't care if the Pope himself assigned Kirie to this mission. They had no business bringing her along. The mere thought of her in danger again filled him with ice-cold dread. The memory of Kirie in the hospital with twilight-colored bruises on her neck after Donovan's attack rose inside his mind like a ghost.

Luca's fists pumped in agitation as he fought to retain control of the shadows dancing dangerously under his skin. "You're a bloody Agent of Light with advanced brain function, Arin; you could've figured *something* out. You might've just ruined the entire mission with your idiocy. She isn't ready for this," Luca growled.

Arin rolled his eyes and folded his arms tightly over his chest. "She handled herself pretty well when Shadowmen attacked two nights ago."

Luca grabbed a fistful of Arin's tunic. "What the hell are you talking about?"

Arin knocked his hand away. "Our girl bumped into one of our Shadow friends in a restaurant. You would know that if you didn't have your head in the sand. The asshole drove her car into the river with her inside it. Then he called a dozen of his buddies to finish the job," Arin said, disgust heavy in his voice. There was nothing he hated more than an unfair fight.

Luca pushed Arin into the wall, and it shook under their weight. "You've got to be shitting me," he growled.

"Dude, stop being such a drama queen," Arin said, pushing him back. "Half the Agents in Rome showed up, and they kicked their asses. Besides, from what I hear, Kirie more than held her own. She electrocuted several Shadowmen at once."

An image of her, glorious and terrifying, standing above a pile of charred corpses rose in his mind. In his vision, her eyes shone like blue diamonds in the noon-day sun, and her long, dark hair blew in the wind. Luca felt a swell of pride and arousal at the thought.

"Was anyone watching?"

"Probably half of Rome," Arin shrugged.

Dread spread through Luca like poison. Kirie continued to expose the immensity of her power to the world. This was so much worse than the attack in the Paris courtyard. Only Luca and a few Shadows witnessed her lose control of her light then. *That* incident was contained. Mostly. Kirie just painted a giant-sized target on her back. The Order would redouble their efforts to find and kill Kirie. If *they* didn't get to her, The Society of Light would use her until there was nothing left. And Luca couldn't do a damn thing about it.

His first instinct was to throw Kirie in a car, head straight back to the airport, and keep her hidden in some undisclosed location for the rest of their lives. But he knew he couldn't do it. He had a job to complete. If The Order was successful in acquiring the uranium, there was nothing he could do to save Kirie or anyone else on planet Earth. Defeating The Order *was* saving Kirie. Assuming she survived the mission ahead of them. Arin was an asshat.

"This is different, Arin, and you know it. We're operating alone. There's no calling for backup this time. Kirie's a liability to the mission and herself."

"I don't know, man," Arin said, smoothing the wrinkles from his shirt. "The Society claims she's special. Gifted amongst the gifted, or some crap," he said, using air quotes. "Mr. Bellamy himself is training her. She'll be alright."

Luca stilled, his fury momentarily forgotten. "Finn Bellamy is her Light Coach? Finn Belemy, the leader of The Society? What's he doing training a novice?"

"Dude, you saw what she did in Paris. Hell, half the city saw her light show. Apparently, that was nothing compared to what she did to those Shadowmen on the river. Rumors are spreading, man, on both sides. They say the Council thinks she's one of the prophesied ones, you know, from the War Scroll. They think her extra light ability could help tip the odds in our favor."

Luca stepped back and ran his hands through his sweat-soaked hair. "Pure bollocks."

Arin sighed and sat on the edge of one of the richly colored queen-sized beds. "They used to say the same thing about you, remember? Many still do."

"We're all the prophesied ones," Luca sighed.

Arin leaned back on his hands and rolled his eyes. It was an old argument. "Come on, Luca. You know that's not the way the Council reads the Scroll."

"I don't want to talk about old men and their religions. This is about *you* bringing Kirie to bloody *Iran* on a rogue mission. This is dangerous, Arin. We aren't messing around. If we're caught . . ." Luca put his hands over his face and squeezed.

"Look. She's already here. Let's just roll with it. Kirie's a smart girl."

Luca grunted through his fingers.

"And who knows," Arin shrugged, "maybe she'll turn out to be an asset."

Luca dropped his hands and stared at his friend. An asset? Was he kidding? They would be lucky to get out alive themselves, let alone a newly trained agent. "If something happens to her, Arin, I'm going to kill you."

Arin tilted his head and studied Luca. "That's a little dark, bro."

Luca leveled him with a dark look. "You have no idea. I'm not kidding, Arin. She better make it out of this in one piece, or it's your ass on the line."

Arin rolled his eyes again, and Luca suddenly needed air. He stalked into the gold-carpeted hallway, letting the heavy hotel door slam behind him. He took the elevator to the main floor to the lobby. At the far end of the building was an exit that led to an interior garden. Pushing through the tall glass doors, Luca could hear the faint city sounds, buffered by the high walls surrounding the verdant courtyard. It was like stepping into a warm greenhouse full of brightly colored plants. Luca breathed in the sweet and spicy scent of the pink and purple hyacinths growing in bunches amidst the ferns. They did little, however, to calm his nerves.

Anger swirled inside Luca as he walked along the path that circled the small courtyard. Lately, his control over the darkness had been slipping, like it found his hiding place and was coming back to claim him. The fear that he'd never be free from his days with Donovan lingered in the back of his mind, stalking him in the shadows.

He couldn't believe *she* was there despite everything he'd done to keep her away, to keep her safe. He'd avoided communication with other Society members, ignored his friends, and buried himself in his search for the Shadowmen's next move. Yet there she'd been, standing on a corner a million miles from where she *should* have been, looking like his very own avenging angel.

Even wrapped up head-to-toe in silks, Kirie took his breath away. Her beauty was painful to him, a constant reminder of what he wanted but would never have. And yet her energy called to him, tugged at him like an impatient child desperate for his mother's attention. The tension between them intensified with every tick of the clock, no matter how many miles or minutes he put between them.

Yet, the Shadows pulled at him also, insistent in their seductive beckonings. The two were at odds, warring inside him for space and attention. Kirie, being as bright as she was, couldn't reside in the same space. One would destroy the other and Luca in the process.

And his *dreams* . . . the voice of rushing waters and endless echoes. The nameless dark entity had invaded his mind months ago. The Void, he believed it was called, though he didn't know how he knew. Devastation beyond comprehension played out in his mind, shown by the ancient deity. People screaming, faces melting from their bones, babies lying dead in the street, trampled over my thoughts like an advancing army.

"Luca?" Her voice stopped him dead in his tracks. Its perfect tenor instantly sent a sharp pain through his chest. Caught up in his tortured thoughts, he hadn't seen her sitting on the concrete bench along the path. She sat under a large fern, its leaves partially hiding her face. She looked like an Egyptian queen, wrapped in silk and surrounded by tropical palms. Her bright blue eyes shone like sapphires. Though she sat in a darkened corner of the garden, her light seemed to chase away the shadows. Luca wanted nothing more than to escape.

Kirie quickly stood up from the bench. "Hey," she said. Her voice had a slight tremor, and her fingers played with the edge of her silk headwrap.

Luca nodded in silence, not trusting his own voice. Kirie's brows tightened and her front teeth bit into her full bottom lip. Luca's eyes caught there, remembering for a moment what it felt like to taste those lips and pull them into his own. Red-hot desire rushed through him, and he broke into a cold sweat.

There hadn't been anyone else since Paris. He'd been too busy to find comfort and pleasure in another woman. If he were to be honest, the idea of sharing himself with someone other than Kirie felt wrong in a way he didn't fully comprehend. He feared she'd completely ruined him for all other girls.

His dark mood must've been written plainly on his face because Kirie retreated a step, like prey sensing danger. "I'm sorry. I can leave if you want."

Luca cursed himself for being a total ass. He put his hands in his pockets and shrugged his shoulders casually, hoping to put her at ease.

"No, It's okay. I just didn't expect to see you here." Kirie nodded, but the crease between her brows remained. "May I sit with you?" The words left his mouth before he could think them through. He wanted to kick himself for not running for the exit while he still had the chance. Instead, Luca found himself sitting next to her on the small, secluded bench, hugged by ferns and fragrant flowers. It was the perfect place where two people could get into trouble. He was an ass *and* an idiot.

"I have to admit, I didn't expect to see you here. In Iran, I mean," she said with a nervous smile.

Luca snorted at the absurdity of the statement. She was the one who was a world away from where *she* should be. "Yeah, I didn't expect to see *you* here either."

Kirie cleared her throat and said in a small voice, "Clearly."

Guilt sucker-punched Luca in the gut. He was being a jerk again, he knew. He took a deep breath to steady his nerves and instantly regretted it. Her vanilla scent, alluring and innocent at the same time, surrounded him, threatening his resolve to remain aloof. Their connection tugged at the center of his chest again, urging him to lean into her warmth and share her light. He wanted to put his arms around her, pull her onto his lap, and do things to her that would make her cheeks flush pink like they had that night in Paris. He wanted her more than he'd wanted anything else in his life, and it scared the hell out of him.

"Luca? Are you okay?" she asked. Her body angled toward him, their knees almost touching.

Luca sprang up from the bench like it was on fire. "I should probably get back to my room. Arin and I have a lot of planning to do for tomorrow."

Kirie's face fell, and she held onto the edges of her head wrap as she stood. "Yeah, of course. You should go."

Luca stepped back from her, unable to bear her disappointment for one more second. "It was good catching up. I'll, uh, see you in the morning."

And then he fled like the coward he was.

Chapter 16

Kirie

We left the hotel early the next morning, silently piled into an SUV, and headed for the desert. Snow-capped mountains gave way to dry, brown land. For hours, we traveled down an unnamed highway that seemed only to lead to more dead landscapes. A trail of dust followed in our wake like the billowing train of a ruined gown. The sun slowly sank low on the dry foothills, sending long, painted shadows across the scorched desert floor.

I didn't sleep well the night before. My run-in with Luca replayed in my mind, chasing away sleep. It was as though I had repulsed him. Had our fight back in Paris put him off so completely? Or, had he heard about what I'd done on the river and was as repulsed by my monstrous actions as I was? My eyes grew as heavy as the setting sun. As they began to close, Abbott called out, "Our target is straight ahead and to the right."

I sat up and peered in the direction he was pointing, my heart suddenly galloping. This was it; there was no going back.

We approached a road that led to a metal fence with bulky stone barricades. Beyond the barriers stood a pair of guards carrying large, black rifles, presumably as a final defense against intruders. Above them was a tall white sign with light blue Persian letters across it in an elegant scroll. Beyond the heavily guarded entrance were several stone-colored buildings and one large gray metal warehouse, each utilitarian in construction.

Abbott drove nonchalantly past the main entrance and down a side road a mile away that led around the backside of the perimeter. Clouds of dust billowed around the SUV as he parked behind a small unmarked concrete outbuilding that seemed to be some kind of utility shed. We silently stepped out of the car. I put as much distance as I could between myself and the others, needing to be free of Luca's electric pull and Alena's oppressive hatred. I sucked in the dirt-flavored air and willed my nerves to calm using the techniques Finn had taught me back in Rome.

Abbott opened the back hatch of the SUV and pulled out four black duffle bags, handing one to each of us in turn. Inside my bag was a blue jumpsuit made of coarse material, a white tank top, and yellow boots, all of which appeared to be several sizes too big. I looked up to ask Abbott where my bag was, but the words quickly turned to dust on my tongue. The oversized jumpsuit slid from my hands as I watched Arin and Luca pull their shirts over their heads and drop them to the ground. It was like a scene straight out of a cologne commercial minus the yacht. Arin was all bulk and pecks, Luca long plains and deep crevices.

Heat flooded my face, and I swallowed hard, struggling to regain my composure. Arin caught my stare and a quirky smile spread across his stupidly handsome face, instantly breaking the spell I'd been under. He pumped his large pecks up in down in show. I shook my head and mouthed, "Dork," and turned my head, attempting to hide my shy smile.

Abbott remained at the back of the car where our gear was stored. Next to me, Alena stripped down to her lacy black bra, not caring who saw. She pulled her cell phone from the back pocket of her jeans and placed it into her duffle bag along with her discarded tunic and headwrap.

An ugly black pit grew in my stomach like it usually did whenever I was in Alena's presence. I both hated and admired her unadulterated confidence and disregard for the feelings or opinions of others. I couldn't help but compare her curvy figure to my small frame. She was all *woman*. I couldn't help but wonder if Luca was watching Alena's little show. For all I knew, it was nothing new to him. I slid my eyes in his direction and saw his eyes firmly locked on the task before him.

Feeling as though I'd won some small battle, I took a deep breath and walked to the other side of the SUV for privacy. I removed the hijab from my head and let my hair tumble over my shoulders, creating a shield as I quickly pulled my long-sleeved tunic over my head. I bent over and grabbed a white undershirt from the bag as Luca walked around the side of the car. He slid to a halt. I stood quickly, dropping the white shirt onto the dusty ground. We stared at one another. Too embarrassed to retrieve the shirt, I crossed my arms over my black sports bra, both embarrassed and relieved that, unlike Alena, I hadn't thought to wear sexy underwear on our super-secret mission.

Luca's eyes widened as they swept down the length of my exposed body. His gaze sparked a fire that engulfed me head to foot as if I were drenched in gasoline, turning my pale skin the color of a tomato. Sucking in a breath, I turned away from him and let my hair fall around me like a robe. Luca cleared his throat and mumbled an apology before returning to the SUV's other side.

I quickly grabbed the T-shirt and jumpsuit from the ground and slipped into them before anyone else decided to join me on *my* side of the car. I stepped into the bright yellow rubber boots that were clearly made for a man with feet much larger than mine. My feet slid inside them like a guppy in a moving fishbowl as I walked back toward the group. By the end of the day, I would have blisters on my heels and toes.

Abbott rejoined our group. He handed each of us a gas mask. I pulled mine over my head, letting it hang from my neck. He then distributed white helmets, gloves, and badges. I studied my fake ID. *Ervin Abed* was written in light blue script next to a picture of a fine-boned young man with dark hair and brown eyes. The muscles in my stomach tightened. He looked nothing like me. I glanced over at Arin's badge. A dark-haired version of Arin smiled up at me from the plastic ID.

"Sorry, it was best I could do on such short notice," Abbott apologized, nodding to my badge.

"It's okay," I mumbled, clipping the ID to the breast pocket of my jumpsuit. I was never going to be able to pull this off.

"So, what's the plan?" Arin asked Abbott. His tone lacked any trace of sarcasm, and I eyed my friend, taken back by this sudden and uncharacteristic seriousness. In a matter of seconds, he'd utterly transformed. He stood feet apart in his too-short mining outfit with his arms crossed over his massive chest. His posture was firm. Confidence and menace radiated off him. Arin looked like a trained assassin waiting for orders. The unexpected shot of fear that skittled across my skin took me by surprise. This Arin scared me.

"I'm about to tell you. Gather around," Abbott said. He waved us over to the car, and I stayed at the back of the group as we followed, uneasy with the change in Arin. Abbott pulled out a map and spread it across the hood of the SUV like I'd seen actors do in the movies my mom used to watch. Alena stood close to Luca, leaning over his shoulder in a familiar way to see the map. Like always, he didn't seem to notice. I forced myself to look away. *Focus,* I chided myself.

"This is our current location," Abbott said, pointing to a spot on the crinkled paper. "Obviously, you won't be entering through the gate here," he said, trailing his finger to a spot near a short road that must've been the main entrance we'd passed earlier.

"Wait," I said, my mind catching on his use of the third person. "Aren't you coming with us?"

Abbott shook his head. "I'm staying behind on the comm in case the mission goes south."

"Where's our entry point?" Arin broke in, his voice still free of his trademark mirth.

"There's a small break in the fence on the south side of the complex," Luca cut in, pointing to a spot near our current position. "It's located behind one of the large warehouses, so we should be able to enter unseen. From there, it's just a matter of merging with the group of men going down into the mine for the night shift." Luca shrugged as if it was the simplest thing in the world. The rolling in my gut disagreed with his assessment.

"You'll need to time it just right," Abbott said, warning lacing his words. "The next crew is scheduled to go in an hour from now, and you need to be ready to go when they do."

We each nodded our agreement. Seemingly satisfied with our compliance, Abbott folded the map and threw it into the back of the SUV.

"One last thing." Abbott pulled another bag from the back of the car. Though it was smaller than the other bags, he carried it with more care. He set it down onto the SUVs hood with a loud thump and unzipped it to reveal an impressive cache of weapons. Arin reached in and pulled out a silver Colt 1911 and a shoulder holster. As he began fitting it beneath his jumpsuit, Alena pulled out twin 9MM handguns and strapped them to her thighs. Luca chose a black vest full of steel throwing blades which he slipped on under his coveralls before stepping back.

All eyes shifted to me, expectation in their business-like faces. I approached the car and peered inside the bag. There was a healthy assortment of daggers and handguns to choose from. With trembling fingers, I picked up a pair of throwing knives and slipped them into the pockets of my jumpsuit. Luca lifted his brows, and I shrugged in response.

We piled into the SUV again. This time, Arin sat in the driver's seat with Abbott beside him. That left Alena, Luca, and me in the backseat. Alena sat in the middle and leaned into Luca, probably as much to get away from me as to annoy me. But even with her separating us, I could feel Luca's energy pulling me toward him. I slid my hands under my thighs and leaned against the car door, the chilled window cool against my heated cheek.

We drove along the tall metal fence surrounding the complex's perimeter for several minutes. The car bounced along the uneven desert earth. Arin cut the engine when we reached the complex's south side, and we piled out of the car for the last time. The sun had set behind the low hills, leaving only a sliver of golden rays lining their low peaks. Anxiety wound around my chest like a boa constrictor, squeezing the air from my lungs as we gathered around in a semi-circle around Abbott.

"Remember, you must keep your masks and helmets on at all

times," Abbott whispered. He looked between Alena and me. "This is especially important for you two. If they see that you're women, your cover will be instantly blown. Do you understand?"

Alena rolled her eyes. "I'm not the one you should be worried about." She turned her head and shot me a glare.

"I understand," I nodded, ignoring her tone.

Abbott nodded once. "According to the reports, this mine produces a minimal amount of uranium, nothing large enough to make weapons of mass destruction. However, recent intel suggests more yellow powder is coming out of this mine than has been reported. Far more." Abbott and Luca shared a loaded look. "Of course, we suspect The Order is involved in its production and distribution. Your mission is to gather information and nothing else. Get in and get out. Tonight, you're not Agents of Light; you're *ghosts*."

Abbott waited for each of us to nod in agreement. He held two small metal devices. Each had a digital display on the front and was small enough to fit in his open palms. "These are radiation detectors. They'll be your only guidance once you're in the tunnel." He handed one to Alena and one to Luca. "There's a vast network of tunnels down there. You'll need to split up to cover more ground."

"I'll go with Alena," Arin broke in.

Alena rounded on him like a mountain cat with its tail on fire. "I don't think so. You can go with your little *girlfriend*." She pointed an accusatory finger in my direction, her Italian accent thickening with her agitation. "I'm with *Luca*."

"Come on, Lena. I'm not that bad to be around." Arin dropped an arm over her shoulders, which she shrugged off.

"You're the one that brought her along, Arin. You take her."

"That's enough, Alena," Luca said. "Let's focus on the mission, shall we?"

"Luca's right. We only have a small window of opportunity here, and we can't waste it squabbling like children," Abbott's paternal tone deflated the mounting tension like a popped balloon. Alena glanced away, her bottom lip protruding like a sulking child. I expected to see triumph on Arin's face. Instead, there was only the ghost of his trademark smile as though it had died on his lips. Like before, I thought I saw a shadow pass over his face. It was there and gone so fast, I couldn't be sure. Unease curdled in my stomach like sour milk, and I was unsure if it was from nerves or Arin's strange behavior.

"Mark your location if you find a spike in radiation and gather as much intel as you can without being discovered," Abbott instructed.

Again, we nodded in agreement. The waning daylight was nearly gone, plunging us into near darkness as we walked toward the fence. I watched the others as they walked ahead, and my limbs began to shake. I still couldn't believe Bert thought I was ready for this.

We lined up at the opening in the fence and slipped through one at a time. I looked back one last time to Abbott. My former teacher gave me an encouraging smile as if to say, "you've got this." I waved to him and tried to smile, wishing I had his confidence.

I followed in the rear as we ran to the metal warehouse in a crouch, twilight concealing our stooped figures. As planned, we gathered in a tight group at the corner of the tall, metal warehouse and waited for the night shift to come by on their way to the mine's entrance.

After several long minutes, a group of dark-haired men of varying sizes and ages walked by. Each wore a blue jumpsuit, yellow boots, and a white helmet. Their gas masks hung around their necks like doomsday necklaces.

"Masks on," Luca whispered.

I pulled my hair up into a tight bun at the top of my head, secured the mask over my face, and set the heavy helmet on my head. There were at least thirty men in the passing group. Once the last one walked by, Luca motioned us forward. My legs screamed at me as I stood from the crouch I'd been holding. I trotted after the men, trying to keep up with their long strides and hoping no one would notice my small feminine gait.

The miners, seemingly unaware of the newcomers to their group, gathered at the opening of the mine shaft. I stood directly behind Arin as the workers began to file into a large metal elevator, counting on his large frame to hide me from the worker's notice. They took turns riding down into the bowels of the earth in groups of seven or eight.

It was our turn last. The elevator bounced up and down with

our weight as we stepped inside. I gripped my hands together and bit my lip until pain shot through it as the elevation jerked downward. There were four other men in the elevator with us. They talked congenially with one another in Persian. I studied a translation book for an hour or so in the hotel the night before, but I could still only understand a word or two of their conversation.

I shrunk back against the gated metal wall, hoping they wouldn't notice me again. One of the men suddenly turned to Luca, saying something in an investigative tone. I held my breath as Luca responded without hesitation to his question in Persian. He spoke in a matter-of-fact voice and moved away from the man, discouraging further discussion. The other man grunted in response and went back to his discussion with the other miners. I breathed a sigh of relief and held onto the metal gate at my back. The air temperature dropped as we descended into the mine, and I shivered under my blue jumpsuit.

The elevator lowered us several thousand feet below the earth's surface before it finally came to a stop. A scratching metal sound reverberated against the wet stone surrounding us as the heavy gate slid open. The group filed out into the dimly lit cavern. There were four different tunnels all leading in different directions, each about as tall and wide as a large man. The same worker who had addressed Luca before turned to him once more. He asked a question, his foreign words obviously laced with irritation. Luca was silent for a moment, as if weighing his response. He finally pointed to the tunnel on the far left. The man spat harsh words and shook his head back and forth, his white helmet sliding across his wide forehead with the movement. Arin took his mask off and threw his hands up in the air, yelling at the man in stilted Persian. I cringed and moved back.

The miner, seeing Arin fully for the first time, stepped back and muttered something before pointing back to the tunnel in question. Luca held out his hands in surrender. The miner nodded in satisfaction and waved a hand at the next tunnel over. Luca nodded, and we watched the four miners walk down the left tunnel. When I could no longer see their blue uniforms, I breathed a sigh of relief.

"What was that about?" I asked.

Arin shrugged. "That guy wanted to know which tunnel we'd been assigned to. Apparently, Luca chose the wrong one because that one," he pointed to the left, "was assigned to them."

Luca spun on Arin. "I had it handled."

"Didn't look like it to me," he tossed back. "I was just trying to help."

"That was helping? Your Persian is shite. That bloke could've called it in."

Arin lifted his hands in surrender. "Whatever. I'll let you take the lead next time."

"We're wasting time fighting like children," Alena huffed, her breath fogging up her mask.

"We need to move," Arin agreed. "Luca, you and Kirie go down that tunnel." Arin pointed the opposite direction than the miners had gone. "Alena and I will go south."

Alena shook her head. "I already told you, Arin. I'm not going with you."

Arin put an arm around her shoulders and began leading her down the southern tunnel. "Come on, Lena . . ."

Alena growled and threw his arm away. Yet, instead of continuing to fight Arin, she marched down the tunnel without a backward glance. Arin shook his head and turned to us. I expected to see exasperation at Alena's dramatics. Instead, a very different man stared back at us. Arin's face was a thundercloud of troubled emotions. Again, my stomach twisted in unease. Something was wrong with Arin.

"See you on the other side, brother," Arin raised one hand in salute. Luca nodded in return, his brows tightly knit. The air was charged as if something unspoken had passed between the two boys, something weighted. Arin nodded to me before following Alena deeper into the Iranian mine.

Luca took a deep breath and turned to me. "Well. Should we be off?" He held a hand toward the opposing tunnel like the quintessential British gentleman. I nodded in response, and we set off down the opposite tunnel.

We walked in silence, surrounded by thousands of pounds of dirt and a million unsaid words. The further we descended into the earth, the more acutely I felt the absence of natural light. The only source of energy in this underground labyrinth came from a string of light bulbs hanging from the stone ceiling.

This was the first time we'd been alone since that night in Paris when he kissed me and then broke my heart. I peeked at him every few seconds, trying to gauge his level of discomfort and measure it against my own, but his face gave nothing away. I searched for something to say, but my lips remained sealed.

I reminded myself that Luca was a player. He was likely thinking of the mission and not obsessed over my every move. I needed to let the past go and move on. Letting go would be much easier if I didn't feel a constant pull toward him. His energy was a riptide I was constantly swimming against, gaining no ground.

When I finally pried open my mouth to say, heavens knew what, my foot caught on something, and I tripped forward. A sudden explosion rocked the tunnel, and Luca and I were thrown forward. Landing on the hard earth, I curled into a ball and covered my exposed neck. A sudden weight pressed down on me, and I realized Luca had thrown himself over me, shielding me with his body. I reached out and clung to his arm as the world around us collapsed. Sharp rocks rained down on us, ripping holes in our jumpers. I squeezed my eyes shut and held in my screams.

The earth stilled, and I opened my eyes. The lights had gone out, plunging us into complete darkness.

"Kyrie," Luca whispered next to my ear as if his voice would set off a new explosion. "Are you okay?" I felt his arms squeeze around me.

"I-I think so. You?"

Luca's weight lifted and light filled the tunnel. His rubber gloves lay on the stone floor, and his right hand glowed. I stumbled to my feet and slipped my own gloves off along with my helmet and mask. I raised my hand, and our combined light filled the crowded space, casting jagged shadows across the broken stone walls. Only a few feet behind us, where a tunnel had once been, was a pile of rocks, floor to ceiling, blocking the way we'd come. I looked at the spot I'd been standing just moments before and shivered. If I hadn't tumbled forward, I would've likely been crushed by the collapsed tunnel.

"What the bloody hell happened?" Luca cursed. He brushed the tiny rocks from his shoulders with his unlit hand, and they pattered like rain to the cave floor.

"I don't know." I swept my hand like a torch across the darkened tunnel, searching for the source of the explosion. "I think I tripped over something just before the explosion."

"Where?" Luca barked. I fought the urge to shrink from his intensity and pointed to a spot just beyond the massive pile of rocks blocking the tunnel.

"Somewhere over here," I replied. Luca and I knelt, sifting through the rocks and debris. Lying in the rubble was what appeared like a metal fishing line. I gently picked it up, and we stared at it for several seconds.

"Tripwire," Luca said, taking it from my hands.

"For us?" I asked.

Luca's troubled eyes met mine. "Who else?"

I considered the implications. If someone set a trap, they must've known where we'd be and when. My mind spun. "But how? Do you think another agent accidentally leaked our position?"

Luca's frown deepened as he rolled the wire between his fingers. "No one but our group knows we're here. This is an unsanctioned mission."

I jerked back. "Wait, do you mean that The Society doesn't know what we're doing?"

Luca ran a hand through his hair and sighed. "I recently discovered there's a mole hidden deep within The Society's ranks. I couldn't risk whoever them learning what I knew and passing the information on. I had no other choice but to keep this mission a secret. We *must* stop the uranium from leaving this facility and falling into The Order's hands at all costs."

I shook my head, trying to clear my confusion. Nothing was adding up. "I still don't understand. Arin said Bert recommended me for this mission."

Luca snorted. "Trust me, if Bert knew about *this* mission, none of us would've made it past the airport."

I bit my lip and stared at the floor, searching for any explanation that didn't implicate Abbott, Arin, or Alena. Was it possible that one of them leaked information? The very thought made me shudder. They loved each other like family. The idea that one of them would turn on Luca was ridiculous.

Male shouts echoed down the tunnel's far end, and we quickly extinguished our lights. Luca grabbed my hand and pulled me to my feet.

"Let me do the talking," Luca whispered in my ear, his warm breath causing me to shiver. "Don't let them see your face."

Bright lights and harsh shouts preceded the mining crew. I pulled my mask and helmet on just before five large men carrying electric lanterns came into view. I kept my head down as Luca called out to them in Persian. I caught several words that sounded like "cave-in" and "help," and once again I wished that I'd had more time to study the language. The men called back with worried tones as they rushed toward us. They surrounded us in a semi-circle. I held my breath as Luca waved off their concern.

A small man stepped to the front of the group. He was about my height and had weathered eyes under bush-like brows. He leaned in my direction as if to view my face, but Luca stepped in front of me, blocking me from view. In loud, urgent tones, Luca pointed toward the site of the explosion. They took off in that direction. The small, wizened man squinted his eyes at me for a moment longer before following the others.

Luca and I watched them disappear down the tunnel, their light going with them. "We need to move," Luca whispered. I nodded in agreement, and we walked into the mouth of the pitch-black tunnel beyond.

Chapter 17

Kirie

It was impossible to mark the passing of time. The lack of sunlight confused my body's internal clock. We'd encountered several more miners in the tunnel as they rushed toward the cave-in, but they paid us little mind. The power was still out, and since it had been a while since we'd run across another living soul, we decided it was safe to use our energy source for light once more. My light was still strong, but I knew it wouldn't last. I would need to find an alternative energy source before the night was over. Given the current circumstances, my prospects were pretty slim.

I pulled off my mask and studied the dark string of bulbs that lined the ceiling of the tunnel. An idea hit me. I took off my oversized helmet and stood below one of the lights. I lifted onto the tips of my toes to closely examine the system. Like a caged bird, each light bulb was encased in a metal grid. The bulbs were in perfect condition, which meant that the explosion hadn't damaged them, just cut off their power source. Luca turned to face me, one eyebrow raised in silent inquiry.

Reaching into the small cage, I touched a finger to the bulb's base. I let a small current of energy flow from my skin to the cold metal ring. The light immediately blinked on, sending shadows across the stone walls. Following my lead, Luca stood below the light next to mine and touched it with the tip of his finger. It, too, flickered on, creating a halo of light above his head.

Luca made a thoughtful humming noise in his throat, reached inside his pocket, and pulled out a switchblade. I jumped slightly when he released the blade with a *shinck*. Though I'd grown used to knives in training, the sound of the sliding metal still took me back to the night my parents died. The image of Donovan slitting my mother's throat shot across my vision like a passing midnight train. I fought to control my fear the way Finn showed me— breathe in, breathe out, breathe in, breathe out—and my heart rate slowed.

With my mind under control, I watched Luca reach up and carefully cut the black rubber surrounding the power cord that connected each light, exposing the wires inside. The thought that Luca had learned to use a knife from the very man who killed my parents rose unbidden in my mind, but I pushed it away, determined not to go there. Luca retracted the knife and stowed it in his pocket.

"Here," Luca said, holding out a hand to me. "Take my hand. We seem to be stronger together."

"What are you . . ."

"Trust me," he said, disarming me with a shy smile.

I lifted my hand, and Luca took hold of it. A familiar hum of energy moved between our palms when our hands connected. Luca reached up again and wrapped his fist around the thin red and blue wires, and our combined power began the transfer. My energy waned slightly as the lights flickered on but continued growing stronger until Luca let go. I looked up at the bright lights lining the stone tunnel and marveled at our ability. He continued holding onto my hand in the fully lit tunnel, the current traveling between us flowed continuously like an infinity symbol. Our joined hands glowed slightly as if the combined energy was creating its own power. The light was a silvery blue hue, a color I'd never seen before in the natural world. It was beautiful.

"Is this normal?" I ask, lifting our linked hands.

Luca cleared his throat. "Not at all."

I searched his face, waiting for him to explain, but he simply stepped closer until our breaths mingled. I could feel the heat of his chest against mine and that familiar pull toward him, urging me to move even closer, to crawl inside him somehow. Pins and needles spread across my nerves, a sensation that was both pleasure and pain.

I knew this moment would later cause me pain. When Luca was

far away again, I'd remember this tunnel in vivid detail, a fact I'd learned the hard way after that night in Paris. If I were to close my eyes and pull up the memory of the night we first kissed, I'd smell the cold grass beneath us, feel the stubble on his chin on my fingers, and the soft breath on my lips. I'd also recall the exact tone of the girl's voice when she picked up Luca's phone. I had re-lived that night more times in the last several months than was mentally healthy. This would be so much worse.

But standing there, in that moment, breathing Luca's air, feeling his warmth, and sharing his energy, I knew no amount of future pain was enough to lessen the draw I felt to him. No amount of anger or distrust was enough to make me stop wanting him. Maybe I was too weak to deny his magnetism. Or maybe I was *choosing* to give in to this desperate need to be close to him despite the emotional danger it posed. Because I *wanted* to.

I gazed into his eyes, and Luca stared back. His normally gem-green eyes were troubled and dark like a stormy ocean.

His brows knit together. "Kirie . . ."

"Do you feel that?" I asked, cutting off the words I feared he'd say. I let go of his hand and put my palms flat against his chest. A shiver ran through me at the feel of the hard planes of his pectorals under my skin. He was as perfectly chiseled as the statue of David but with infinitely more warmth and light. I let the pull of his energy, so much stronger at my touch, draw mine into his. As his light flowed back into me, tension left my body, like release of a breath I didn't know I'd been holding.

"Tell me I'm not crazy. Tell me you feel this too," I whispered.

Luca's eyes closed, and his head fell forward to meet mine as if in supplication. "You're not crazy."

For one ridiculous moment, I regretted standing in front of him in my formless jumpsuit and helmet hair, but when Luca opened his eyes again, the fire in them burned all thoughts and insecurities from my mind. He *wanted* me, perhaps as much as I wanted him. Luca closed the distance, and his lips crashed into mine. I wrapped my arms around his neck, desperate to eliminate the space between us.

Luca wrapped his arms around my waist and lifted me until my feet barely grazed the floor. Every part of Luca was hard plains and sharp edges, but his lips were soft and pliable beneath my own. I shivered again from the heady energy flowing between our joined skin. As our kiss deepened, Luca pushed my back into the stone wall. My legs instinctively lifted to his hips, and he pulled them tightly around his waist. Liquid fire pooled in my lower belly, and I could hear the damp stone crack and sizzle under our combined heat.

His lips trailed down the side of my mouth to my neck, where he left a string of kisses along my collarbone. I let out a moan, and my head fell back against the stone wall, now as warm and dry as the desert above. Luca arched into me in response, and I swore the world around us lit on fire.

The lights above flickered, startling us apart. Luca put a hand flat against the wall behind me, and my body sliding down his until my feet touched the ground. Panting, we watched the string of lights flicker again. *Did we cause the disturbance?*

I continued watching as the pattern changed, the lights blinking longer and slower. Luca's body grew tense against mine as we silently watched the lights slowly dim, threatening to go out altogether. Holding a hand in front of his face, Luca breathed out a puff of air. It clouded around his fingers like wisps of smoke. The liquid fire in my stomach turned to stone.

Not here.

Not now.

Tendrils of cold air began to slither up my exposed neck and into my hair leaving a trail of goosebumps in their wake. The shadows in the far corners of the tunnel began to move while feelings of desperation and loss settled over me like a cold, wet blanket. The situation was both familiar and terrifying.

We were no longer alone in the tunnel.

"Conserve your energy," Luca said in a low voice.

With quick precision, Luca unzipped his jumper and shrugged out of the sleeves. He tied them around his waist, exposing his vest of knives. I did the same, my fingers fumbling through the motions. I frantically pulled Bert's lessons on underground combat training from my memories. Just as Luca said, I needed to conserve my limited energy and rely on my weapons training. I worked to steady myself as I assumed a fighting stance.

"Luca," I whispered. My breath puffed out in big, white clouds.

He gave me a hard look and turned to face the southern side of the tunnel. "Get ready."

The lights blinked out. We were plunged into darkness, thick and alive.

Two long heartbeats. The lights blinked back on. A man dressed in black stood completely motionless at the far end of the tunnel—a scarecrow of a man. His black raven eyes stared unblinkingly at Luca. I raised my fists in a defensive position like Bert taught me. Luca's hands remained firmly at his sides as he moved between me and the Shadow. The expression on Luca's face was dark, dangerous, and almost alien in its sharpness.

Blink

Three more breaths. My heartbeat was the only sound in the stagnant blackout. The lights flickered back on. The man was several feet closer, perfectly still as if he hadn't moved. Behind him stood another man, shorter and heavier but a Shadowman like the first. Their faces, devoid of emotion, zeroed in on Luca. Luca pulled the switchblade from his pocket and released it. *Shink*. Adrenaline shot through my veins.

Blink

Four terror-filled seconds. I swung out at the darkness, but my fists connected with nothing but frigid air. The lights blinked on. A third man stood behind the first two, unmoving. The line of Shadows had somehow moved closer again, though none showed signs of movement. Helplessness and despair crept into my heart. I shook them off. The darkness was a poison I had to resist at all costs.

Blink

Five shallow breaths. The darkness stroked my skin in an unwanted caress. Despite Bert's firm instruction to hold my ground, I slowly backed away. Tripping on my oversized boots, I landed hard on my butt. The impact sounded like an explosion in the silent tunnel.

Lights on. Another foot closer. I jumped to my feet and raised my fists, my feet planted shoulder-width apart.

Behind me, I heard a rustling sigh like dead leaves. I pivoted, my feet slipping again in my ill-fitting books. A girl stood at the other end of the tunnel. About my age, blood-red hair, muscular frame, black, shark-like eyes focused only on me. The blood drained from my face as I stared into the face of Satan's handmaiden.

Ciara.

Blink

The lights flickered back on almost instantly, shining dimly in the dank cavern. Ciara and the three men surrounded us. Their forms were immobile like the undead. The silence was filled with despair so thick I could taste it on my tongue.

Ciara broke first. She stepped forward, shadows seeping off her pale skin like a slow-rolling mist. She cocked her head to one side.

"Hello, little doll," she said in a childlike voice. "It's nice to see you again."

"I'm afraid I can't return the sentiment," I said. My voice shook, undermining my forced bravado.

Ciara threw her head back and let out a sultry giggle. My breath froze in my chest. Wait. I *knew* that laugh. It was flirtatious and dangerous and utterly *unique*. It had been a highlight of my waking nightmares since that night in Paris. This was the laugh of the girl from the horrible phone call. It had been *Ciara* on Luca's phone.

The realization snapped me from my fear-induced paralysis, and hot anger coursed through me. I slid my throwing knives from my pockets. I itched to blast her with my light, but I knew I had to conserve my waning energy as long as possible.

Behind me, there was a *whoosh* and a *thud*. I turned my head and saw a knife sticking out of the scarecrow man's neck. Luca already had another blade in his hand, poised to throw. The man faltered for only a moment. He reached up and wrapped his fingers around the knife's hilt and pulled it out with a sickening sucking sound. With a mocking smile, the scarecrow dropped the knife to the stone floor and stepped forward. Blood ran down the front of his shirt in rivulets.

I quickly turned my attention back to Ciara, who had moved closer.

"Stay back," I warned, lifting my daggers.

"Go ahead, little Bright One," Ciara said with a sideways grin. "Cut me." Her black eyes glinted in the low light.

She didn't have to tell me twice. I pulled my right arm back and released the dagger.

Ciara dissolved into mist. The blade passed through her noncorporeal form and ricocheted off the stone walls. I heard another *whoosh*, and a man grunted behind me. I turned to see the scarecrow fall, this time with a blade protruding from his eye. His body twitched on the ground as Luca grappled with the two other shadows. Each held a blade, slashing in and out in an inhuman blur of movement.

In my moment of distraction, Ciara rematerialized and rushed forward. She was on me in an instant, knocking the other blade from my hand. We fell backward together onto the stone floor as if in an embrace. She landed on top of me, knocking the breath from my lungs. I struggled to suck in a breath, but her clammy hands wrapped around my throat. I clawed at her face and kicked my feet, completely forgetting every one of Bert's combat rules.

Poisonous thoughts began to fill my mind. Ciara's dark gift was potent, her poison strengthening ten-fold at her touch. Slithering self-doubt wound around my heart. Dark whisperings filled my mind.

I was no Agent of Light.

My training taught me nothing.

It would be so easy and sweet to give in to the darkness.

To be free from this constant struggle.

To no longer strive to live up to everyone else's expectations.

It would be. So. Easy.

My will to fight seeped from my body like blood from an open wound. My inner light was waning, shrinking in the presence of the darkness flowing into my pores. I thought of my mother, cold and rotting in the ground. For the first time in months, I longed to be with her.

NO!

I pushed back against the seductive lure of letting go and succumbing to the serenity of darkness. Low male grunts and curses buzzed in the peripheral as Luca fought his own battle. I bucked against Ciara's weight, but she held tight. None of my sparrings with Dawn or Eden had prepared me for hand-to-hand combat with a Shadow as powerful as Ciara. My vision faded around the edges, vignetting the redhead's maniacal face.

Like the first rays of dawn, Finn's steady voice rose in my fading consciousness. *Calm your mind. Focus your energy.* I let his soothing words settle over me, reminding me who I was. I stopped struggling and closed my eyes. I let my arms and legs fall to the cold stone floor and willed myself to focus, to force the darkness from my mind and body.

Thinking I'd passed out, Ciara let out a mirthless laugh. "I still can't comprehend *why* they're so threatened by you," she whispered, her cold breath washing over my face. "You're. Just. So. Damn. Fragile." Her hands squeezed tighter around my throat with each word.

The clamor around me disappeared as I pulled my remaining energy into my center. A sense of warmth and calm flowed through my veins, slowly burning away the darkness. I imagined my small store of energy concentrating and strengthening within my chest the way Finn had taught me. It formed into a sphere of pure light, though not nearly as bright as I'd produced in training.

I directed the last of my power from my chest, down my arm, and into my right hand. As the darkness began to close over me, I opened my eyes and lifted my now shining hand to her cold, clammy cheek. Her skin sizzled on contact. Falling backward, Ciara held her hands to her scalded face. Her screams reverberated off the stone walls.

I sat upright, gulping in the frozen air. My lungs spasmed with sudden relief. I scrambled across the slick floor, grabbed my daggers, and looked to Luca. Two Shadows still surrounded him. The scarecrow man lay in a bloody heap, his sightless eyes blown out.

I aimed my dagger at the Shadow nearest me and sent it flying. The Shadow dematerialized, but not in time to avoid my blade. Another scream, this one rough and animalistic, echoed down the tunnel. The Shadow solidified into human form, and fell to the ground, my blade protruding from his heart. He coughed and blood sprayed from his mouth.

A force hit me from behind, knocking me to the ground once more. Still holding tightly to my remaining dagger, I landed face-first. My cheek smashed into the hard ground, and stars exploded across my vision.

"You stupid bitch!" Ciara growled as she bore down on top of me.

She tore at my hair and clothes, forcing reckless waves of hate and sadness haphazardly into my skin with each hit. I wriggled out from beneath her body and sat up, swinging my blade at her. Ciara swatted my hand away as if it was nothing more than a pesky fly, knocking the blade from my grip. She lunged for me again and grabbed hold of my ankle, tugging me onto my back again. I kicked out, and my free foot connected with her face.

Ciara howled in rage as I scrambled crab-style out of her grasp toward Luca who was trading blows with the short, stalky Shadowman. He threw a series of punches, but the man vaporized, and his fists hit nothing but smoke. Within seconds, the assassin rematerialized and tackled Luca to the ground. The two became a writhing heap of grunts and fists.

Locked beneath the Shadowman's weight, Luca roared in frustration, the force of it vibrating off the stones surrounding us. Dark Shadows began amassing around the men like a gathering storm, but this time, the darkness seemed to be coming from Luca, not the Shadow. His emerald eyes dimmed until they were nothing but black pits. Behind me, Ciara laughed maniacally as the lights above flickered once more. Panic flared through me as Luca began to give in to the darkness.

"Luca, NO!" I screamed.

I lifted my palm and threw out a burst of light. Luca's sightless eyes swiveled in my direction. He stared into my eyes with the desperation of a drowning man.

"Luca, focus on the light," I pleaded.

He gritted his teeth as if in pain and let out a mournful moan. Slowly, his eyes cleared, and the black receded into his irises. He elbowed the Shadow in the face and kicked him off. Luca surged toward me, hand outstretched. Ciara grabbed hold of my leg again and pulled me away from him, growling like a rabid animal. The male Shadow reached for Luca once more and dragged him several feet back.

A desperate energy came over me, infusing my aching body with renewed power. I screamed and lunged out of Ciara's grasp. I grabbed Luca's outstretched hand, and every vestige of energy left within me flared to life at our touch. The light bulbs above shone brightly before exploding in a shower of sparkling glass. Ciara and the man cried out in pain as a radiant arch of light bowed over our joined palms. It grew in intensity with each passing second. Every energy cell within me multiplied exponentially. The Shadows scurried from the intense light like frightened sewer rats.

I met Luca's eyes. His emerald gaze held an intense desperation as if he was barely hanging onto his sanity. The tunnel began to sizzle, steam rising off the hot stones. The male Shadow fell, shrieking as he writhed in pain on the floor. Just before our energy peaked, a blur of red hair disappeared down the tunnel. The light flared so brightly that even Luca and I closed our eyes against its brilliance. The man's cries were cut off like the flip of a switch, and the air filled with the smell of burning flesh.

With a cry, I pulled my hand from Luca's, and we were plunged back into utter darkness.

Chapter 18

Kirie

Luca," I cried out.

"Here, love," he replied in a hoarse voice. I felt his hands reach for mine in the darkness and we wove our fingers together. This time, only a soft light emitted from our joined palms. I breathed in a relieved sigh and let the warmth surround me. My momentary relief vanished when I noticed the charred remains of the Shadowmen surrounding us. Their ashes hung heavy in the air like a cloud of dust motes. I put a hand over my face to avoid breathing the human remains floating around me, and I wished for the darkness again.

Luca let go of my hand and stood. With an outstretched palm, he walked from pile to pile, illuminating the remains strewn across the floor. He kicked aside pieces of charred bones and shoes as if searching for something. A small, white object rolled across the dust-covered floor, stopping at the sole of my rubber boots. In a daze, I bent down and picked it up, turning the smooth surface over in my fingers. Horror swept over me as recognition dawned on me. It was a tooth. I dropped it and doubled over, heaving over my people-dust-covered boots.

When I emptied the bile from my stomach, I sat down hard with my back against the stone wall, which was still warm from our light. I watched Luca check the rest of the shadows, looking for who knew what.

"It was Ciara, wasn't it?" I said to his back. My voice came out raspy and broken.

Luca pulled a piece of fabric from the charred form on the ground, turning it over in his hand. "No. This one appears to be another one of the males." He sighed and ran his free hand through his hair. "Ciara must've escaped through another passage."

"No, Luca. It was *Ciara*," I said, cutting him off.

Luca glanced over at me, his brows knit together in confusion. A fresh wave of heat spread up my neck and face. "What do you mean?"

"She was the one who answered your phone the night of the bombing." The charred fabric slipped from his fingers and floated to the ground like a descending ghost. "How did she get your phone?" I asked, my voice shaking.

I both wanted an answer and didn't. Did Luca have a relationship with the Shadow? Was it even possible to get close to someone that evil and dangerous? Shadowmen were so dead inside, it was hard to imagine they could have relationships.

Was it really so *impossible*, though? He *was* raised by Donovan, after all. He could've introduced them before Abbott recovered Luca in London. Perhaps Luca hadn't put his past in the past. Not entirely. I thought about the Shadows shrouding him during the fight. They'd been coming from him.

"That," he said with a heavy sigh, "was Donovan's doing."

"Donovan?" I flinched back as if his words had fangs. "What could he possibly have to do with that call?"

Luca sighed heavily again and stood. His eyes shone in the dim light like flickering jade candles. "He, um, stole my phone."

I squeezed my eyes shut and shook my head. "How the *hell* did you get close enough to that psycho for him to steal your phone?"

Luca peered down the tunnel and then back at me. "Can we talk about this later . . ."

"That man killed my parents, Luca!" My raised voice echoed back at me . "He nearly killed me. If you're still in contact with him . . ."

"Shhhh," he hissed, putting a hand on my arm. "Someone will hear you."

"I don't care!" I threw his hand away and took a step back. Was it possible that Luca never really left Donovan behind? Was it possible he was working for the Shadowmen all this time? Was *he* the mole? My skin grew cold at the thought. "I want answers. Real ones this time, not these bullshit half-answers you're always giving me. I have a genius-level IQ, too, Luca. Stop treating me like I'm an *idiot!*"

"Look, I'm not telling you anything until you calm down," he said in a harsh whisper. "I've had a long day, and I don't want to add detention by Iranian officials to the list of shite I have to deal with tonight."

I took another step back and folded my arms over my chest. "Fine. I'm calm. Now, explain."

Luca dragged his hands through his dark hair and sighed again. "I met with Donovan in the catacombs after the attack in the courtyard."

My eyebrows shot up. "You *met* with him?"

Luca pointed a finger at me accusatorially. "Hey. You said you'd stay calm." I rolled my eyes but shut my mouth. Luca continued. "I met with him to give him a *warning.* Donovan is a proud man, and you were the one who got away. I knew he wouldn't stop hunting you until you were dead."

"So why . . ."

"Let me finish," he said, raising a hand. I sighed, closed my lips again, and mimed locking them with a key. "I'd hoped I could convince him that you were off-limits. Somehow, during the course of our conversation, however, he lifted my phone from my pocket. I imagine that call between you and Ciara was her idea of a joke."

I watched his face for the lie, but his gaze was steady, and his words rang true. The fight drained out of me all at once, leaving me feeling deflated and guilty for jumping to conclusions and assuming the worst. "Did you know? Did you know it was Ciara when I confronted you in the hallway?"

Luca stuffed his hands into the pockets of his jumpsuit and spoke to the floor. "I had a pretty good idea, yeah."

"Then why did you let me believe she was your girlfriend?"

"To be fair, love, you made that assumption on your own. I'd thought to correct the misunderstanding," he said, shrugging his shoulders. "But then you said you deserved better. There was really nothing left to say after that."

"Luca, I didn't know . . ."

Luca straightened his shoulders and met my eyes. "No, you were right. You simply reminded me who I was. I'm damaged, Kirie. Irrevocably. Just look at what happened tonight. The darkness is still inside me," he said, stabbing a finger to his chest. "It's a part of who I am."

"But you're one of the brightest talents in The Society. Everyone says . . ."

Luca shook his head hard. "Stop, Kirie! Just stop. If you knew the things I've done."

I threw my arms up in frustration. "But none of that was your fault. Donovan forced you to do those awful things."

Luca opened his mouth to protest when male voices echoed from the far end of the tunnel, cutting off his retort.

"Come on," he signed, brushing past me. "We've got to keep moving. We still have a mission to complete."

We picked up our masks and helmets, brushed the ashes off them, and walked down the tunnel in loaded silence. His words played over and over in my head. *It's part of who I am.* There was no denying the shadows that lived inside Luca. I'd seen them forming around him with my own eyes. His darkness seemed to equal his light in strength. Yet, I could feel the quality of his light when we touched. It was pure and unspoiled. He was fundamentally *good,* regardless of the darkness lurking beneath the surface. I knew it.

I ached at the knowledge of his self-loathing. I wanted to close the gap between us and wrap my arms around him. I wanted to make him know what I knew, that he was *not* beyond saving. Deep down, I knew our combined energy had the power to vanquish the shadows inside him. I itched to say something, but the set of his rigid shoulders told me now wasn't the time.

As we walked, I became aware of a pulsing energy coming from the other side of the tunnel wall. I paused and put my hand on the stone. Luca stopped, giving me a questioning look.

"Do you feel that?" I whispered.

He placed his hand next to mine for a moment and nodded. Unlike the rest of the mine, the wall at this spot was warm to the touch and nearly vibrated with energy.

"There's a lot of electricity just on the other side of this wall," he whispered back. I nodded.

We walked slowly on, our hands trailing along the stone wall. A sudden spike in energy caught my attention. I stopped and closed my eyes, letting it flow through my hand. A powerful vibration thumped in my chest as if I were standing next to a giant subwoofer at full volume. I felt Luca's presence next to me. I gazed up, and our eyes met. Luca slipped the hand-sized radiation detector Abbott had given him from an inner pocket and turned it on. The screen lit up, and a small arrow slid from green to red along the color bar indicator. The device let out a sharp beep.

"I think we've found what we are looking for," he whispered, sliding the device back into his pocket. "We just need to find a way in."

We inched forward. Several feet ahead, the tunnel curved slightly in on itself. The closer we got to the curved section, the stronger the vibration became. It took three passes until we found a door-sized outline cut into the stone. The hidden doorway was set into the curved wall, so it was nearly invisible to passersby from both directions.

Luca and I searched for a handle or lever, but the door was flush against the wall. I could hear and *feel* the electric activity beyond the panel, and I knew this was an entrance to a larger space. We ran our hands up and down the rough surface for several more minutes. My hand brushed against something smooth and cold. A panel lit up. The electronic screen had displayed a perfect picture of the wall like a chameleon, hiding it from view.

"Luca, look at this," I said under my breath.

Luca leaned into me and traced the screen with his finger. Six lines appeared in the middle of the screen above an electronic keypad. We stared at each other, brows raised.

"We need a code," Luca said, biting his bottom lip. My gaze lingered there for a moment before I forced myself to focus on the task at hand.

He placed a palm over the keypad, and a slight glow emanated from his skin. Luca closed his eyes and numbers began to scroll across the screen.

"You're going to have to teach me that trick," I breathed in awe.

The door slid back into the wall with a *swoosh*, revealing a metal landing on the other side. We were immediately hit with a wall of noise. Men called to each other, and motors ran and revved. Luca and I sprung back and flattened ourselves on either side of the doorway. My heart raced in my chest. Had they seen us? We stared at each other and waited for any sign that we'd been spotted, but there was no raised alarm or stomping feet in our direction.

After a moment, Luca nodded once, and we slowly peeked inside. Directly to our right was a flight of stairs leading down into a massive underground warehouse full of people, containers, and machines. On the far wall was a ramp ending in giant garage-style doors, presumably leading to the surface. Stacks of containers were lined up across the floor.

Their combined energy washed over me in waves, filling my depleted cells. The rough-cut stone ceiling was at least a hundred feet high, giving the space a cavernous feel. Luca ducked back into the tunnel and threaded his arms back into his jumpsuit. I followed his lead.

"Put your helmet on and hide your hair," he instructed.

"We're not going down there," I squeaked. Unlike the dim tunnels, this warehouse was well-lit. Even in my disguise, my small feminine frame would easily stand out amid the larger male workers. If we strolled out onto the warehouse floor, we'd be caught within minutes.

"Don't worry. We'll stay near the perimeter walls," he replied as he zipped up his jumpsuit. "We just need to get a better look at those containers. We'll be in and out before anyone notices we're there."

"What if they see us?" I asked, zipping my own formless jumper.

"Just stay behind me and don't say a word." He turned toward the door and paused. He looked back at me with a frown. "You better put that back on," he said, pointing to the mask still hanging from my neck. "No one who sees your face will believe you're a boy."

We slowly descended the metal steps. Unlike the wet, musty tunnels, this subterranean warehouse smelled of grease and diesel fuel. I held my head up and tried to walk like Luca, with long, sure strides. No one paid any mind to us as we casually skirted the perimeter of the room. A forklift drove by, transporting a pallet of boxes across the concrete floor. The driver nodded to us, and we nodded back.

Luca led us to a tall wooden crate, and we crouched behind it. I peeked around its corner and let my eyes wander. The immense interior was a beehive of activity. The men wore formless jumpsuits and helmets, making it difficult to differentiate them from one another. Still, I sensed darkness wafting off many of them like a bad smell. Chills ran down my arms. There could be dozens of Shadowmen there.

In the center of the space, shiny steel drums sat on pallets. The drums were huge and likely large enough to carry a couple hundred liters of material. A black and yellow sticker instantly caught my attention.

"Uranium," Luca whispered.

I swallowed against the lump rising in my throat. Dozens of containers filled the warehouse, all easily the size of three grown men. Just beyond them was a long row of blue trucks topped by metal platforms. An Iranian worker in an orange jumpsuit matching ours drove a forklift to one of the drums and slid it under the pallet, lifting it several inches from the ground. He transported it to the waiting trucks with quick, smooth movements, and lifted the heavy steel drum onto the platform. Steal met metal with a loud *clank*.

Luca stood and pulled a tiny black camera from his pocket. He took pictures of the drums—click-click-click—before crouching down beside me again.

"What do you think The Order wants with all that uranium?" I whispered. Luca leveled me with a knowing stare, and the stupidity of my question sank in. The image The Void showed me of the nuclear bombs detonating across the globe came to mind. Was this where it all started? Bile rose in my throat, and I put a hand to my mouth.

As if reading my thoughts, Luca said, "I need to stop those trucks from leaving this mine."

I glanced around. We were in a giant underground cavern full of our enemies. What could we do? I shook my head. "Abbott said to get in, get proof, and get out. We did what we came to do."

Luca pointed toward the line of trucks. "There isn't time." One of the truck's engines roared to life, emphasizing his point.

My heart thrust its way into my throat. Luca wasn't thinking straight. I had to stop him. "But there are at least two dozen Shadowmen out there. They're going to see us before we can even get close. It's impossible."

Luca turned his back on me and whispered, "Stay here."

As Luca began to rise, I grabbed his hand, hoping to anchor him to me. The energy between us sizzled. "Luca, please," I pleaded. "We'll find a way to the surface and call Abbott. If we get enough agents here in time, we can stop them from transporting the containers."

Luca twisted out of my grip and shook his head. "They'll be gone before then. We have no idea where they're headed next. This may be our only chance to stop them. I need to act *now*."

Without another word, Luca sprung to his feet and sent a bolt of light at a drum on the other side of the cavern. I stared in shock and horror as the curved steel burst open and the yellow contents inside burst into flames.

"Fire!" Luca yelled in Persian. Instantly, pandemonium broke out in the underground warehouse. Men shouted and ran toward the fire with panicked expressions. Luca followed them, yelling unintelligible words, adding to the chaos.

Heart pounding in my ears, I rolled forward on my toes, posing to run after him when I heard a shuffling noise behind me. I turned my head toward the sound, and something hard and heavy came down on top of me. My vision exploded into stars just before everything went black.

I have been one acquainted with the night.
I have walked out in the rain—and back in rain.
I have outwalked the furthest city light.

I have looked down the saddest city lane.
I have passed by the watchman on his beat
And dropped my eyes, unwilling to explain.

I have stood still and stopped the sound of feet
When far away an interrupted cry
Came over houses from another street,

But not to call me back or say good-by;
And further still at an unearthly height,
One luminary clock against the sky

Proclaimed the time was neither wrong nor right.
I have been one acquainted with the night.

"Acquainted with the Night"
by Robert Frost

Chapter 19

Kirie

When I woke, I was lying on a damp cement floor. Pain radiated through every limb. I looked around the room. All four walls of the small space were made of patinaed metal. There were no windows, no light, except a single light bulb hanging from an old wire that swung slightly, casting moving shadows about the room.

My vision swam, and my head pounded with the beat of my heavy heart. Thu-dum, thu-dum, thu-dum. I tried to sit up, but my arms and my feet were bound to my sides. Someone had stripped me of my jumpsuit and weapons, leaving me lying on the gunmetal-cold concrete floor in nothing but my tank top and jeans. I shivered violently against the shock and cold.

To my left, an office desk, chair, and metal armchairs flanked a gray metal door. Everything was utilitarian and age-worn. I racked my brain for clues as to where I was, but I last remembered watching Luca run toward the fire he'd started in the warehouse.

I strained my neck, searching for him, but the office was small, and I was obviously alone. I hoped he'd found his way out of the mine and that he'd been able to destroy the uranium before it had been moved. The alternative was too horrifying to consider.

The door opened and shut with an ear-piercing screech of rusty metal. A gust of cold air swept in, sending chills skittering across my skin like a thousand tiny spiders. A dark figure appeared above me. Hands braced on knees, Ciara leaned over me, her pale lips quirked up on one side. The flickering light above created a blood-red halo around her pale, angular face.

"Ah. The little bird has finally been caged." She ironically tilted her head sideways in a bird-like motion.

I pushed against my heels, attempting to scoot away from the Shadow. I only managed about a foot of distance.

"Where do you think you're going?" Ciara said with a laugh, clearly enjoying herself. She stepped over me again. "I've been waiting to get my hands on you for months."

Ciara reached down and pressed a corpse-cold finger firmly to my chest. Inky tendrils weaved their way into my core, and my internal light instinctively shrank away.

"D-don't t-touch me," I stammered, squirming against my restraints. Fresh pain shot up my arms and legs as the coarse ropes dug into my exposed skin.

"What's the matter, little doll? Are you sa-scared of the d-dark?" she said in a mocking baby voice.

I gritted my teeth and glared up at her. "Get away from me."

"But I finally have you right where I want you," she said, leaning closer. The light in the room began to flicker. Ciara's blood-red hair fell around my face, enclosing us like a curtain. The ends of her tresses tickled my cheeks as she whispered, "Besides, someone wants to talk to you."

She placed the palm of her hand over my heart and darkness poured into me, thick as smoke. My vision darkened and my thoughts turned black. A familiar black presence washed over me like a tsunami, swallowing me whole.

"No," I cried, pulling again against my restraints. I tried to summon the light, but the darkness was too vast. I was instantly lost in it.

I was floating in a vast and empty space. A voice, formless and endless in its depth, spoke.

The days of darkness are near. Give in to the darkness, Bright One, The Void said.

"I will not," I ground out through teeth tightly clenched.

You are not made for this hateful world. Give into your weak, submissive nature and become one with the darkness.

"I'm *not* weak," I cried out.

Light flooded my mind, and I was pulled into a vision. I saw a young girl sitting on a crowded school bus as if from a spectator's view. It took only a moment for me to recognize my younger self.

Small and pale, I couldn't have been no more than eight at the time.

In the vision—memory, I realized—I sat alone in the front row, arms folded tightly over my stomach as the other students dashed in and out of rows and seats, yelling and laughing despite the bus driver's stern warnings. Always the good little girl, I remained quiet, distancing myself from my overactive peers despite the fun they were having. I couldn't risk acting out or losing control. Mommy said no one could know my secret.

The vision melted away in smoke, and I saw a slightly older version of myself standing in the center of my old kitchen in Colorado. I remembered that moment vividly. Mom stood before a thirteen-year-old me, arms folded tightly over her chest. My throat tightened at the sight of her—healthy, young, and *alive*. My arms ached to reach out to her, but I was unable to move, even within the vision.

"I promise I'll be extra careful and stay in the background." I held my hands in front of me, squeezing them tightly together as I waited for her answer.

The corners of Mom's lips dipped, and I sensed her decision before she spoke it. "I'm sorry, my love. I can't let you go to a conference meant for adults."

"You could come as my chaperone," I said without much hope.

Mom sighed heavily. "You know that's not what I mean."

"But I've learned all I can at school. I need more. There'll be a class about biophotonics, and all the leading scientists in the field will be there. It's an incredible opportunity."

"A thirteen-year-old middle schooler will stand out like a beacon at a medical conference. We can't risk that kind of exposure." She shook her head firmly. "I'm sorry, but it's a no."

I felt anger and frustration at her insistence that I stifle my ambitions for safety's sake. I wanted to fight, to explain that I was suffocating under all the layers of mediocrity she kept piling on top of me to disguise what I truly was. But, like always, I gave in and shuttered my negative emotions. "Okay, Mom. Just thought I'd ask."

Her eyes filled, and pain and regret swam in her unshed tears. "I'm sorry. I love you."

Stomach acid climbed up my throat as I whispered, "Love you, too."

I was pulled into vision after vision, times when I'd so easily given in or given up on myself and my dreams. *You are not a fighter,* The Void repeated. *Give in to your submissive nature, and I will end your suffering.*

The Void was right, I wasn't a natural fighter. I hated training with Bert despite the gains I'd been making. Eden was right, too, when she insinuated that I didn't have the stomach for it. And yet.

. .

I thought of my Light Training sessions with Finn and the breakthroughs I'd made in biophotonics at such a young age. I might not have a killer instinct, but I flourished under Finn's tutelage and Paris's guidance. I may not be the bravest warrior the world has ever seen, but I was something more. I was a *thinker* and an *innovator*. That was just as important, maybe more so.

I'd changed since my parents' deaths. I was more resilient. I believed in myself. I *was* brave, if only for confronting my fears. I could've run away at any time and hidden from the Shadowmen for the rest of my life. But I didn't. I was still there, determined to use my light for good despite the discomfort it caused me.

Anger rose in The Void's suffocating presence, and the light from my memories was quickly replaced by gloom. I cried out as a bone-white hand appeared out of the darkness. It reached toward me, stopping mere inches from my chest, palm out. An intense pulling sensation flowed inside me. My back bowed and my head jerked back as the hand extracted the darkest parts of my inner self. Pain, jealousy, grief, and anger—heavy things I'd been struggling to carry since my parents' murders were extracted from me in one big jerking motion. They formed together in an inky-black orb that hovered in the ghostly palm. One by one, flickering images of gray and blue smoke floated across its surface like an eight-ball telling horror-filled fortunes.

An image of my mother's pale and lifeless body lying in a pool of blood on the living room floor floated to the forefront. It was a scene I'd never been able to unsee, a stain that could never be erased. I waited for familiar grief to consume me as it did each time I remembered that night, but I felt nothing. I was utterly numb to the grief and trauma.

Another image appeared of my own heart-sick face the night I called Luca's phone and Ciara picked up. Again, I waited for the stabbing pain of jealousy and betrayal to assault my chest, but nothing happened.

My mind snapped to a different scene of me standing on the shallow banks of the river surrounded by lifeless, charred bodies, yet the horror and disgust I'd felt for myself were missing. All my negative emotions lived outside of me now, leaving me utterly numb and empty. It was something akin to peace . . . only colder.

I understood then. This was what The Void offered—an escape from pain and fear. I would never again have to feel that overwhelming grief of losing my mother. Never again have to worry if Luca would ever want me the way I wanted him. Never again have to hunt another Shadow, take a life, or hold a weapon. How could that be possible?

"Who *are* you?" I called out, my voice echoing across the expansive space like waves on a tranquil ocean. It had been the unanswered question living alongside my fear of this faceless threat. The Void embodied darkness in a way no other Shadow I'd encountered had. And its presence felt ancient and lifeless.

I am dark energy, The Void replied.

I gasped. I'd studied dark energy. Though little was known about the mysterious force, scientists believed it made up over 70 percent of the universe. It had been theorized that dark energy was stronger than any energy we knew of and kept getting stronger as the universe expanded. It existed in empty space, filling it with its immeasurable power.

My darkness surrounds the light, ever ready to consume it. I am the refuge from meaning and pain.

I shook my head. Each time The Void had invaded my mind, I experienced a loss of identity. It was as though he was stripping me of my energy, leaving me nothing but an empty shell. "You offer a refuge, but at what cost?"

There is no cost, only liberation from the meaning you mortals create. Surrender to me. Give up your light and find peace.

Peace. I couldn't deny that the idea of being numb and letting go of all the disappointment, sadness, and fear was seductive, like the lure of alcohol or drugs to a tortured soul. True, The Void had taken my pain, but it had also taken my dreams and passions—all the things that make me uniquely me. Though my grief and pain were difficult to bear, they were an inseparable part of who I was. And I was beginning to like *me* for the first time in my life.

"Surrendering oneself isn't liberty. And taking someone's inner light isn't benevolence."

A burst of frigid air laced with intense anger blasted over me. The Void's voice surrounded me, large and loud. *You are fighting the inevitable, Bright One. Six long battles have been fought between Light and Darkness. It all ends with your surrender. No more war. No more pain. Just a return to silence. You must submit to me.*

The orb of my negative emotions slammed back into my chest, filling me once more with fear, pain, and sorrow. I gritted my teeth against the onslaught. "I will not," I ground out.

Then your loved ones will suffer greatly.

I was pulled into a new vision, this one dark and smokey. I was in a Roman courtyard. The buildings surrounding the cobblestone streets were smoldering, and black smoke hung over an orange sky. Rome was burning. Still dressed in her training gear, Dawn lay on the ground surrounded by black-eyed Shadowmen. Their hands were outstretched, and their lips were spread in feral smiles as she writhed on the ground, screaming in pain. Her inner light visibly faded by increments. I tried to rush forward and call out to her, but I was paralyzed and voiceless. The scene dissolved around me into another setting.

I stood on the road outside my apartment. Aonani was standing with her back against the stone building. Male and female Shadows of varying ages stood in a semi-circle around her. Darkness radiated off their pale skin as they focused their dark energy on her tiny body. She held her hands over her ears, eyes squeezed tightly shut. Her mother lay dead on the street at her feet. Aonani fell to her knees, her tiny voice crying out in pain and sorrow for her dead mother.

Over and over, the Void assaulted me with more images I'd never be able to forget. The loss of each friend and colleague filled me with stabbing grief as if they'd actually died.

Submit, and their deaths will be quick.

I gulped in oxygen as my heart thumped wildly in my heaving chest. "Why are you doing this? What do you want?"

The end of light. A return to darkness.

Suddenly, I was floating in space. Laid out in front of me was a dark universe with charred orbs floating lifelessly in the lightless space. My mouth dropped in disbelief as I recognized the swirling design the orbs formed. It was the Milky Way. In the center was our sun, dead and dormant. My stomach dropped. It was a planet graveyard.

In the beginning, there was darkness. In the end, the same, the voice whispered across space.

"The end of life in the universe," I translated. It's an ending where *everyone* loses. Good and bad. Light and dark. "Why would the Shadowmen help you do this? What's in it for them if everyone is dead?"

Corrupt men and women have heeded my whisperings for centuries without question. From kings to common criminals, all embraced darkness without thought of consequence. And my Shadowmen are the most depraved of them all. Each saw nothing but their hatred of light and love of power. They seek a reward that will never come.

"So, you use them to create their own destruction?"

A puff of frigid air blew across my face like a sigh. *Not destruction. All will be converted back to dark energy for energy never dies.*

The law of conservation of energy.

I learned it years ago in an online AP Physics class. All organisms were made of energy, Bright Ones most of all. I'd never forget when Abbott spoke of it in that little cafe in Paris. How could I? It was the day my entire worldview shattered, and my old life officially ended. The Void wanted to convert all ordinary matter to dark energy, extinguishing all light and life from the universe.

Sensing my thoughts, The Void pressed forward. *There will be no hate, no fear, no treachery. All beings will live in peace for eternity.*

Again, I felt the tantalizing tendrils of his logic harkening to my broken parts. My sorrow-weary soul leaned into the promise of numbness. I'd longed for a reprieve from the pain, a moment to breathe without sorrow constricting my lungs. At the same time, the thought of living without the light terrified me. Giving in would be to live forever in the darkness that I'd always feared. I'd never feel the sunlight on my face or the tingling warmth of Luca's hand on my bare skin. That wasn't peace. It was nothing.

I tried again to push The Void from my mind, but Ciara must have been actively weakening my light with her touch because it didn't stir when I called on it. I searched my core for my connection to Luca, but it was as if it had never been there. Panic ripped through me. What had they done to him? Was he already gone?

As if sensing my thoughts, The Void whispered. *You are drawn to the boy. Like negative and positive charges, you are a pair. There is nothing in the living universe like you two. I need you both.*

Relief washed over me. Luca was still alive, then. Despite my distrust of The Void, what it suggested hit true. Luca had always felt like my other half. Not in a cheesy soul-mate kind of way, but on a deeper, molecular level. I finally understood why. Like a battery's positive and negative charges, our uncommonly strong energies were drawn together by an invisible force.

My teeth chattered against the cold. "W-why us? There are h-hundreds of other Agents of Light who will continue to fight the Shadowmen if we're gone."

Together, you are the strongest living force of light in the universe.

The *only* matching pair. Strong. Unique. No wonder the Shadowmen hunted us so fiercely. They were afraid of us.

Yet, there I was, still breathing. Why? The Void seemed only to have power over the mind and spirit. Like a ghost, it had little influence over the physical world. But Ciara could do whatever she wanted to my body. She'd tried to kill me in the past, yet there I was, completely at her mercy, and she hadn't harmed me yet. *Physically.* Why was she letting me live?

"Why not just kill me?" I said through gritted teeth.

Since light first shone in my darkness, shattering peace, my attempts to eradicate it have failed. The Bright Ones are cunning and difficult to kill. You and the boy will ensure their final destruction. For there is nothing more effective at leading self-righteous humans to their doom than a false prophet.

A new vision appeared. Luca and I stood to the right of The Society's leaders in front of an assembly of Agents. Finn, my father, gazed down at me with pride as Daiko introduced us as The Society's greatest hope. The chosen ones. Saviors. The vision darkened, revealing a scene where Luca and I handed over key information revealing The Society's locations and movements to a group of faceless Shadowmen.

I pulled against my restraints in vain. "I'll never turn on my friends!"

You will, for I have already turned many Bright Ones toward the Dark.

I was swiftly pulled into another vision. When Arin's face appeared in my mind, I gasped. He was walking down the street in some strange, gray city I didn't recognize. Turning a corner, he approached a cluster of black-eyed men and women. Shadows swirled around them, obscuring their faces. A man stepped out of the darkness and approached Arin. My stomach twisted when I saw his face. It was Donovan, the author of my worst nightmares. What was Arin doing with *him?*

Arin looked left and then right as if searching for something. "Where's my sister?"

Sister? What was he talking about?

Donovan shrugged. "Don't worry, mate. She's safe, I promise. But we have another job for you."

Arin fisted his hands at his sides and shook his head. "No! I did what you asked. I gave you The Pantheon. Now, it's your turn. Hand over my sister."

Shock shot through me like a bolt of lightning. It was Arin? *He'd* been the one to reveal The Paris Center of Light's location? Impossible. The vision was a lie. It *had* to be. Arin was an Agent of Light. He'd never betray his own like that.

Besides, Arin didn't have a sister. Not anymore. On the night of the bombing, he'd told me that his little sister, Arabella, died along with his parents when the Shadowmen attacked his farm. Hadn't he? I thought back on the conversation we had as we lay beside each other on my bed. I pulled the memory from my mind, still perfectly intact.

"She was just a baby at the time. They found my parents' bodies in our barn. They never found Arabella's remains," Arin had said.

They never found her body.

Bile climbed up my throat as the puzzle pieces began to click into place. His sister wasn't killed after all. She was *taken.*

Two young female shadows stepped forward, revealing twisted faces. Their dark and soulless eyes focused on Arin, and he fell to one knee with a grunt.

Donovan looked down at him. "Don't worry. This assignment will be easy."

Arin lifted his head with seemingly great difficulty. "What more could you possibly want from me?"

A crooked smile crept up on Donovan's face as he said two simple words. "Kirie Sorenson." My blood ran cold at the sound of my name coming from *his* mouth.

"Kirie?" Arin said, brows knit in confusion. "What could you possibly want with her? She's untrained, hardly a threat to The Order."

"Don't worry about why, mate. You just focus on the mission. For your sister's sake, yeah?" Donovan raised his brows, clearly expecting full obedience.

I waited for Arin to argue with Donovan, to demand his sister's safe return once again for the service he'd already performed. Instead, my heart broke as Arin dropped his head in defeat and whispered, "How? When?"

"That's a good bloke," Donovan said, patting his shoulder. Arin flinched away from his touch. "Luca has found one of our key locations of operations. He's planning a mission to foil some important plans as we speak. Naturally, you'll go with him like the proper mate you are. Your mission is to take Kirie with you. Nothing more, nothing less. Get her to the location and leave the rest to us."

"And then you'll release my sister?" Arin pressed.

Donovan's smile had an edge. "Sure, mate. Deliver Kirie to us, and she's all yours."

The vision disappeared into smoke, and I was again floating in space. My physical body shook, and hot, stinging tears trailed down my temples and into my hair. Arin, my gentle giant, had led me to Iran like a lamb to the slaughter. I could hardly believe it.

Join me. You and the boy will be the harbingers of Darkness to the universe. This is your calling. This is your destiny.

Sickened by it all, I pushed against Ciara's darkness once more. "Get. Out." I growled. Her sharp nails dug into my skin as The Void pressed even further into my core. I tried to find a spark of light left in me, but how could I find the light amidst so much darkness?

If you resist, you will suffer. And the boy will suffer, too.

From a distance, I heard Luca scream.

Chapter 20

Luca

"UGH!"

Luca's throat was raw from prolonged screaming. It was impossible to mark how long they'd tortured him. The Shadow bastards had captured Luca not long after he'd set the fire and locked him in a small office somewhere in the mine.

Though his body lay half-naked on the cold cement floor, his mind floated somewhere between sorrow and pain for hours, perhaps even days. He could hear Kirie's screams coming from somewhere in the distance, a discordant track set on replay. Her tortured voice grated painfully on Luca's skin.

"It's not real, it's not real, it's not real," he chanted between panted breaths. He had to keep it together. He had to maintain his sanity—for her.

Submit to me, young Bright One, the fathomless voice whispered again in Luca's mind. A nameless shadow stood above him, pouring his inky-dark magic into Luca's chest. His light, depleted and worn thin, struggled feebly against it.

"Never," Luca growled through clenched teeth. He hadn't survived Donovan's "lessons" all those years ago to give in to the darkness now.

The Void's whispers turned to shouts, deep and powerful as the seas. *The world will burn. Submit to me, and their deaths will be quick. Defy me, and those you love will suffer long.*

Ugly visions of death and mayhem accompanied Kirie's tortured cries. Images of Kirie burning in the eventual attack were The Void's favorite tools to use against Luca. The other visions it displayed were equally gruesome and graphic. Millions of people's skin melted off their bones in the heat of the blasts. Different faces. Different cities. All the same. Destruction, sorrow, and pain. The Void was showing him the end of the world as if it had already happened.

"NO!" Luca screamed at the disembodied entity. "We will not allow this to happen!"

It has already begun.

Luca clenched his fists and sought the light, but the darkness was as complete as the deepest cave. The shadows clung to him like a second skin, pressing into him. Luca's inner shadows revealed in The Void's presence, making it nearly impossible to keep them in check.

Months ago, The Void began torturing Luca with his visions, though he'd never spoken of the visions, not even to Abbott. He'd always suspected it was some manifestation of the darkness inside himself. So, he hid The Void's visitations like he hid his shadows. Deep. But Luca was beginning to suspect this disembodied entity was something much more menacing than a mere Shadowman.

For millennia, The Society had assumed The Order was led by the world's top leaders, ever rotating with the changing of the guard, so to speak. It was understandable. Men like Hitler and Stalin were evil enough to fit the bill. For centuries, kings, politicians, and czars had all employed Shadowmen to get what they wanted—power and destruction. However, Luca was beginning to wonder if The Void was pulling the strings all along, not the corrupt elite. Luca had never encountered an entity quite like The Void. It was beyond time and form. It was darkness itself, deep and vast as space. The Shadowmen were simply his puppets. How daft they'd all been not to see the bigger picture.

The metal door screeched open, and booted feet strolled in. Luca's tormentor silently walked out, closing the door behind him. Luca instantly recognized Donovan's stride, each step full of over-bloated pride and undeserved confidence. Hatred for the man swirled inside his gut like acid.

"'Ello, my boy," Donovan said in a cheerful voice.

The shadows swirling inside Luca responded to their creator. He tamped them down and glared at the filthy man. "Fuck you," Luca spat.

Donovan's ungroomed brows shot up. "Good to see you, too," he said with a chuckle.

He walked over to Luca and crouched down, cocking his head to the side as he studied him. "Seems I was right about you."

Luca pulled against his restraints, straining away from the man's disagreeable breath. "I can't imagine what you mean."

"When I saved your life. I knew it, I did. You're different than the other Society scum. Special."

"Sod off, Donovan. I'm not going to play your little puppet this time."

Donovan laughed. "Yes, you will. Just like before."

The small spark of energy left in Luca's core flared. "I was a child then. You'll find I'm more difficult to persuade now."

Donovan considered Luca for a moment. Searching his face for the Shadows he'd help create. "You, my boy, are a survivor. Like a sewer rat, you'll do anything to pull through, won't you?"

Luca looked away from his childhood tormentor. "It's not about me this time. There's more at stake now."

"Ah, yes. Your little bird," Donovan said with a harsh laugh.

Luca's eyes zeroed in on Donovan, both his shadows and light shrieking at his mention of Kirie. "I swear to God, if anything happens to her, I *will* kill you. And I'll take my time doing it."

Donovan leaned forward. "Have you told her? About that little girl? You remember, don't you? She was just a wee one. Only five years old."

"Shut up!"

Donovan leaned even further in. "Does your girl know you're a baby killer?"

Instead of shrinking away, Luca lifted his head until their foreheads touched, his emerald eyes on fire. "Fuck. You."

Donovan lifted his hand and placed a finger on Luca's temple. The onslaught was immediate. Luca squeezed his eyes shut as Donovan's familiar darkness rushed into his mind, greedy and searching.

Luca pulled against his restraints again as the image of the little girl's dead body lying on a filthy city street filled his mind. "Get out of my head!"

"Did you tell her how many you've killed?" Donovan pulled each face from Luca's memories, one by one. Luca had spent years forgetting these faces and the guilt attached to them. He was weak from a lack of food and energy, and too depleted to force Donovan from his mind. Shame burned Luca's soul as his sins were replayed in his mind.

"Just imagine what you can accomplish working with The Order. We're building a new world order, and you can be a leader, revered and feared by all."

"I'd rather die," Luca panted.

Donovan dropped his hand and leaned back, searching Luca's face once more. "I believe you would." For a split second, a desperate expression flashed across Donovan's face. He quickly slipped his familiar, sardonic mask back into place. Luca had always suspected Donovan had developed a fatherly affection for him, as much as anyone without a soul could. Luca could never return the sentiment.

Donovan rocked back on his heels, towering over Luca. "Consider your position, my boy. You're running out of time." Donovan stomped out of the room, sealing Luca alone in the cold, utilitarian room.

Hours passed in silence. Kirie's cries quieted some time ago, as had the voice in his head, giving Luca a much-needed respite. Abbott taught Luca to lock the worst of his sins and traumas away in a mental vault. Months of training on the secluded island in the Caribbean, all for nothing. Donovan had broken down his defenses with a single touch and set Luca's demons free. The visions Donovan had raised from his dark memories were living ghosts in the room, keeping him company as the cold hours dragged on.

The room began to swim. He hadn't had anything to eat or drink for what felt like days. His stomach cramped in painful want of substance. Luca curled in on himself, his arms and legs still tightly bound, and fought against his hunger and emotional anguish. He drifted in and out of consciousness, never truly awake, never fully asleep. It was as if he were in purgatory awaiting his judgment day. His ghosts waited with him.

Finally, a metal grating sound shattered the silence as someone entered the room. Several pairs of booted feet entered. Luca looked up, his eyes painfully dry and gritty. Donovan had returned. This time, he was surrounded by several Shadowmen, all wearing black tactical gear. Each black-eyed monster wore an emotionless mask of indifference as they stared down at Luca.

"Time to go, my boy," Donovan said.

He reached down and wove his arms beneath Luca's. Pain shot through his shoulders as Donovan yanked him to his feet. Luca bit his tongue, determined not to make a sound as Donovan dragged him to the open metal door into a dark, dank tunnel. The other Shadows surrounding Luca and Donovan acted like midlevel sentries. As they forced him forward, a growing sense of doom settled over Luca. He knew in his gut something big—something terrible—lay in wait for him.

He stumbled on unsteady feet as they led him back into the cavernous warehouse where he'd been captured. The trucks full of uranium were gone, presumably already on their way to a secret facility where they'd be used to create a nuclear arsenal. Luca's failure to stop the Shadowmen settled over him, a cloak of self-loathing threatening to topple him to the ground. His failure would cost millions of lives.

As if he could hear Luca's thoughts, Donovan leaned into him and whispered, "It's over, my boy. You've lost. Before long, the whole bloody world will bow to The Order."

He'd wanted to believe the visions The Void had shown him were only possible outcomes, not visions of a certain future. He couldn't believe there was no hope for mankind. But as in the final hours of the day, the Shadows surrounded him, ready to snuff out the light. Luca was beginning to fear a return to total darkness had been inevitable all along.

Luca felt her before he saw her. Though greatly weakened, their bond tugged at his chest as she approached from behind. Luca turned his heavy head toward her and nearly fell to the floor. She'd visibly lost weight in the few days they'd been underground, and her long hair hung limply in front of her pale, drawn face. The light that had shined from her like a visible aura, was dull and nearly lifeless. She was a corpse walking. Luca itched to move to her and give her whatever light and life he had left inside him to sustain her. He pulled against Donovan's hold, and his black-eyed guards placed their hands on his shoulders, their heavy palms anchoring him in place.

At the top of the ramp, a giant metal bay door opened, momentarily revealing the night sky. Two black trucks drove through and descended into the subterranean warehouse. The metal overhead door quickly closed, sealing them inside once more.

The twin trucks stopped in front of the grave gathering. The doors of the one in front opened, and several black-clad Shadows stepped out. One stood tall above the rest. His fair hair and bulky size instantly gave him away. Luca's breath caught in his throat. Arin. They must've captured him too. And Alena . . . was she in the other truck? Luca's eyes burned. Everything had gone so spectacularly wrong. He'd led his second family to their deaths. *How much pain and loss could one soul withstand?* He hoped their deaths would be quick.

The back door to the next truck opened, and a middle-aged male Shadow with a paunch slid out, pulling a small, hooded figure from the backseat. The man led the child-sized captive to the center of the room to stand several feet in front of Arin. Luca watched in surprise as Arin folded in on himself, and his body began to shake with silent sobs. In all their years together, Luca had never seen his adopted brother cry. His pain was unbearable to witness.

Luca studied the faces around the room, searching for answers. Evil intention hung like a cloud above them like a gathering storm. Who was the small figure beneath the hood? Luca shook his head, unable to think straight.

"Arabella!" Arin cried out, his voice that of a drowning man. The small child jumped as if she'd been electrocuted. The Shadow tightened his grip on the girl's arm. Luca's mind spun. Arabella was Arin's baby sister's name. He'd spoken of her in the past, always with great sorrow and regret. But she was dead, was she not? Killed along with Arin's parents on their Kansas farm.

Donovan let go of Luca and stepped into the center of the gathering. He stopped in front of Arin and placed a fatherly hand on his shoulder. Arin shrank back in disgust. Luca tensed for the inevitable attack, knowing he was too weak to save his brother from the pain and sorrow he was surely about to endure.

"Relax, mate," Donovan said to Arin in a placating tone. "You've done well. Consider our arrangement complete. You have our thanks."

His strange words were like bullets to Luca's gut. Donovan's meaning was impossible to decipher. Was Arin working with the enemy? Unthinkable. Luca looked to Kirie, expecting to see the same shock and confusion etched on her face, but she simply stared lifelessly at the small figure, no signs of outrage on her drawn face. Had she known?

Arin sniffed and pulled himself up to full height. Donovan suddenly appeared comically small standing in front of him. "I did what you asked. I brought Kirie to you. Now, let my sister go."

Luca's mind darkened like a stormy sky. His brother. His mate. A traitor.

Chapter 21

Kirie

I couldn't tear my eyes from the tiny captive. The shadow guarding her pulled the hood from her head, and I nearly gasped. Arabella. Arin's sister. The small slip of a girl had to be around eleven years old, yet her malnourished form made her appear much younger. Her greasy blonde hair hung lifelessly around her shoulders and dark circles the color of plums ringed her eyes, making them appear bruised and sunken. A dirt-covered dress hung loosely on her small frame. It looked as though she hadn't bathed in weeks. Her body visibly shook as she eyed the monsters surrounding her.

I wanted to rush forward and shield the poor thing, but Ciara held my arm so tightly that my fingers tingled from lack of circulation. I could feel Ciara's desire to kill me in the rigidity of her grip. If she could snap my bone in half, I'm sure she would have. After hunting me for so many months, letting me live must've been driving her mad. I was too weak from lack of food and light to muster up any return feelings for the horrible girl.

Of course, I was aware of Luca's presence in the room; our connection was weak but unbroken. His normally steady energy was chaotic and tinged with something else. Something dark.

"Let my sister go, Donovan," Arin demanded. I waited for the hurt and outrage I felt when The Void first revealed Arin's betrayal to resurface, but all I felt for my false friend was sympathy. What would I have done to save my mother's life had I been given the chance? What had it cost him to trade his sister's life for Luca's? A brother for a sister.

In response to Arin's demand, Donovan glanced at the Shadow holding Arabella and nodded. I didn't like the crooked smile that played on Donovan's thin lips. The man holding Arabella thrust the unfortunate creature forward and she stumbled into the center of the gathering. Arin's sister was as exposed as a fawn in a forest clearing surrounded by hunters. The dark energy in the room stilled, and the hairs on my arms stood on end. The tension was tight and bloated.

Arin reached out to his sister, his movements slow and careful. "Arabella, come here." Her tiny body shook violently, and her vacant eyes remained downcast. She was too afraid, it seemed, to move even an inch. Arin's eyes swept the surrounding Shadowmen wearily as he stepped into the open space.

Something heavy pumped through my veins. Something like dread. As Arin walked forward, none of the Shadows moved, yet danger hung heavy in the air. I snuck a peek at Luca from the corner of my eye. His face was thinner, and his normally golden-brown skin lacked color. I was sure I didn't look much better. Like me, Luca seemed to be holding his breath.

Arin stepped closer to his sister, and she shrank away from his outstretched hand. "It's okay. It's me, Arin. Your brother."

She didn't acknowledge the giant standing before her. Her reluctance wasn't surprising. She'd likely been given little reason to trust anyone in her short life. Plus, Arabella had been only a year old when The Order took her from her parents' Kansas farm. I wondered if she even knew she had a brother.

"It's okay," Arin repeated softly. "I'm here to take you home."

Arabella's eyes darted up, and she stared up at her brother with an intensity that defied her frailty. "Home?" she repeated, her voice small and reedy.

"Yes. I'm going to take you home to America," he replied, emotion thickening his voice.

Arabella swallowed, lifted a rail-thin arm, and placed her trembling hand in Arin's upturned palm. He wrapped his hand around hers with obvious care and turned toward the line of waiting vehicles. His movements were slow and cautious as if he smelled the ill intent polluting the stagnant air, too. I darted a look at Luca once more. His face was paler than before.

I glanced between Luca and Donovan. And I knew. Donovan

never intended to let them leave.

I opened my mouth to call out a warning, but several loud pops drowned out my voice. Arin and Arabella dropped in unison. Their bodies made sickening thuds as they landed side-by-side on the gray, concrete floor.

Luca threw off his captors and rushed forward. "No!" It was a primal cry, full of grief. The sound was a punch to my gut.

Luca threw himself atop his brother's prone form, shielding him with his own body. My heart squeezed in my chest as I waited for more gunfire, but the middle-aged man to my left lowered his gun, obviously satisfied with the outcome of his dirty work. Bile rose in my throat as a mixture of copper-scented blood and gunpowder filled my nose.

"Arin!" Luca cried. The bullet had gone through his stomach, and a pool of blood spread beneath his body. "Brother, talk to me." Arin, eyes wide and unblinking, remained still. Stunned or dead, I wasn't sure.

I pulled away from Ciara, and she let me go without a fight. I stumbled into the center of the room and fell onto my knees next to Arabella. A crimson stain was quickly spreading across her chest. I slipped in her blood as I crawled on my hands and knees to her side.

My hands trembled as I placed them over the gaping hole in Arabella's chest as if I could hold the lifeblood inside her. Her breaths came in and out in tiny gasps, and her large brown eyes were wide with fear. I searched for the entry wound and my stomach dipped. There was a hole in the center of her grimy dress. Chest wound. How could anyone so frail survive such an injury?

"Hold on, honey. It's going to be okay." She must've heard the lie in my words because she began to cry.

I looked at Luca for help, but he was fully focused on Arin. He pressed his hands to his belly, and a light glow emanated from his palms.

"No!" Arin gasped, pushing his hands away. "Not me. Save *her*."

Luca shook his head. "No." Tears rolled down his face. "Don't ask me to make that choice."

I waited for someone to step in and pull Luca away from Arin, but the surrounding Shadows just watched us, seemingly content that Luca and I weren't threats in our current states. The sick bastards even seemed to be enjoying the show. Ciara, most of all. Her black, soulless eyes watched us intently, a smirk lifting one side of her mouth.

Arin reached up and pulled Luca down by his shirt front. A thin stream of blood ran down the side of Arin's mouth as he struggled to speak. "P-please. Save her."

"Luca, I think I can help her," I said. Luca looked up and met my eyes. The grief already pouring out of him shocked me. His pain felt like my own. "I can do this," I said.

Luca nodded. "Do it." He pressed his palm back over Arin's stomach. Arin grunted in pain.

Turning back to Arabella, I arranged my hands over her wound and tried to still my mind as Finn had taught me. I closed my eyes and attempted to conjure up a happy memory of my mother, but the warm blood leaking through my fingers forced me to think only of her death. It didn't help that her mother's killer stood mere feet away.

I tried to pull up childhood memories spent with Rylie instead, but the sorrow and malice in the room crowded out all positivity. I let out a grunt and opened my eyes. I peered at Luca still crouched over Arin, who writhed in pain on the blood-slick concrete floor. I reminded myself that Luca was still alive and breathing despite it all. It was a speck of light in an otherwise dark night. I held onto that ember and willed my energy to the surface, but my energy stores were nearly empty, and I was physically exhausted from a lack of food. Nothing more than a weak glow emanated from my hands, not nearly enough for the job. A female, probably Ciara, snorted derisively from behind me at my feeble show of power.

Tuning her out, I focused on Arabella's fatal wound and willed her internal organs to mend and her skin to close. Several seconds passed, but nothing happened. I tried again and again, but the injury was too great. Arabella stilled beneath my hands, and her eyes lost focus. She was slipping away.

"Hold on. Stay with me," I said, frantically pressing my meager energy into her chest. "It's not working!" I yelled to Luca. The light beneath his palms was no brighter than mine had been. We were both too weak.

Arin pushed Luca's hands away from the gaping hole in his

stomach with surprising force. "G-go. S-save her," he whispered between labored breaths.

Luca shook his head. "No. I can't."

"Please, brother. F-for me."

Arin's softly spoken words broke a dam in Luca. He smashed his face into Arin's neck and let out a guttural cry. Though painful for me to hear, the soul-shattering sound was likely nourishment for the surrounding Shadowmen.

Luca's pain, sharp and hot, shot through our connection, strengthening it. I gasped out loud as it flared alive. The energy inside me reached for the cord that tied us together, and I became acutely aware of the electricity powering the lights and machinery in the room. I reached out to it, and the ambient energy readily flowed to me. I soaked it in, letting my sorrow and desperation amplify my need for it. The lights above us flared, and a bulb popped. A tiny shower of glass tinkled as it sprinkled onto the concrete floor. The Shadowmen finally stirred, and Donovan took a step forward. We didn't have much time.

"Luca, grab my hand," I said, reaching for him. "We need to do this together."

He straightened and met my eyes. Arin's blood coated his face and neck. "Hold on, mate," he told Arin. "Don't die on me."

Luca reached over Arin's body. Our palms connected, sticky from the sibling's shared blood, and a bolt of power shot up my arm, raising the hairs on my arms. Light and power flowed through me unimpeded, healing and feeding my depleted cells. The

Shadowmen tightened their circle around us, raising their hands to shield their eyes from our growing light.

Luca's eyes darted to and from Arin, who lay still on the concrete floor, no longer writhing in pain. "Hurry!"

I repositioned my free hand over Arabella's open wound and did my best to clear my mind from the chaos surrounding us. Skipping the happy thoughts, I envisioned her organs and skin stitching together, pulling our shared energy to my core. Before it fully formed, I sent a stream of energy down my arms and into the girl's frail chest. The light shot into her, aided by Luca's and my shared connection. Her tiny body jolted, lifting her back several inches off the floor.

Arabella's eyes shot open, and she gasped. I lifted my hand from her body and ran my fingertips over the entry wound. Despite being streaked with blood, the skin was smooth, perfect, and new. It worked! The girl's chest rose and fell as she greedily sucked in breaths. I felt a tug on my arm.

"Now Arin!" Luca grabbed me away from Arabella's heaving body so we could both reach Arin. Crouching at his side, Luca placed his free hand on Arin's stomach. The pool of blood surrounding him soaked into his clothes and darkened his corn husk hair. Though his chest still slowly rose and fell, Arin's skin was pale and waxy as if he were already dead.

With gritted teeth, Luca pulled the energy from our connection and the ambient light so forcefully that I gasped out loud. I felt him send it into Arin's body. Donovan darted toward Luca, arm extended as if to stop him. I raised my free hand and shot a bolt of energy, driving Donovan back. Another man stepped forward and I sent another bolt in his direction.

"Luca! Hurry!" I yelled.

"I'm trying. It's not working!" Luca cried. Tears cut trails down his blood-soaked face.

Pulling more energy from our shared stores, he sent another stream of light into Arin's wound. Still, blood flowed from the gaping hole in Arin's stomach, soaking into the fabric at our knees. I searched Arin's face for any sign of fight left in him but found resignation instead.

Arin lifted a limp arm, touched Luca's hand, and mouthed, "I love you."

"NO! Brother, fight!" Luca screamed, slamming a fist to his chest.

Arin's body suddenly stilled. His irises exploded into multi-colored stars. I felt his energy leave the room the moment his spirit left his body. The warehouse visibly darkened with his passing.

Luca let out an inhuman cry. He dropped my hand, and the light surrounding us evaporated. I shivered, cold from lack of energy and shock. My core was an empty pit. Arin was dead. I could hardly think the words.

Chapter 22

Kirie

Luca laid his forehead on Arin's and let out a loud cry of anguish. A Shadow standing somewhere behind us laughed. Another joined in. Then another.

"Shut up!" I turned and glared at the soulless bastards, amazed at their depravity even after all they'd done. The Shadow guards' appearances had changed in the horror-filled minutes since shots had been fired. Darkness hung heavily over them. Their pupils were huge and shark-like, and parts of their bodies had begun to evaporate into a shadow. There was an eagerness in their forms, too. *This* was why they killed Arin. Their darkness fed off our sorrow. It was food to them.

"Hold back," Donovan said, gesturing for the group to recede. "They'll be weak as babes now."

I watched, expecting them to obey, but the Shadowmen only tightened the circle they'd formed around us. I turned and pulled Arabella, wide-eyed and confused, to a sitting position. Luca fisted his hands in Arin's bloody shirt and bared his teeth at the Shadowmen. Like me, he must've sensed the subtle shift in the atmosphere. Blood was in the water, and the sharks were circling their prey. Though The Void had plans to use us against The Society of Light, I didn't trust these agents of darkness to not give in to their growing bloodlust.

A twenty-something-year-old male suddenly dissolved into smoke and darted toward Arabella. I pulled her into my side, and the Shadow's smoky figure passed her by inches. It hissed menacingly as it swung back around.

I surged to my feet and held my hands up. "Stop! Don't touch her." More laughter from the darklings as they tightened the circle around us like a noose.

"Hold your ground," Donovan growled, but several additional guards dissolved into shadows, more eager to spill blood than listen to their leader.

"Luca." I grabbed his sleeve. He still held Arin's lifeless body close to his chest. Tiny wisps of shadow played around his body as his inner demons clawed from beneath his skin. "Luca. Look at me!"

He turned his head toward me. His eyes were dark green orbs the color of a murky lake. They met mine. Immersed in his grief, he didn't seem to recognize me. I leaned down and put a hand to his face. "Luca. Please. I need your help."

He shook his head, and a small whimper escaped his lips. I needed to pull him away from the dark cliff he was poised on. I opened myself up to the energy in the room once more, siphoning electricity from the lights above. I pushed a stream of light through my hand into Luca's cold cheek. His skin brightened for a moment, and his eyes cleared. "Luca, focus. We're in danger. Pull from the lights," I said.

Luca blinked once. Twice. He broke eye contact and finally looked around. The Shadowmen had formed a tight circle around us, malice written on their eager faces. Awakening to the encroaching danger, Luca gently placed Arin on the concrete floor and stood. He tilted his head up to the large halogen lights. They surged as he pulled electricity from them. When his eyes met mine, they were a bright emerald green once more. And yet, the dark, wispy shadows still clung to him. He was a dark angel, both shadow and light, glorious and terrifying. His otherworldly beauty nearly knocked the breath from me.

He put his palms on either side of my face, conveying his determination and resolve with a single look. Luca was with me, and this stopped now. His fierce conviction flowed through our bond, strengthening my own.

By unspoken agreement, we turned to face the threat, our connection flaring to life. The remaining ambient energy in the room flowed into us like a river as we surrendered to our connection. Inside that connection now was a shared grief, intensifying the strength of our bond. The lights above exploded into a shower of glass, plunging the room into darkness save the halo of light surrounding our glowing bodies. Our light grew stronger with every sorrow-laden breath. The Shadow guards dissolved fully into smoke and retreated to the room's dark corners like cockroaches.

A small cry rang out. I peered down to see Arabella cowering on the floor. Her big eyes, so similar to Arin's, were twin mirrors reflecting our light. I reached down and pulled her to her feet. "Get behind me," I told her. She shivered in a blood-soaked dress as she quickly cowered behind us.

I heard a *crack,* and a bullet zipped past my ear, missing me by mere centimeters. My hand blurred as I raised my hand in the direction of its origin and shot a bolt of light. Metal screamed as it connected with a truck parked just outside the reaches of our light. It lit on fire, illuminating the dark corner. A semi-solid Shadow holding a gun darted away from the blaze, dissolving back into smoke.

Another crack and whiz. Another bullet. It sliced through Luca's arm, tearing his sleeve. Luca shot a bolt of light toward the opposite side of the room, lighting a wooden crate on fire. The nearby Shadow shrieked. I shot several bolts into the darkness, setting more vehicles and crates on fire. The Shadowmen shrilled as they darted toward the nearest exit. I zeroed in on the keypad next to the metal door and shot a bolt at it. It instantly melted.

An explosion shook the ground as the fire in the truck I'd hit reached the fuel tank. The force of the blast lifted the large vehicle off the concrete floor, slamming back down with a *crunch*. Thick black smoke billowed into the air, quickly filling the underground warehouse. Together, Luca and I had nothing to fear. Together, we could level this mine and everyone inside it.

I tugged Luca's hand, and he looked down at me. "Let's finish this," I said.

He nodded, and our shared energy quickly intensified as we siphoned power from the growing fire. My unwashed, unbound hair lifted off my shoulders and flowed in the windless air. The glass windows of the surrounding vehicles shattered, and our light pulsed brighter, exposing every dark corner, every crevice. The shadows darted to-and-fro, trying to shy away from the light, but there were no more dark places to hide in. One by one, they reverted to their solid human forms. Men and women lay writhing on the floor, shrieking in pain. Angry red blisters began to form on their pale skin, turning red.

In the corner of my eye, I saw Donovan, Ciara, and a few other Shadows escaping through a side door I hadn't seen before. I was beyond caring. They could run but they couldn't hide from the fire that would soon consume this mine. The ground grew hot and the metal trusses supporting the room's structure began to glow red. One by one, the injured Shadowmen dropped like flies, their bodies quickly turning into blackened husks.

Arabella let out a little whimper behind me.

"We need a way out of the mine," I said, holding tightly to his and our bond.

Luca pointed to the concrete ramp that led to an industrial-sized overhead door. "We need to find a way to open the bay door. It's the most direct route to the surface."

As if in answer, the massive garage door exploded inward. Black smoke poured out through the jagged opening into the night air beyond. A sand-colored Humvee burst through the opening, screaming down the ramp toward us. I pulled Arabella closely behind me and stepped back, ready to take on this new threat.

The military vehicle skidded to a halt several feet from us. The passenger door swung open and a hellcat with caramel hair emerged.

Chapter 23

Luca

lena, glowing and glowering, held twin guns aloft as she scanned the burning warehouse for active threats. "Get in!" Abbott yelled from the driver's seat.

Kirie guided a stunned Arabella toward the Humvee. The young girl watched Alena in awe or fear as she passed her.

"Who's she?" Alena asked, gesturing to the girl with the barrel of her gun.

"She's Arin's little sister. The Order has been holding her captive," Kirie replied, helping Arabella slide across the long backseat bench in the Humvee.

Alena spared a fleeting glance at the girl before scanning the warehouse again for Shadowmen. "Fine. We'll talk about *that* later." She turned to Luca, and he braced himself for her next question. "Where's Arin? We lost track of him hours ago."

A sharp pain pierced Luca's chest. Unable to say the words, Luca stepped forward and placed a hand over Alena's outstretched arms, lowering her guns to her side.

She shook him off and lifted her weapons again. "Stop it, Luca. Where's Arin?"

The self-contained fires surrounding the perimeter grew with surprising speed, belching thick black smoke as they began to merge into one. Behind him, the girls began to cough. Time was running out. With a trembling hand, Luca pulled Alena to him, pools of tears forming behind his eyes, pressing on his already-pounding skull. She stumbled to his side. "Alena, get in the car," he choked out in a raspy voice that lacked volume and strength. Behind him, Kirie leaned into the Humvee, presumably to deliver the news to Abbott.

Alena pushed Luca away with the butt of her pistol and glared at him. "What the hell is wrong with you? We can't leave without Arin." He turned Alena to Arin's still form lying on the floor. Her guns fell from her grasp, clattering into the hot concrete.

"NO!" Alena screamed. She lunged forward, but Luca wrapped his arms around her waist, pulling her back to the Humvee's open doors. "Let me go!" Alena clawed at Luca's arms. He choked on a sob and held tightly to his last remaining found sibling, unwilling to lose her too.

A red-hot steel beam above them groaned, breaking in two, and sparks rained down on them. "Get in NOW!" Abbott demanded from the driver's seat. "This place is filled with flammable materials. We need to leave!"

"We can't just leave him here," Alena cried. Luca wanted to let her go and run with her to their fallen brother. Instead, he lifted Alena off the ground and swung her into the backseat. Kirie climbed in after her without missing a beat, pulling the heavy steel door closed with a bang. Luca slid into the front seat, and Abbott hit the gas.

The choking stench of smoke and gasoline filled the truck's interior as Abbott swung the Humvee around. Luca's eyes stung as he looked through the low rear windshield at the lone mound lying in the center of the warehouse as they raced up the ramp to the exit. The flames devouring the warehouse walls crept toward Arin's body with greedy fingers. Luca lost sight of Arin's corpse as they drove through the opening in the bay door. He had an instinctual urge to jump out of the vehicle and run back to him, to shake his brother awake and take him home. The two of them had been joined at the hip since they were children, and leaving without Arin was killing him.

As they emerged from the mine, they were greeted by a line of emergency vehicles. The desert compound was alive with flashing lights and blaring sirens. It was night, though having been underground for days, Luca could only guess the time. Mine workers and firefighters in respirators and jumpsuits ran toward the mine's opening, frantically dragging hoses and axes from the fire trucks' side compartments. Abbott wove through the chaos, barely tapping the breaks. No one paid them any mind.

The ground shook as a series of explosions rocked the mine. The massive Humvee bounced off the ground, and Luca bit his tongue from the jarring motion. He swung around in his seat. The entire mine was imploding, burying Arin in the process. Luca fell back into his seat and doubled over as waves of fresh grief washed over him. Abbott let out a strangled cry of his own. The sound of his adopted father's pain only compounded his own.

The road out of the mine led to a rear exit. Without pause, Abbott aimed straight at the low metal security gate and the Humvee tore through it with little trouble. No guards remained at the gate to pursue them. The dark desert folded over them and the glowing mine, sirens and explosions fading in the rearview mirror. Luca knew he'd left a piece of himself in that hellhole that he'd never get back.

The cab was silent as they sped back toward Tehran. Alena held Arabella close as the girl cried. She rocked Arabella back and forth, making little shushing noises. Her own tear-soaked cheeks were pale from grief. The small girl curled into Alena like a duckling with its mother. Numb from shock and pain, Luca watched her comfort the little girl. Alena had never shown such warmth in all the years he'd known her.

Luca could feel Kirie's quiet presence in the seat behind his. She was grieving too. Though, how he knew, he couldn't tell. Luca could *feel* Kirie's emotions through their link, something he hadn't been able to do before. It was as if their shared horror and grief had deepened their bond to a near-telepathic level. He couldn't even begin to guess what that would mean for their relationship going forward.

Luca put his head in his hands and breathed deeply. The mission had gone wrong in ways he could never have fathomed. Not only did The Order have the uranium, but he also had no idea where they'd taken it. It would take weeks, maybe months, for The Society to catch up with them. By then, they'll likely have created enough nuclear bombs to put their world-ending plan into action.

At least this time he'd have The Society's help as Luca no longer had to hide this intel from his superiors. The mole had been identified and eliminated. A lump rose in his throat. It would likely take years for him to process Arin's betrayal and death—maybe a lifetime. Add days of torture onto *that* pile of shit, and he was one big cocktail of messed-up emotions. Luca could feel the shadows inside him reveling in his anguish. He told them to shut the hell up and forced them back into their box.

Chapter 24

Kirie

The private jet waited for us at the Tehran airport. We shuffled zombie-style up the stairs into the softly lit cab. Ash and blood mixed with the pine scent of a freshly cleaned cabin like a poisonous cocktail. Luca collapsed in a captain's chair near the front. I fell into the seat across from him as Alena gently guided an exhausted Arabella to the couch at the back of the plane.

Abbott stepped through the open cockpit door and sat in the co-pilot's seat. The stoic pilot sat at the flight controls, ready to go.

"Destination?" he asked.

"Rome," Abbott replied in a weary voice. Grief hung heavily on his stooped shoulders.

The man looked back as if to do a quick head count and

frowned. Without a single question about Arin, he turned around and began pushing buttons on the flight board. I bit down on the inside of my cheek as tears pricked my eyes. Perhaps losing agents on a mission was commonplace when you worked for The Society of Light. Was that my future? Would I be that desensitized as the pilot one day?

Abbott pulled the cockpit door shut as the engines roared to life. I fastened my seatbelt with a *click* and let my body sink into the soft leather. I hurt from the inside out. My arms itched beneath the dried blood that still covered my skin, and I longed for a bath. Guilt hit me like a punch to the gut at wanting something so basic when Arin was dead.

The plane taxied down the runway, and I sighed in relief when we were finally in the air. I laid my head back as the engine's whirring filled the silent cabin, grateful for the growing miles separating me from Iran. If I never returned to that country again, it would be too soon.

Across from me, Luca sat with his arms folded loosely over his chest. His eyes were closed, though I doubted he was sleeping. After all we'd been through down in the mine, I doubted either of us would sleep soundly again.

At the back of the plane, Arabella had rested her head on Alena's lap, and promptly fell asleep. Alena rested a soft hand on her head and closed her own eyes, the crease between her brows easing slightly. I stared in wonder at the care she was taking with the little orphan. Arabella must've been some kind of magician because, within a few hours, she'd softened all of Alena's hard edges. It was the kind of magic I'd likely never possess.

Exhaustion pulled my dry eyes closed. As my body finally relaxed, a deep sadness slowly settled over me. Though I felt sorrow for Arin's death, this emotion was sharper than my own and laced with deep shadows. It was Luca, I realized. I'd felt something similar when Luca and I held hands just after Arin died. Something about our connection had changed down in that mine.

I looked up and studied him. The blood that still covered his face and neck had dried to a dark brown and was beginning to flake off in places. Arin's blood. It was all that was left of the boy Luca loved as a brother. *Would he feel more loss when he washed the last of Arin's blood down the shower drain?* An intense need to cross the aisle and wrap my arms around him, to take some of his pain into myself and ease his suffering, if only for a little while, came over me.

Luca opened his eyes and met my gaze as if reading my thoughts. I was stunned by the myriad of intense emotions that suddenly flowed across our connection. Luca always seemed so calm and collected. Impervious, even. How could I ever have guessed how *much* he felt? I tried to pull apart the different emotions and put names to them. I sensed sorrow, grief, weariness, pain, and defeat, but that wasn't all. As he stared at me, an even stronger emotion cut through the rest. I gasped out loud when I recognized it.

Love.

I put my blood-stained hands over my face and began to cry.

Salty tears stung my raw throat as I tried to hold them in. I hardly dared believe what I was feeling. I never dared hope my love for Luca could ever be returned, let alone surpassed. Yet, there it was, coming through our connection clear as day. Luca *loved* me. The joy and relief were so intense that my chest hurt from the sheer weight of it.

"Kirie," Luca said it like a benediction. I wanted to hear him say my name like that every day of my life.

I dropped my hands and tried to still my sobs.

"Come here." Luca opened his arms wide. I unclipped my seatbelt and crossed the space separating us. Luca pulled me onto his lap and wrapped his arms around me. We were both several days past the need for a bath, but I didn't care. There was nowhere in the world I wanted to be than wrapped in his filth-covered arms. His complex tangle of emotions flowed through our connection, wrapping around me like a web. It was both comforting and intoxicating.

I rested my forehead against his and tried to return my love back across our connection, still unsure how this new ability functioned. "Do you feel that?" I whispered.

His breath caught and he held me tighter. Fisting his hands in the back of my shirt, he buried his head in the crook of my neck. "God, Kirie," he whispered back.

I soaked in his warmth for a moment before pulling back to search his face. "How's this happening?" I asked, the words burning my smoke-singed throat.

His emerald, green eyes shined in the dim light. "I don't know. No two Agent of Lights have ever had this kind of connection."

"What does it mean?"

"I don't know," he repeated.

I settled into him, and we fell asleep encased in each other's warmth. This time, there was no endless beach or fathomless voice with taunting threats filling my dreams. There was only Luca's loving embrace, keeping the darkness at bay. It was the first time I'd felt warm and safe in months.

Sometime later, the cockpit clicked open, startling us awake. Abbott stepped out, cell phone in hand. His eyes widened when he saw our entwined bodies but said nothing. I sat up and slipped into the seat next to Luca's, my face aflame. Abbott sat across from me and held the phone out. "It's for you."

I pointed to my chest. "Me?" Abbott nodded and slipped the phone into my upturned hand. He held my gaze as I lifted it to my ear. "Hello?"

"Kirie?" It was Finn.

"Yes, this is Kirie."

He let out a huff of breath. "Are you okay?" Fear was evident in his trembling voice. I paused, not knowing what to do with his fatherly concern since he'd been my dad for about a week.

"I'm okay," I finally said. Luca watched me carefully, likely reading my messy emotions. I turned away, feeling exposed.

Finn let out a puff of air. "Thank God. I've been worried sick for days. I'm going to meet you at the airport. You'll need to be debriefed, but I was hoping you and I could talk afterward."

I cleared my stinging throat. "Yeah, sure. Of course."

"Good. I'll see you soon." Finn ended the call.

I waited for the anger I'd felt when Finn told me he was my father to resurface, but all I felt was relief. How could I complain that I had a birthfather who cared for me when, just last week, I'd been an orphan? There was nothing like torture and death to put things into perspective. I may not know Finn well, and he may have abandoned my mother while she was pregnant with me, but I could understand why he did it. After all, Arin was willing to sell his soul to protect his sister. Love made people do desperate and stupid things.

I looked up and met Luca's questioning stare. "It was Finn," I said.

"Finn?" Luca's brows rose. "Finn Bellamy?"

"Yeah." I shrugged. "He's my . . ." I paused, unsure whether I should call him my Light Coach or my father. I had no idea if Finn planned to tell anyone about our relation. What would people think? Would the news that I was the daughter of one of the world's most powerful leaders ruin the tenuous truce I'd made with Eden? Did I even care at this point? My head began to hurt. "He's been, um, been helping me with my Light Training."

Luca cocked his head to the side. "Yeah, I'd heard about that. But it's more than that, isn't it? I can feel it."

Abbott raised his brows. "You can feel what? What are you talking about?"

"Later," Luca said, waving him off.

Abbott appeared as if he were about to press the issue, so I cleared my throat and deflected his attention. "Finn said he'd meet us at the airport."

He nodded. "Of course. You should be prepared, though. He won't be alone. Daiko and Delgado are in town, and they'll likely be with him. They aren't going to take us going rogue lightly. They're going to ask us all some pretty tough questions."

I looked back at the couch where Alena and Arabella were still sleeping. "Should we wake them?" I asked, hitching a thumb in their direction.

"No, let them rest." Abbott turned to Luca. "I've filled Mr. Bellamy in on the basics. They want to debrief us when we get there. I told them you all need at least eight hours to sleep and recuperate, but they sounded pretty anxious to speak with you in particular."

Luca let out a heavy sigh. "Yes, I imagine they are."

"Obviously, they'll want to know why you didn't report what you found in D.C. and how you convinced several Society agents and employees to aid you in an unsanctioned mission."

Until that moment, I hadn't considered that this mission would have consequences beyond losing the uranium. Why would I, really? What could be worse than torture, death, and an eventual nuclear war? And Arin. The weight of the situation bore down on me, and I dreaded arriving in Rome. Though I hadn't known the mission was unsanctioned, I *was* part of its failure and Arin's death.

Luca and I weren't strong enough to save him. We couldn't withstand the Shadowmen's darkness. My first mission was a spectacular failure, and the last thing I wanted was to relive every detail of it for the most powerful leaders of the free world.

"The blame is on me," Luca said.

Abbott shook his head. "We all agreed to come."

"No. It was my plan. I'll take the heat."

I put a hand on Luca's arm, and his muscles tensed beneath my palm. "We all messed up, Luca. No matter what, we're in this together."

The pilot's voice filled the cabin. "Please fasten your seat belts. We are preparing for our final decent."

After the plane touched down and the engines shut off, I stood at the door, reluctant to pass through. But there was no hiding from this. I took a deep breath and ducked through the door frame.

A line of black SUVs met us, and a contingent of agents escorted us to separate vehicles. Luca and I made eye contact just before we slipped inside our individual SUVs. His energy still surrounded me, soothing my frayed nerves a bit.

Chapter 25

Kirie

Back at the Rome Center of Light, we went straight to the locker room attached to the training center to wash up. I stood at the entrance, staring awkwardly at the coffered ceilings as Alena helped Arabella find the supplies she needed. I nearly snorted at the exquisite classical art painted there. Even in their bathrooms, The Society of Light had spared no expense. Craftsman mosaic tiles stretched across every surface of the gold-trimmed space, every inch a masterpiece. I supposed that when an organization had thousands of years to accumulate wealth, it needed to find ways to spend it. For the first time since joining The Society, I was disgusted by its extravagance.

Alena cooed over the younger girl like a mother hen, guiding her into one of the dozen shower stalls, an ivory towel draped over her shoulder. I followed suit, slipping into the closest stall to the exit—a habit I'd picked up in recent months. I turned the tap to hot and stepped under the spray when the water began to steam. Resting my head against the warming tile, I let the water wash the remnants of pain, torture, and grief from my body. I wished it could be as easy to cleanse it all from my soul.

It wasn't long before I sensed him. The men's locker room sat adjacent to the women's, and Luca's energy radiated through the tile wall. The image of him showering naked in a stall identical to my own popped into my head unbidden. It set my already hot skin ablaze. I wiped my hands down my face. With all we'd been through, lust was the last thing I should be feeling. Yet, there I was, burning for Luca. I felt like I was losing my mind.

I pushed away from the wall, and furiously scrubbed dried blood and dirt caked my hair and body. The lavender-scented soap did little to calm my racing heart.

When I finally stepped out of the stall wrapped in a towel, Alena and Arabella were already clean and dressed in the black training attire The Society always kept on hand. Arabella's thin blonde hair was pulled back from her freshly scrubbed face, and despite her small stature, I could see Arin in her. His strong jawline. His cornhusk hair. The shape of his eyes. I swallowed hard.

The training uniforms were made to fit close to the body, but Arabella's hung off her skeletal frame. When was the last time she'd had a full meal? A fresh surge of hatred for the Shadowmen washed over me. Poor Arin never had a chance at saving her. It was clear from the hollows beneath Arabella's eyes that The Order broke her years ago.

"They're going to be tough in there," Alena said, pulling me from my morbid thoughts. I glanced up to see her watching me. "Good luck."

"You too," I said, surprised by the lump forming in my throat.

Alena held her hand out to the little girl, and Arabella grabbed hold of it without hesitation. She nodded to me as she led Arabella out of the locker room. Somehow, loss and grief had broken down a wall between Alena and me. Perhaps we'd never be friends, but I could no longer feel the searing hatred pouring off her.

I turned to retrieve training clothes from a tall cabinet in the corner when my connection with Luca snapped tight.

"Kirie?"

I spun around, nearly dropping my towel when I saw Luca standing in the locker room doorway. A towel hung low on his otherwise naked form. With a yelp, I grabbed the edges of my towel, securing them beneath my arms just in time. My skin was hot and sticky despite having just showered.

"Hey," I squeaked like a startled mouse. My eyes ran over Luca from head to toe as if they had a mind of their own. He was all peaks and valleys, hard edges, and long planes. I could study the topography of his body for days. I shook myself. I was definitely losing my mind. "W-what are you doing in here?"

Luca leaned into the wall, and his eyes swept over me, too. The temperature in the steamy bathroom rose another few degrees, and

I knew I was minutes from starting a fire. "I just wanted to check on you before our interviews." His smooth British accent did little to calm my racing heart.

"I'm okay. How are *you*?"

Luca ran a hand through his wet hair, spraying tiny drops of water around him. "I've been better," he sighed. "Look, I feel terrible about all of this. I told them you weren't involved."

Through our link, I could feel his anxiety on my behalf. "It's not your fault. You had no idea I'd show up."

I wanted to walk over, smooth his rough edges, and tell him we'd be okay, but my utter lack of clothing kept my feet rooted in place. "But it was *my* mission. My responsibility," he said.

"I'm not worried about being interrogated. What's the worst they can do, put us on probation?" I had no idea what they did to rogue agents, but I was fairly certain they didn't put them in some secret dungeon.

He shrugged. "You're innocent, so they won't do anything to *you.*"

"What are you worried about?" I asked, trying to read the web of emotions coming through our connection.

"That they'll throw me out on my arse, make me fend for myself against an army of Shadowmen."

Anger flared in me. *Like hell, they will.* "They can't do that. I won't let it happen," I said.

Luca let out a sad chuckle and stepped forward until there was only a foot between us. "My Kirie against the world," he whispered, a sexy smile kissing his lips.

My Kirie.

Like a moth to a flame, he drew me in. I closed the distance between us and rested my palms on his chest. His warm muscles twitched in response to my touch. "Say it again," I whispered. His brows drew together in question. "Call me yours."

Luca reached up and wrapped his hands around my wrists. "I don't know how to make this work, Kirie. I'm fucked up. I'll only drag you down with me."

"But this connection between us . . ."

Luca shook his head. "No! You didn't choose to be tied to me in that way. You aren't obligated to be with me because of it."

My eyes dropped to his lips, and I leaned in until our chests touched. "Obligation is the last thing I feel for you." I let my desire for him travel across our link. His pupils widened until his eyes were nearly black.

Luca sucked in a sharp breath. "You're going to be the death of me, my love."

Someone cleared their throat, and we sprang apart. Heat crept up my neck when I saw Finn, of all people, standing in the doorway. He didn't look pleased.

Luca folded his hands in front of him and dipped his head in deference. "Mr. Bellamy, sir."

Finn stared him down, a deep frown carved into his face. "Shouldn't you be getting dressed, Mr. Durant?"

"Yeah. Of course."

Finn watched Luca retreat until he was out of sight. He turned to me, his disapproving frown loosening only a fraction. "You too, Ms. Sorenson. We're waiting for you in the hallway."

I wanted to roll my eyes and tell him he didn't have the right to act like my dad after seventeen years of absence. Instead, I sighed and turned to grab a training outfit from the cabinet. "Yes, sir."

Chapter 26

Kirie

A pair of armed guards escorted us to the executive wing of the underground compound. Alena and Arabella were in the lead, followed by Luca. Finn and I walked several feet behind the rest of the group. The silence between us was weighted. I could tell he was wrestling with what to say about my relationship with Luca. I let him struggle. Whatever was going on with the two of us was none of his business.

Finn slowed down. "I, um, have an apartment in Rome. It has three bedrooms and looks out at Saint Peter's Cathedral." I met his slower pace, confused by why, of all things, he was telling me about his home.

"That sounds . . . nice," I edged.

Finn cleared his throat and adjusted his shirt collar. Was he . . . nervous? "Yes, well it has more rooms than a bachelor like myself needs." His words tripped haphazardly over themselves. "I'd like you to stay with me . . . if you want."

"Oh." I didn't know what to say. Training with Finn was one thing, but living with a man I hardly knew?

Finn put his hands in his pockets, affecting nonchalance. "It just isn't safe for you to live alone anymore."

"I don't know," I began.

Finn put a hand on my forearm, and we stopped walking. We stood facing one another as the others continued down the hall. Luca glanced back at us, worry evident in his pinched brows. I gave him a slight smile, letting him know not to worry.

"Look, I know this whole father-daughter thing is new for both of us, but I'd like to do what I can to keep you safe. Plus, it will allow us to get to know each other better."

I folded my arms over my chest to hide my shaking hands. Finn was offering me something I never thought I'd have again. A home. A family. It was all too much.

"When you went missing . . ." Finn let out a heavy breath. Pain was etched into the lines around his mouth and eyes, making him appear older. He rubbed a hand across his forehead, wiping away tiny beads of sweat. "When I found out you were gone . . . it was the longest week of my life. I can't explain it. I just *need* to keep you safe. Will you let me try?"

I wanted to argue that I'd been keeping *myself* safe, thank you very much, but after everything I'd been through, the offer of shelter and safety was tempting. I was *bone tired*, and the novelty of living alone had faded long ago.

Then, there was The Void to consider. It would stop at nothing to possess Luca and me to use us as weapons against the light. Who was I in the face of such immense and ancient power? Perhaps Finn had a point. Perhaps a little protection would be a good thing.

"Okay," I said finally. "I'll consider it,"

"Thank you," he said with a relieved smile. My chest warmed slightly.

With that, we caught up with the rest of the group. As we rounded a corner at the end of the hall, the warmth that had bloomed in my chest moments before popped like a balloon. Mr. Daiko and Ms. Delgado were waiting outside a line of office doors. My skin crawled at the sight of that small, horrible man. I knew Daiko would be there for the interviews, I just wasn't emotionally prepared to come face-to-face with him. All my internal sirens were blaring. *Warning. Warning. Warning.* The man was repugnant; I felt pity for whoever had to interview with *him*.

Finn walked over and stood next to his fellow leaders. My stomach clenched at the formidable force the three of them made. Power poured off them so strongly it was nearly visible to the naked eye. I couldn't help but feel intimidated.

Mr. Daiko stepped forward, always the self-proclaimed spokesman of the three. "Mr. Durant," he said to Luca. "Mr. Bellamy will conduct your interview in his office. Ms. Delgado will speak with Alena and Arabella." Mr. Daiko put a hand to his chest and turned to me with a slight bow. "Ms. Sorenson, I'll conduct your interview."

No.

I broke out in a cold sweat. The very last place I wanted to be was inside one of *his* offices again. I turned to Finn. "Can't you interview me? I'd much rather be with you."

Luca, standing in front of Finn's office door, lifted a brow to ask if I was okay. When I shook my head, he began walking back to me. Finn put a restraining hand on Luca's shoulder as he passed and leaned in to whisper something in his ear. Luca stood down immediately. A wave of betrayal washed over me. Didn't Finn *just* *say* he wanted to protect me? Could he not see the panic in my eyes?

Finn turned to me again, an apology written on his features. "Sorry. It was decided that it would be a conflict of interest if I conducted your interview. Don't worry; Mr. Daiko is very capable." I glared at him in response. For a genius, he was being pretty dumb.

Finn guided Luca into his office with a firm hand, and the other two followed Ms. Delgado into hers. Alena threw me a questioning glance as she passed, but I could only shake my head. Then it was just Mr. Daiko, me, and the two guards who had escorted us there. Daiko motioned me into his open office, a faux smile plastered to his self-important face. I wanted to make a run for it, but the guards stood on either side of me. Were they there to protect me or trap me?

Imaginary spiders skittered across my skin in warning as I passed Daiko into his office. I reminded myself we were on the same side as he shut the door behind us and locked it.

Diako's office was the definition of ostentatious. His giant wood desk, a Louis XV antique with bronze inlays, sat in the center of the plush room. The cream-colored carpet was so thick it muffled our footsteps. Expensive vases and paintings were displayed perfectly throughout the room, suggesting a designer's touch. Of all the items in the room, it was the marble bust in the center of his desk caught and held my attention. Like much of the art in Italy, this piece was obviously ancient. I examined it closely as I sat in one of the armchairs. The name Marcus Junius Brutus was etched on a golden plaque at its base. The warning sirens blaring in my mind were now deafening.

My eyes darted to Daiko, who, instead of sitting at his seat across from me, chose the chair beside my own. I sat back in the deep red velvet cushions, trying to put as much distance between us as I could.

"It is lovely to see you again, Ms. Sorenson, though I wish it was under better circumstances. I'm sure I don't have to tell you how serious the situation is."

A flair of anger rose in me. Did *I* know how serious the situation was? The real question was, did *he?* Daiko hadn't been down in that mine. He had no idea what Luca and I had been through or what The Void wanted us to do. All that uranium gone and untraceable, "serious" didn't come close to what this was.

"No, sir. I'm very aware of how serious this is."

"Great. Let's get started, then."

With the speed of a viper, Daiko lunged forward and grabbed hold of my face with both hands. My body froze in shock as he forced his venomous energy into my mind. He began rifling through my memories. I willed myself to fight back, but my body wouldn't cooperate. I was paralyzed in shock and fear. No! *This can't be happening again.*

Like last time, Daiko helped himself to my most intimate thoughts and feelings. Unlike last time, however, I could sense he was searching for something specific as he riffled through my memories. He had no interest in my childhood or school days, choosing to focus only on the events following the river attack.

Gray images of the dark tunnels filled my vision when he found my memories of the Iranian mine. My shoulders crumpled forward as he forced me to relive the days-long torture. Thankfully, he played those events in fast-forward, never lingering long on any singular moment. That was, until he reached Arin's death. Daiko plucked that particular memory from the others and played it again in slow motion as if he were studying every detail.

My head spun when he suddenly went back and began cherry-picking every interaction I'd had with Arin in the past month. It was as if he'd pressed control-F in my head and searched only for memories with Arin in them. But why? What was he looking for? He lingered on the moments leading up to our flight to Iran, combing through each spoken word between us as we stood in my apartment.

"So. Where are we going, then?" I asked him.

"I'm taking you on your first mission!"

"Wait. Seriously?" I was so shocked that I wasn't thinking straight.

"Seriously," he'd confirmed.

"But I'm still in training. Did Bert really agree to this?"

"It was his idea, actually. I came by the training center to see you and ran into your sweetheart of a trainer. When I mentioned that I was going on a quick mission, he suggested I bring you along. He thinks you're ready."

Looking back, the red flags were everywhere. Bert agreeing to send me on a last-minute mission without talking to me first made no sense. None of the other trainees had ever been on their own missions. I'd let my love and trust in Arin cloud my judgment. Now, I could clearly see the shadows in his eyes, the moments of desperation when he thought I wasn't looking. Watching it all on replay was physically painful.

Again, I commanded my body to run, to fight . . . to do *something*, but my arms and legs remained listless. Daiko's invasive power paralyzed me as effectively as Ciara's darkness had. I could sense a thread of shadows in Daiko's energy that must've always been there. It was edged with secrecy and ill intent. Something was very wrong. I had to do something *now!*

"Get out of my head!"

I pushed against his energy with my own, determined to expel him from my mind, but I must've pushed too far. I gasped out loud when foreign images flooded into me. As if I hit a download key, Mr. Daiko's mental files began transferring into my mind. At first, it was pure chaos. Memories swirled inside my head like a tornado of both light and shadows. I tried to retreat, but the onslaught was too much.

My own face flashed across my mental screen, and I grabbed hold of the memory, if for no other reason than to make the madness stop. A scene took over my vision. I saw myself standing outside the back entrance of the Rome Center of Light waiting for Jaques to pick me up. With a start, I realized that it was Daiko's memory of the day my bodyguard died. Only, instead of seeing it through my own eyes, I was seeing it from Daiko's point of view.

"Hello, Kirie." The words seemed to be coming from my mouth, but they were in Daiko's voice.

"Sir," I had replied. My voice sounded strange from another person's perspective. *"I didn't realize you were in Rome."*

"I've only just arrived. I met with Mr. Bellamy tonight and he tells me your light training is going well."

"I'm glad he thinks so."

I–no, *Daiko*–reached up and placed a hand over my shoulder. I remember the revulsion I'd experienced in that moment, my body instinctively reacting to his unwanted touch. I felt my own small shoulder in the palm of his hand, but that wasn't all. There was something small and metallic there, too. Daiko attached a metal disk to my training jacket. I read the thoughts and intentions overlapping his memory, and I gasped. Mr. Daiko had planted a tracker on me. But *why?*

My heart began to race as the answer became glaringly obvious. The shadow from the cafe. I'd wondered how he'd found me so quickly. I'd never fully accepted it had been just bad luck or horrible timing.

That meant . . . *no.*

Mr. Daiko, a leader of The Society of Light, had worked with The Order. *He* was responsible for Jaques's death, not me. Hot tears pricked my eyes. Relief washed through me like a cool wind as I was able to let the guilt since that night go. That relief, however, was quickly replaced by searing anger. That *bastard!*

Things were quickly going from bad to worse. Arin wasn't the only mole in The Society, nor was he the highest ranking. Who else was selling secrets to The Order? If one of our leaders was a traitor, no one in The Society of Light could be trusted. Any number of people in that underground building could be working for The Order, too.

Luca and I had to go. We were no longer safe in its fold.

I wrenched my hands away from Daiko's head and stumbled out of my seat, tipping the chair onto its back.

He stood and puffed up his small man's chest. "How dare you enter my mind, child?"

I stood facing him, my hands balled in fists at my side. "How dare I? How dare *you!*"

Mr. Daiko aimed an accusatory finger at me. "Listen, girl. I don't know what you think you saw, but . . ."

My face was hot. "How could you do that to your own people?!"

Mr. Daiko took a step forward. I took a step back. "You know nothing of the complexities of war, little one."

"I know Jaques is dead because of you. I know that you tried to hand me over to that Shadowman." I shook my head. "It isn't *complex*. You're a traitor, pure and simple."

Mr. Daiko lunged forward with incredible speed. He slammed into me with the weight of a wrecking ball, knocking the air from my lungs. We fell to the floor in a heap. Daiko pressed me into the plush carpet and wrapped his arms around me. Although he was surprisingly heavy and strong for an old guy, I had the best trainer in The Society of Light. I was no longer easy prey.

In a move I'd practiced a hundred times, I wrapped my own arms around Daiko's torso. Digging my heels into the carpet, I lifted my back off the ground. Pulled by gravity and momentum, Daiko rolled off my chest and landed head-first on the floor. In a blur of action, I sprang to my feet and sank into a defensive stance.

Arms up.

Knees bent.

Daiko pushed to his feet and lifted his palms to the ceiling. Like the switch of a light, his energy surged to the surface. I shielded my eyes as the room filled with a sudden, blinding light, and my own energy flared to the surface in response to this new threat. The hairs on my arms stood as my skin began to glow. Our combined power merged, and the temperature in the room rose several degrees.

"Stand down, child," Daiko commanded.

"Never," I growled, righteous anger coursing through my shining veins. "I will not let you get away with this."

Daiko's energy surged hotter momentarily before he shot a bolt of energy directly at my chest. I spun to the right, and it missed by inches. The smell of burnt hair filled the air. I looked down at the ends of my singed braid. Unbound, it fell in loose waves around my body, several inches too short.

Fury tore through me then. My waist-length hair was a final reminder of my mother. With a shriek of outrage, I shot a bolt of energy at Daiko. He ducked and it missed him by inches. I shot bolt after bolt at the traitor, managing only to singe the edges of his suit jacket and pants as he ducked and dodged with the agility of a much younger man. I gritted my teeth in frustration.

Daiko grabbed the back of the armchair and flung it at me as if it weighed no more than a feather. It hit me in the shoulder, knocking me onto Daiko's desk. My breath was knocked from my lungs with an *oomph*, my hair falling around me like a curtain. All the items on the desk were smashed and scattered to the ground. All but the bust of Marcus Brutus, which lay on its side inches from my face.

I wrapped my hands around the cold marble and swung around. Daiko was right behind me, hands reaching for my throat. I lifted the bust and brought it down hard. It connected with the side of his head with a sickening thud, and Daiko folded to the floor like a ragdoll. He lay still as blood ran down his face into the cream-colored carpet, the thick fabric soaking it up greedily.

I dropped the bust with a gasp. This was *not* good. I'd just assaulted a leader of The Society of Light in his own office. What would I tell the others? That I'd read his mind and that he was a traitor? Who would believe me?

I held my breath and waited for the guards standing just outside the door to rush in and arrest me, but the door remained firmly shut. I looked around the ruined room. Surely the guards heard our struggle and raised voices. Why hadn't they intervened?

Unless . . . I swallowed hard. Unless they'd been commanded to guard the door no matter what they heard. Unless Daiko had planned to attack me, and the guards were in on it all along. It would explain why they'd chosen this door to guard instead of staying in the hallway.

I was so screwed.

Squeezing my eyes shut, I reached out to Luca through our connection and projected my fear and anxiety with all the energy I had left. Within the space of a breath, his alarm and concern answered back.

Chapter 27

Luca

Luca sat across a teakwood desk from one of the most powerful men in the world. Mr. Bellamy leaned back in a camel leather chair. He steepled his fingers beneath his chin as he stared Luca down. The man didn't fit the role of a Society co-leader. His sun-bleached hair and easy-going attitude gave him the appearance of a regular bloke. Even his office decor belied his station's weight with its beachy colors and eclectic furniture. His casual persona encouraged one to drop one's guard. Luca fought the urge to relax in his presence just then.

He waited for the inquisition to begin. From the second he called Abbott with the plan, he'd dreaded this moment. He'd gone rogue, and despite his reasons, he knew there would be consequences.

Luca also knew some in The Society would feel vindicated by his fall from grace. After all his years in service, many still believed he was unfit to be an agent. When Abbott saved him from The Order, The Society elders decided to hold an unprecedented vote on whether Luca should be allowed to train as an Agent of Light. Some argued he'd spent too much time under the influence of The Order, that he couldn't be trusted. Others said he had too much darkness within him to be a Child of the Light. The decision to let him stay hadn't been unanimous. Ever since, many in the upper levels of the organization watched him, waiting for him to muck it all up.

Ultimately, he'd gone and proved them right. Withholding classified information and carrying out a covert mission outside the bounds and knowledge of The Society was a serious offense. He may even be expelled from the only home he'd known since his family was butchered. But what choice did he have? The mole could've been anyone. Telling The Society might've meant telling the Shadowmen he was on to them. He couldn't take the risk. Not that it made a difference in the end.

Mr. Bellamy cleared his throat and began. "I'm sorry for your loss. I know you and Arin were close." Luca watched the other man closely. Mr. Bellamy *sounded* earnest, but after Arin's betrayal, He'd lost faith in his ability to read people.

"Thank you, sir. It's been . . . difficult." Luca's throat worked to choke down the grief and anger crawling up his throat. His emotions were a jumbled mess. After all of this was over, he'd have serious baggage to unpack regarding Arin's death and betrayal.

Mr. Bellamy's chair squeaked as he sat forward, leaning his forearms on the desktop. "Well, are you ready to get started?" Luca straightened in his seat and nodded. "Good. Tell me about the intel you received from the Shadow in D.C."

Luca recalled how he identified the female Shadow in the President's circle and tricked her into revealing where she was staying. The thought of that night still made him sick. At the mere mention of Kirie, he'd let his inner shadows slip out. The enemy had to be dealt with, true, but the way he'd done it . . . Donovan would've been proud.

"I procured the laptop and eliminated the threat," Luca summarized, praying Mr. Bellamy wouldn't ask for more details.

Mr. Bellamy's brows furrowed as he studied Luca's face. "Why didn't you follow protocol and turn the computer over to the tech department?"

Luca had anticipated this question, of course. After the Paris Center of Light attack, suspicions had formed in his mind. How did they find its location after all those years? Shadowmen had been bumbling around Paris searching like blind mice for months, leaving small, haphazard fires in their wake. Yet, the hit on the Pantheon had clearly been planned and executed with precision.

Luca also couldn't understand why the attack happened when most of the agents were at home. The Order typically preferred to inflict maximum damage.

"I had reasons to suspect the Paris attack was an inside job,"

Luca explained.

Mr. Bellamy hummed and rocked back in his seat. "I see. Tell me about the intel you were able to extract from the Shadow's device."

Luca gave him the cliff notes version of the files' contents. He described locating the uranium stockpile using a few grainy photos and a reverse image search.

Mr. Bellamy regarded Luca with skepticism. "So, you decided to keep this highly sensitive information to yourself simply because you *suspected* there was a mole within our ranks? You'll have to give me a little more than that, son."

Luca sighed. He was exhausted, and he wanted this interview to be over. He wanted to get back to Kirie. "It wasn't mere suspicion at that point, I'm afraid. I found an incriminating email hidden within the files. Someone had provided the location of the Center just hours before it was bombed. The email was sent from inside the building."

Bellamy raised a brow. "Arin?" It was more a statement than a question.

Luca dipped his chin and pressed his lips into a tight line, struggling to confirm his adopted brother's part in the attack verbally. Tears pricked the back of his eyes, but he forced them back.

"I know this is difficult for you," Mr. Bellamy said kindly. "We can take a break if you need time to compose yourself."

"No. I'm fine." Luca took a deep breath. "Yes, Arin sent the email, though I didn't know it then. I later found out that The Order was holding his little sister hostage and forcing his hand, which you are now aware of."

"I see. Then what happened?"

Luca related the events in the uranium mine, omitting only the kiss Kirie and he had shared in the tunnels moments before their attack. He admitted that they'd been unable to prevent the Shadowmen from transporting the uranium to another location. He then gave a detailed description of the crates and transport trucks, hoping they could be tracked via satellite images. As for the days of torture and Arin's death, Luca gave only the most basic of details.

"Thank you for your candor, Luca. I know this ordeal has been a challenge for you. I just have one more question." Mr. Bellamy leaned forward once more. "What are your intentions toward Kirie?"

Luca frowned. "I'm sorry. Sir?"

"I saw how close the two of you were just now. I want to know what's going on there."

Luca felt as if he'd fallen into a funhouse room of mirrors. What did Mr. Bellamy, of all people, care about his love life? True, the man had trained with Kirie these past few weeks, but Luca had never heard of a trainer asking personal questions before, let alone someone as senior as Mr. Finn Bellamy. It pissed Luca off, actually. Weren't they there to talk about the mission?

"Pardon me," he said with as much British poise as he could

muster. "I wasn't aware I was required to report with whom I was involved to The Society."

"Normally, that's true. But Kirie's different. I guess you could say that I am . . . personally invested in her well-being."

"Because you two have been training together?"

Mr. Bellamy sighed. "Not exactly. This isn't widely known, so I'd appreciate it if you kept it to yourself." Confused, Luca nodded. "I've recently discovered that Kirie is my biological daughter."

Luca jerked back in his seat. What? He must be joking. Kirie was an orphan like the rest of them. Donovan would've made sure of that. "I thought Kirie's birth father was dead," Luca said.

Mr. Bellamy shifted in his seat, visibly uncomfortable. "Yes, well, it was a surprise to us both. And although I've been a father for only a few weeks, I've developed this deep-seated need to protect my only child from threats like Shadowmen." Mr. Bellamy waved a hand at Luca. "And boys, it seems."

Luca searched Bellamy's face for similarities to Kirie. It wasn't obvious at first. The man's face was long and thin, while Kirie's was heart-shaped. His hair was light, and hers was midnight dark. It was in his eyes . . . almond-shaped and Caribbean blue. The color was as unique as it was beautiful. Luca had been a fool to not see it before.

Without warning, a surge of fear and adrenaline slammed into Luca.

Not his own. Kirie's.

He jumped to his feet. Mr. Bellamy stood, too.

"Something's wrong," Mr. Bellamy guessed.

Luca nodded, and they rushed into the hallway. Outside Mr. Daiko's door, stood the two guards. Luca had wondered about their appearance in the hallway earlier but had assumed they'd expected trouble from *him*. Their presence in front of Mr. Daiko's door made no sense. Kirie was no threat. He'd assured anyone who would listen that she had been tricked into going on the mission.

"You're dismissed," Bellamy told them without explanation. The guards looked at each other in uncertainty.

"Sorry, sir. Mr. Daiko ordered us to stay right here," the man without a neck said with a thick Russian accent.

The leader stared him down, and Luca nearly laughed when the guard, who was easily twice Mr. Bellamy's size, began to sweat. "Y-yes sir." He turned to his comrade and jerked his head. Together, they walked down the hall, throwing uncertain glances back at them until they were out of sight.

Mr. Bellamy tried the door handle. Locked. He stepped back and nodded once to Luca. Luca raised his hand and blasted the door handle off with a burst of light. Mr. Bellamy kicked the door in. They were instantly hit by an overwhelming stench of burnt wood and blood.

Luca rushed into the room and froze in shock at the scene before him. Mr. Bellamy joined him and gasped. The walls all around them were scorched black, and a pair of armchairs lay on their sides. Small knick-knacks littered the floor, and Mr. Daiko lay prone and bleeding on the ground. Kirie stood in the eye of the tornado, visibly shaken.

"What happened?" Bellamy asked, rushing toward her.

Kirie stepped around Bellamy's outstretched arms to Luca. She grabbed his hands and stared up at him with wide eyes.

"We need to leave. Now!" she whispered.

Luca saw the warning of danger in her stormy blue eyes. He wanted to sweep her up and get her as far away from that building as possible, no questions asked. But he was rendered mute by the confusing scene before him. Had Kirie really just fought one of the most powerful men in The Society? And won? And *why* had they fought?

Mr. Bellamy grabbed Kirie's elbow and swung her around to face him. "Kirie, tell me what happened."

She lifted her chin and glared at the man. "Your jerk friend over there tried that mind rape thing on me again. Only this time, I pushed back and saw *his* memories. Turns out, Mr. Daiko isn't who you think he is."

Bellamy shook his head. "What do you mean?"

"Daiko planted a tracker on me the night I was attacked. That's how The Order was able to find me so quickly."

Mr. Bellamy turned and peered down at his colleague who still lay unconscious on the floor. The blood from his head wound had slowed to a trickle. Luca could see the disbelief in Bellamy's expression. He clearly didn't want to believe his closest ally had betrayed him. Luca understood how he felt. He wouldn't have believed it of Arin had he not witnessed it himself.

Bellamy looked back at Kirie, eyebrows tightly knit. "I—are you sure?"

Kirie lifted her chin higher, anger flashing in her eyes. "I can't believe you left me with that creep."

Mr. Bellamy's gaze bounced between Kirie and Mr. Daiko. "Kirie, please. Are you *sure* Mr. Daiko placed a tracker on you?"

Kirie folded her arms tightly over her chest. "I don't know why that's so hard to believe. Am I the only one who sees how awful the guy is?"

Luca's mind was whirling. If The Void had infiltrated the highest levels of The Society, nowhere was safe for them anymore.

Kirie was right. They had to run.

Luca held out a hand to her. "Time to go, my love."

Bellamy stepped forward and grabbed hold of Kirie's shoulder. "Hold on. We need to talk about this."

Luca pulled her from his grip and leveled him with a glare. Luca would lay him out flat like his colleague if it came to blows.

Bellamy put his hands up. "Hold on. I just want to help. You need to plan. I have a safe house. It has everything you need to disappear for a while."

Luca shook his head. "No. There's a list of every safe house owned by The Society. It wouldn't be difficult for another mole to find us."

"This one isn't owned by The Society. Only I know its location. You'll both be safe there, I assure you."

A personal safe house unknown to The Society? If that were

true, then Mr. Bellamy had his own fears and suspicions about the agents and leaders serving under him. Or . . . Luca's mind spun. Was he conducting his own traitorous missions for The Order? Either way, he didn't trust Mr. Bellamy's intentions.

Luca squared his shoulders. "Why should we trust you?"

Bellamy turned to look at Kirie. "She's my flesh and blood. Trust that I'd never put her in danger."

Kirie returned his stare, biting her lip as she considered his words. "I think we can trust him," she said finally.

Mr. Bellamy let out a sigh of relief and rounded Mr. Daiko's desk to pull a piece of paper and a pen from a top drawer. He quickly scribbled something down and handed it to Kirie.

"This is the address of the safe house. Take public transportation and keep your heads and faces covered at all times. There are cameras everywhere, and it wouldn't be difficult for them to trace your movements." Bellamy pulled a wallet from his back pocket and extracted a stack of euros.

Kirie tucked the money and address in her pocket and threw her arms around her birth father. "When will I see you again?" she asked in a thick voice.

Bellamy pulled back and held her face in his hands. Luca grew uncomfortable as tears began rolling down the older man's face. "You look so much like her," he said. Luca could only imagine he was talking about Kirie's mother.

Kirie began crying, too. "She never stopped loving you."

He took an unsteady breath. "Nor I her. We'll make them pay

for what they've done to our Claire."

A fierce glint lit Kirie's eyes.

"Count on it," she said, nodding resolutely. They all had scores to settle before this war was over.

Mr. Bellamy stepped back and took a steadying breath. "You both need to go before anyone discovers what happened here. I'll cover for you for as long as I can."

Luca reached out and shook Mr. Bellamy's hand. "Thank you, sir. I'll take good care of her."

"You mean, we'll take care of each other," Kirie corrected.

Luca couldn't help but smile despite their dire circumstances.

Mr. Bellamy squeezed his hand meaningfully. "You better. Now go."

Luca reached out for Kirie, and she slipped her hand into his. As they walked toward the door, Luca felt Kirie's regret at leaving her father behind. She'd just found him, only to have him taken from her again. It wasn't right. It wasn't fair. She deserved so much more.

Theirs was a cursed life, one full of unending danger and grief. Their very nature made them a target for the world's most evil creatures. Fair or not, Luca had learned early on that he only had two choices in life. He could lie down, let the darkness consume him, or fight to stay in the light. When he met Kirie, she became his light, his reason to fight. There was no going back. There was no backing down. There was only keeping Kirie safe.

Hand-in-hand, they disappeared into the night.

Donovan

The assassin stood on the other side of a large pane of glass, arms folded tightly over his chest. A beehive of men and women in white lab jumpsuits hurriedly worked to assemble the cone-shaped objects. There were dozens of them lined up on shiny metal tables.

These bombs would lay waste to the world.

For the first time since joining The Order, the assassin felt uncertain about his mission. World domination had always been The Order's edict. By extension, it was also his. He'd fought long and hard to eradicate The Children of Light, to create a world where shadows reigned. Success was within their grasp.

His stomach twisted as he watched the technicians turn the yellow uranium they'd taken from the Iranian mine into weapons of mass destruction. Nothing would remain after this. The world would be nothing but smoke and ash.

They would be the lords of death and desolation.

Ciara joined him, facing the glass wall with a twisted smile on her red lips.

"Beautiful, aren't they?" she purred.

"Fucking gorgeous," he replied.

J.B. Tucker is a novelist and short-story writer living in the Rocky Mountains with her bearded husband, three game-loving teenagers, and a small pack of doxies that follow her every move. She earned a master's degree from Weber State University in English (cohort in creative writing). By day, J.B. Tucker teaches high school creative writing, and by night, she crafts complex worlds and characters in both long and short forms.

Please visit her author page at www.jbuckerbooks.com